Nicola Cornick
Claimed by the Laird

HARLEQUIN® MIRA®

Published in Great Britain 2014
by Harlequin MIRA, an imprint of Harlequin (UK) Limited,
Eton House, 18-24 Paradise Road,
Richmond, Surrey, TW9 1SR

© Nicola Cornick 2014

ISBN 978-1-848-45312-8

59-0814

Harlequin's policy is to use papers that are natural, renewable and recyclable products and made from wood grown in sustainable forests. The logging and manufacturing processes conform to the legal environmental regulations of the country of origin.

Printed and bound by
CPI Group (UK) Ltd, Croydon, CR0 4YY

Dear Reader,

Welcome to *Claimed by the Laird*, Book Three in the Scottish Brides series! This is Christina's story. Christina has always been in the shadow of her younger sisters, but now she is swept up into a shocking upstairs-downstairs whirlwind romance—with the new footman at Kilmory Castle!

Lucas Ross is a very unusual footman indeed. Tall, dark and handsome, Lucas is surely too commanding to be a servant, and his affair with Lady Christina MacMorlan is bound to cause scandal. But Lucas has other, secret reasons for being at Kilmory and, when they are revealed, can their love survive the ensuing disgrace?

Like the other books in the Scottish Brides series, *Claimed by the Laird* is inspired by real-life events. I thoroughly enjoyed researching the background of whisky smuggling in the Scottish Highlands!

I have loved writing all the books in this series and would like to thank all my readers very much for their wonderful support through so many writing years.

Happy reading!

To Andrew, my own hero,
who was there at the beginning.
With my thanks and all my love.

PROLOGUE

"I DON'T KNOW why I am helping you," Jack Rutherford said.

Lucas Black laughed. "Because my club serves the best brandy in Edinburgh?" He topped up his friend's glass.

"It does," Jack allowed. "But that isn't the reason."

"Because you owe me money?"

The cards lay abandoned on the cherrywood table between them. This was one of the club's private rooms and empty but for the two of them. Beyond the door lay the gambling hell's main salon, packed tonight with a clientele representing the richest men in Edinburgh society. Lucas cared nothing for a man's antecedents, but he did care that his guests could pay their debts. He was in a position to be selective. An invitation to The Chequers was one of the most sought-after privileges in Scottish society.

Jack took out his pocketbook. "Twenty-five guineas, wasn't it?" he said.

Lucas waved the debt away. "I'd rather have your help."

His friend was frowning, watching the brandy swirl in his glass. He did not reply.

"A conflict of loyalties?" Lucas asked. He and Jack were business partners; they had helped each other out of more difficult situations than Lucas could remember. Which made it interesting that this time Jack was refusing to commit himself.

"Hardly that." Jack glanced up. "I have little time for my father-in-law," he said. "He tried to push both my wife and my sister-in-law into the sort of marriages that could have damaged them irreparably. People think him charmingly eccentric, but that is too kind a judgment." He shifted in his chair. "No, it's the element of deception that concerns me. I thought you were the sort of man who would walk in and state his terms rather than masquerading as a servant to spy on people."

"I am the sort of man who prefers a direct approach," Lucas agreed, adding drily, "but can you imagine what would happen if I walked into Kilmory Castle and said that I suspected someone there of killing my brother and I had come to find the culprit and bring him to justice? They would throw me out—or have me clapped in bedlam."

He stopped. His dry tone had masked all kinds of emotions, but Jack had not been fooled. Lucas saw the sympathy in his eyes.

"I'm sorry about Peter," Jack said, a depth of sincerity in his voice that Lucas could not doubt. "I understand that you want to know what happened—"

Lucas cut him off with a sharp gesture. "I want

justice," he said through his teeth. "It was no accident."

He could see that Jack was struggling for a response.

Don't, Lucas thought viciously. *Don't say that you understand how I feel. Don't tell me that Peter's death was investigated, that if others could not find a culprit, neither will I.*

Rage and frustration welled up within him and he clenched his fists. He had met his half brother only once as an adult after years of estrangement. They had laid a foundation that they had both hoped would develop into a strong bond. And then Peter had died, robbing them of that chance and that future. He had been nineteen years old, no more than a boy.

When his half brother had first written to say that he was coming to Scotland and wanted to meet, Lucas had ignored the letter. He had had no contact with his family since his mother's death and had wanted none. His childhood memories of life in Russia were not happy ones.

You're a bastard and your mother is a whore, the other children had whispered to him, the ugliness of the words so incongruous amidst the opulent beauty of his stepfather's palace.

Bastard, bastard...

The taunt echoed in his head and he pushed it away, shutting it out, closing down the emotion, the response, as he had done since the time the words first had a meaning for him. His parentage did not matter. In fact, he was grateful for those taunts because in the end they had given him the incentive he needed to prove himself. He had worked tirelessly to build a business empire that would give him wealth and influence to outstrip anything his family possessed. His hatred of his relatives had inspired him.

Then Peter had come and all that had changed. He could still see his half brother standing on the doorstep of his house in Charlotte Square, a tall, lanky youth who had not yet fully grown into his own skin but whose bearing showed the man he would one day become. Peter was hunched against the wind that whistled down from where Edinburgh Castle stood stark against a cold blue autumn sky.

"Dear God, but this country is cold!" His brother had walked straight in without invitation. He had spoken in Russian, and had embraced Lucas, who had stood there in astonished silence. Very few things had the power to surprise him; Peter had achieved that within five seconds.

"I wrote!" Peter had said enthusiastically.

"I know," Lucas had said. "I did not reply."

But there had been no resisting Peter, who cloaked a steely determination behind an irrepressible spirit that reminded Lucas of a puppy. Lucas recognized the determination because he had it, too, and he could not withstand his brother's affection. They spent a riotous fortnight together in Edinburgh; Peter got gloriously drunk and Lucas had to rescue him from the tollbooth where he had been locked up in order to sober up; Peter threw himself into the social round of parties and balls and dinners—as a Russian prince he was much celebrated. Peter's tutor, a long-suffering fellow who was trying to escort the boy and three companions around Europe, also insisted that they attend the talks and exhibitions for which Edinburgh's academia was famous. Peter slipped out of one lecture halfway through to visit a brothel. Lucas had to rescue him from there, as well.

After two weeks, Peter and his companions had set off for the Highlands.

"I must see Fingal's Cave!" Peter had exclaimed. "So wild, so romantic." He had written after the boat trip to the island of Staffa, waxing lyrical about its beauty and telling Lucas that they were visiting Ardnamurchan on their way south. He wanted to see the most westerly point on the British mainland.

Then the news had come of his death. His body had been found by the side of a coastal track at Kilmory, a village at the end of the Ardnamurchan Peninsula. He and his companions had dined the previous night at Kilmory Castle with the Duke of Forres and his family. After that Peter had apparently returned to the Kilmory Inn, only to go out later, alone. No one knew why or whom he was meeting, but his body was found the following morning, half-clothed. He had been beaten and robbed. Robbery and murder were unusual in the Highlands despite the wild reputation of the land and its people, but that was no consolation to Lucas, who had lost the half brother he had barely had chance to know.

The fall of logs in the grate recalled him to the

room and he realized that Jack was speaking. He forced down his grief and anger and tried to listen.

"I truly believe that Lord Sidmouth is using you for his own ends, Lucas," Jack was saying carefully. There was something in his eyes that was almost but not quite pity. "He's using your grief to manipulate you."

Lucas shook his head stubbornly. "I offered to help Sidmouth of my own free will," he said, "in return for information and resources."

After Peter's death, the home secretary had sent men from London to try to find his murderer, but they had drawn a blank. Lord Sidmouth was certain that the case was connected to the illegal trade in whisky distilling with which the Highlands were rife. It was his contention that Peter had inadvertently stumbled over the notorious Kilmory smuggling gang and had been killed to ensure his silence. Lucas had no reason to doubt the home secretary's assessment and he had a burning desire to avenge himself on the gang of thugs who had taken Peter's life.

"I know it's a long shot," he said, "but maybe I can discover something that those fools from London could not. If the whisky smugglers were responsible for Peter's death, then I have a better chance of learning of it than Sidmouth's men had, and to do that I cannot approach Kilmory openly." He fixed his gaze on the fire. It burned low in the grate, filling the room with heat and light. Yet Lucas felt cold inside. He could not remember the last time he had felt warm, could not remember if he had ever felt warm, not inside, where it mattered.

He was the illegitimate son of a Scottish laird and a Russian princess, the product of a night of youthful passion when his father had been traveling through Russia. His birth had scandalized Russian society and disgraced his mother. She had made an unhappy dynastic marriage five years later to a man who had been prepared to overlook her sullied reputation because he was dazzled by her dowry.

Lucas had gone with his mother when she had married, but he had been a changeling, unwelcome in his stepfather's house, keenly aware of the difference between him and other children. His grandfather had asked Czarina Catherine to legitimize him, but that had made matters worse rather than better. His cousins and his stepfather still called him a bastard; his mother still had such grief and shame in her eyes when she looked at him. Peter had been the only one unaware of the dark shadow cast by Lucas's existence. He was little more than a baby, open, trusting and loving.

His little brother, his life snuffed out by a stranger in a strange land. The coldness swept through him again and with it an ice-cold determination to discover the truth.

"Peter deserves justice," he repeated. "I can't just let it go, Jack. He was the only family I had left."

"No, he was not," Jack corrected. "Stop feeling sorry for yourself. What about your aunt?"

Lucas smiled reluctantly. "All right, I'll give you

that." His father's sister was a force of nature. She
had come into his life when he was living rough on
the streets of Edinburgh. Even though he had told her
to leave him alone, she had refused to abandon him.
He had been a sullen, ungrateful youth, eaten up with
bitterness of his father's family, but she had driven
a coach and horses through his resentment. She had
forced him to pull himself up out of the gutter and
he loved her fiercely for it. She was the only woman
he did love, the only one he could imagine loving.

There was silence in the room. "You never speak
of your father," Jack said after a moment.

Lucas shrugged. There was discomfort in it. He
could feel the tension knotting his shoulders again.
"There's nothing to say about him."

"He left you his estate at the Black Strath," Jack
said. "That must count for something."

To Lucas, it counted for absolutely nothing. He
could feel the anger and hatred stir within him. These
days he seemed to be angry all the time: angry that
Peter had died, angry that no one had been brought
to justice for it, angry that no one really cared. Jack
was right; he knew that Lord Sidmouth *was* using
him. Sidmouth wanted to bring an end to the whisky-
smuggling gangs who ran rings around his excise officers. He wanted the members identified and jailed.
Peter's death was a convenient means by which to
engage Lucas's help. But that did not matter if they
both got what they wanted.

"I've always wondered why your mother waited

so long to tell you about your inheritance," Jack said. "Your father died when you were only a baby."

"I think she was afraid," Lucas said slowly. He could still remember the clutch of his mother's fingers, clammy and cold, and see the desperation in her eyes.

Don't blame your father, his mother had said. *He was a good man. I loved him.*

But Lucas had blamed Niall Sutherland. He had never forgiven his father for abandoning his mother, for his cowardice and weakness. Their romance had been secret, her pregnancy only discovered months after Sutherland had left. Although Princess Irina had written to tell him, he had never returned to Russia. Lucas felt nothing but contempt for him for condemning Irina to the shame and stigma of bearing an illegitimate child, and Lucas to the endless taunts and mockery that went with bastardy. If he had anything to be grateful to his father for, it was that his example had taught Lucas to be the opposite of him: hard, ruthless and strong.

Jack was watching him. Lucas took a mouthful of brandy. It tasted bitter and he put the glass down abruptly.

"She was unhappy," he said. "I think she was afraid I would leave her and go to Scotland to claim my inheritance. Even as a child I was headstrong." He smiled ruefully. "She was wrong, of course. I would never have left her."

"But you went when she died," Jack said.

"There was nothing to keep me in Russia then."

Lucas crossed to the fireplace, tossing a couple of logs onto the glowing embers. There was a hiss and a flare of flame. "My stepfather had me horsewhipped from the house on the day she died." He kept his voice level, even though in his memory he could still feel the bite of the whip through the thin material of his shirt, hear the sound as it ripped, feel the sting across his back. His chest felt tight as he remembered the black panic as the thongs snaked about his neck, choking him. He had fled to Scotland only to find that the trustees of his father's estate were unimpressed by a fifteen-year-old boy who had no means of proving his claim.

He shook his head sharply to dispel the memories of the past. His aunt had ensured that he received his estate, but he was no laird; he had rented out the Black Strath ever since he had come into his inheritance. His interest was in business, not the land.

"Peter hero-worshipped you," Jack said. "Evidently his father was unable to poison his mind against you."

Lucas smiled reluctantly. "Peter had a loving spirit," he said. "He was like our mother."

Jack nodded. "I understand." He corrected himself. "That is, I understand that you feel the need to bring his murderer to justice." He let out his breath on a long sigh. "You will make a spectacularly poor footman, by the way."

"I don't know what you mean," Lucas said. "I can work hard."

"You can't take orders," Jack said, draining his glass. "You are accustomed to giving them."

"You don't think that I fit the advertisement?" Lucas sat, and tapped the newspaper that was folded on the table in front of them. He read aloud, "'Footman required at Kilmory Castle. Must be diligent, reliable, well trained and deferential.'"

"You are an impressive fail on almost all counts," Jack said.

Lucas laughed. "I won't get you to write my references, then." He picked up one of the playing cards, toying with it, turning it idly between his fingers.

"Tell me more about the household," he said. "So that I am prepared."

"I've never been to Kilmory," Jack said, "but I understand it to be a fourteenth-century castle that has no proper plumbing or heating, so it is probably as uncomfortable as hell. The duke prefers it, though." He shrugged. "He always gets his own way."

"Do any of the family live with the duke at Kilmory?" Lucas asked. He knew that some of the MacMorlan clan had been there when Peter had died. Sidmouth had told him.

"There's a houseful at the moment," Jack said. He ticked them off on his fingers. "You'll be tripping over them at every turn. Angus and Gertrude are staying there at present—that's Mairi's ghastly elder brother, the Marquess of Semple, and his even more horrible wife. He is heir to the title and full of self-importance. I believe they have their daughter, Allegra, with them."

Lucas grimaced. "And I'm supposed to wait on these people?"

"Your choice," Jack said unsympathetically.

"Hmm. Who else?"

"Lachlan." Jack grinned. "The younger brother. He is an utter waste of space. His wife left him some months ago and he has taken to drink for comfort."

Lucas gave a soundless whistle. "Never a good solution." He raised his glass in ironic toast. "Is there anyone else?"

"No," Jack said. "Yes." He corrected himself quickly. "There's Christina, the eldest daughter." He frowned slightly. "We always forget Christina."

"Why?" Lucas said.

"Because…" Jack paused. "She's easy to overlook," he said after a moment. He sounded slightly shamefaced. "Christina's self-effacing, the old spinsterish sister. No one notices her."

Lucas found that hard to believe when both Lucy and her sister Mairi MacMorlan, Jack's wife, were stunningly pretty, diamonds of the first order. He felt an odd, protective pang of pity for the colorless Lady Christina, living in their shadow, the duke's unmarried daughter.

He let the playing card slip from between his fingers and it glided down to rest on the carpet.

There was a discreet knock at the door, and Lucas's manager, Duncan Liddell, stuck his head around.

"Table four," Duncan said. "Lord Ainsley. Can't

pay his debts. Or won't pay. Not sure which." He was a man of few words.

Lucas nodded and got to his feet. It happened occasionally when sprigs of the nobility had a little too much to drink and felt they were entitled to play for free. A few discreet words in the gentleman's ear usually sorted the matter out.

"I'll leave you to it," Jack said. He stood up, too, and shook Lucas's hand. "Best of luck. I hope you find out the truth." He hesitated. "I don't care what happens to the rest of them," he said, "but don't hurt Christina, or Mairi will have my balls for helping you."

Lucas grinned. "I know your wife is a crack shot. I wouldn't want to get on the wrong side of her." He sobered. "You have my word, Jack. I've no quarrel with any of Forres clan. I doubt I will have much to do with them. All I want is to infiltrate the whisky gang and find out what really happened to Peter."

As he followed Duncan into the salon, Lucas caught sight of the playing card resting under the table. He bent to pick it up. It was the jack of diamonds. He laid it on top of the pack. It seemed appropriate for the bastard son of a laird and a princess who had made his own fortune and was as hard as the diamonds themselves.

CHAPTER ONE

Ardnamurchan, Scottish Highlands, May 1817

IT WAS NOT the way Lucas was meant to die, blind-folded, tied up, on his knees in a smugglers' cave, with the pungent smell of rotting fish in his nose and the roar of the sea in his ears as it crashed onto the rocks several hundred feet below.

One minute he had been strolling along the cliffs in the evening twilight to stretch his legs after an interminable journey from Edinburgh, the next this nightmare of ambush and capture. He had heard that the Highlands in May were very pleasant, but he had been mistaken in that. The Highlands in May was no place to be if there was a knife at your throat.

He had been careless. The thought made him angry. Lord Sidmouth would be so proud of him, he thought savagely. His spy caught by the very men he had come to investigate. But he had been tired and the last thing he had been expecting was to stumble on the whisky smugglers moving their cargo. He wondered if this was why Peter had died. He wondered if his brother, too, had seen something he should not, had stumbled disastrously into a situation he could not control. The irony would be if he discovered the truth so quickly, so easily, and then did not live to prove it.

The smugglers were arguing. Their Scots accents were so thick Lucas found it hard to understand some of them, but the general thrust of the conversation was not in the least difficult to follow.

"I say we throw him over the cliff, no questions asked."

"I say we let him go. He's seen nothing—"

"It's too dangerous. He could be a spy. I say he dies."

"And I say we wait for the lady. She will know what to do."

There was a short, angry pause.

"I told you not to send for her." The first man swore. "Damn it to hell, you know what she will say."

"She doesn't like unnecessary bloodshed." The second man sounded as though he was quoting. Lucas could not help but wonder if the shedding of his blood would nevertheless be deemed necessary.

Lucas kept silent. He was cold, wet, tired to his bones and starving hungry.

Who was the lady? Some ruffian as brutal as her trade?

Sidmouth had briefed him on the illegal Highland whisky trade. The government in London demanded that every Highlander who distilled whisky should pay tax on it. The Highlanders declined. The government sent excise officers to hunt the smugglers down, which was no doubt why this gang suspected him of being a spy. Which he was. A very incompetent one.

Damnation.

Lucas remembered the whisky he had tasted on the back streets of Edinburgh. They called it the *Uisge Beatha* in Gaelic, the water of life, but he had thought it was rougher than a badger's backside.

A faint drift of a salt-laden breeze stirred the noisome press of air in the cave, and the smugglers fell silent. It was a wary silence. Lucas felt the hair on the back of his neck rise and his skin prickle. He found he was holding his breath.

The air shifted as someone walked past him. The lady. She had arrived. Lucas had heard no footsteps. Nor could he see anything from behind the blindfold. The material was thick and coarse. He was wrapped in darkness. Yet he could feel her presence. She was close.

He tried to rise to his feet and immediately one of the smugglers placed an ungentle hand on his shoulder and forced him back down on his knees.

"Evening, ma'am." The tone of the men's voices had changed. There was respect in their muttered greeting and a note of caution. Lucas realized that they were on their guard. They could not predict her reactions. And in their uncertainty lay his hope. Suddenly the moment was on a knife's edge between life and death.

"Gentlemen."

Lucas's heart was beating violently against his ribs. All his senses were straining. One word from her and he would be dead. A knife between the ribs, quick, lethal. He fought back the suffocating fear that beat down on his mind. He had nothing in particular to live for, but no particular wish to die, either.

He sensed the lady was very close to him now. He could hear the shift and slip of a material that sounded rich and fine, like silk or velvet, and then he caught the most elusive of scents, a fragrance of bluebells—very sweet, very innocent. The incongruity of it almost made him smile. The infamous leader of a band of criminal renegades and she smelled of spring flowers.

Someone kicked him hard in the ribs, and the thought disintegrated in a blaze of pain. Lucas toppled onto his side under the force of the blow. They were crowding in on him now like a pack of wolves. He could sense their malevolence. There was another blow, and then another. He twisted and rolled in a vain attempt to avoid them, hampered by his bound wrists, blinded, utterly at their mercy. He was too proud to beg a pack of ruffians to spare his life. Perhaps that was a weakness that would kill him but he did not care.

"Stop."

It only took the one word from her to halt them. She spoke sharply and with such an edge of authority that they all fell back. For a moment Lucas could focus on nothing but the hot flare of pain in his ribs. Then as it dulled to an ache, he drew in a labored breath.

"Here…"

She was helping him to sit; his back was against the wall of the cave. It was cold and damp, but the solid rock helped to steady him. Her touch was gentle but firm. He sensed she was between him and the men, shielding him, protecting him. He felt a wave of shame that he could not defend himself and a fierce, hot tug of emotion toward her that he did not understand.

The silence in the cave was absolute, but the atmosphere still simmered with violence. Lucas could feel it in every cell of his body. He could sense, too, some ripple of feeling in her that belied her confidence.

Fear? No. She was not afraid of these braggarts and bullies.

Revulsion.

Lucas's heart bounded. Extraordinary as it was, he sensed in her a hatred of brutality.

The smugglers' words made sense now. This was why the more bloodthirsty amongst them had not wanted her to know of his capture.

They were afraid she would save him.

He felt as close to her as though he could read her thoughts, closer, as though he shared the sensations and emotions that drove her.

He had never felt like this before. He hated the intimacy of the feeling and he hated that he did not understand why he felt it. Most of all he hated his own powerlessness.

"Begging your pardon, ma'am." One of the men sounded abashed, like a naughty schoolboy, but there was rebellion beneath his brusque apology.

"We caught him on the track above the bothy. He was following us—"

"Spying," one of the others put in.

"We need to get rid of him." There was a rumble of agreement.

"Over the cliff," the first man said. "Now."

"Is that so?" Unlike the men, her voice held no trace of a Scots accent. It was low and smooth, as rich and soothing as honey. She truly was a lady born and bred.

"Stand back." There was a rustle of skirts as she shifted beside him. Lucas could not rise as he was once again pinned by the large boot of one of the men, which was lodged in his aching ribs. The boot pressed harder and he sucked in his breath on another wave of pain.

"If you could restrain your tendency toward violence, please." She sounded weary now but the boot eased its pressure a little.

Her hand was beneath Lucas's chin. He imagined she was turning his face to the light. She wore no gloves; her skin was soft and her fingers felt gentle against the roughness of his stubble. For a moment they brushed his cheek in a sweet caress. Lucas felt a shiver down his spine of something that was not fear. He fought it back angrily. His life was on the line and all he could think about was her touch.

Get hold of yourself, Lucas.

"What sort of a spy would be caught so easily?" There was mockery in her voice.

"A bad one," one of the men said dourly.

"Or an innocent traveler," the woman said. Her tone was sharp. Her hand fell. Lucas sensed she was sitting back on her heels.

"Innocent or not, the sea is the place for him," the man growled. He seemed to be the spokesman. The others were content to let him talk. "It's the only thing to do, ma'am."

"Nonsense." She sounded angry now. "Our quarrel is not with the likes of him and you know it."

"And you know he's a danger to us." The man was curt. "We've no choice." He was standing his ground and the others supported him. Lucas could smell their stubbornness and their fear. It was in the air and on their unwashed bodies as they pressed closer. They wanted him dead.

He knew the woman could feel it, too. One false step and they would both be in trouble. It was extraordinary to sense with absolute certainty that she was on his side.

"No one will know," the man said. "Who's to miss him?"

"Only he can tell us that." Her voice betrayed no feelings, nothing of the quick, careful calculation Lucas could sense behind the words. "Perhaps it's time to learn a little more about him." Her hand touched Lucas's arm, conveying a warning even as her tone warmed into mockery again. "What's your name, handsome?"

"Lucas," he said. He was aware that as repartee went it was far from sparkling.

One of the men laughed. "We could spoil his pretty face. That would teach him a lesson."

"Don't you dare," the woman said. Her voice was light. "I need something nice to look at around here." Her words were dismissive, as though he counted for nothing. Lucas hated being treated so casually, but he could see how clever she was. She made him seem unimportant, no threat.

"What's your other name?" she said.

Lucas cleared his throat. "Lucas Ross, ma'am," he said. "At your service." It was only half a lie.

"Your speech is as pretty as your looks." Her voice was cool. "What are you doing in Kilmory, Lucas Ross?"

"I'm after a job," Lucas said. "At the castle. Footman. I've come from Edinburgh."

"Fancy city manners," one of the smugglers said, and it was not a compliment.

"I want to be a butler one day," Lucas said.

"Let us hope you live long enough to achieve your ambition." The lady sounded dry. "Where are you staying?"

"At the inn in the village," Lucas said. "I booked a room and ordered supper. The landlord will notice if I don't return."

"Tom McArdle won't give us any trouble." Another of the smugglers spoke this time. "Very likely he'll dispose of your belongings for us. Where do you think he gets his whisky from, laddie?"

The others gave a low rumble of laughter. They were closing in again now, going for the kill. Lucas knew he had not made a strong enough case to be allowed to live. There would be no loving wife to miss him, no parents and no siblings. He should have invented a few and told an affecting story of how they depended on him. His lips twisted into a bitter parody of a smile.

"We're wasting time." One of the men hauled him to his feet.

"Wait." The woman spoke again, the sharpness of authority back in her voice. "You are too hasty, my friend. Another body around here will bring the gaugers back down on us faster than a sniff of the peat-reek, and the dragoons with them. Have you forgotten that it is only a six-month since the last time?"

Another body…

Lucas felt his blood run cold. She was speaking of Peter.

The silence prickled with tension. Lucas waited, all his muscles wound up tight. He heard the shift and mutter of the men all around him.

"That was nothing to do with us." The leader sounded defiant. "We know nothing of it."

"Whether it was your doing or not," the woman said patiently, "two bodies draw unwanted attention. Do you understand me? Besides, if Mr. Ross here has applied to work at the castle, too many people will know who he is. We cannot take the risk."

"Be damned to it." The man's patience was exhausted. "I say he dies and the others stand with me. We can get rid of the body so they'll never find it."

"Enough!" Lucas heard her move, heard the unmistakable click of a pistol being cocked, heard the intake of breath as the men froze into immobility. He felt a shiver of fear, for her, not for himself. Absurd, extraordinary, but the bond between them seemed tighter still.

"You are dangerous fools," she said. She still spoke quietly, but with an undertone of iron. "Do you really want to take this risk? Do you want to throw away all your profits because of some poor benighted city boy who gets lost in the Highlands? Think again, my friends, before it is too late."

Once again Lucas found himself holding his breath. Violence bred violence, and she was taking a terrible risk to save his life. There were at least four of them. They could overpower her easily enough. One bullet was all she had to stand between him and death.

Time spun out. He felt each second pass.

Then everything changed. Lucas felt it first in the uneasy shift and shuffle of the smugglers' feet, then in the muttered words he could not catch, then finally in the easing of the tension. It was the money, he thought, as much as the show of force, that had changed their minds.

"She's right." One of the men spoke grudgingly. "Think how much we made on the last few barrels. We don't want the gaugers sniffing around again…"

There was a mutter of agreement, surly, resigned. Someone sighed as though the denial of his right to mete out a violent death was particularly disappointing.

Relief whipped through Lucas; his legs shook. If they made him walk now, he would not need to pretend to weakness. He felt the lady's relief, too, though she masked it well.

"Bring him." Her voice told Lucas that she had walked away as though she had already taken their capitulation for granted.

"My lady—" It was the spokesman, fighting a rearguard action. Then, correcting himself, "Ma'am—"

"Yes?" Her voice was light and cold. "If you still have concerns about my clemency, then console yourself with the thought that we will know exactly where to find him if he is foolish enough to say a word about tonight." She turned back to Lucas. "No loose words in the inn after a few drams, Mr. Ross," she said. "And no misplaced thoughts of spilling what you know to the authorities. A fine fool you would appear telling such a cock-and-bull story. My advice is that you should give up on the job at the castle, hurry home to Edinburgh and forget all about us."

"Yes, ma'am," Lucas said again. He caught the bluebell fragrance again, sweet, stirring his senses. There was no way he was going to forget her. He willed his body not to harden into arousal. Christ. Who *was* this woman who could do this to him when he could not even see her?

"Bring him," she repeated. Her tone was autocratic and this time no one argued.

The men half carried, half pulled Lucas as he stumbled to the mouth of the cave. Outside it was full night, the darkness pressing against his blind-fold. The cold air was like a slap in his face, fresh and sharp with the sting of the sea. The sound of the waves was suddenly loud, boiling on the rocks below. He sensed that he was very close to the edge of the cliff.

"Untie him." She was taking no chances that when her back was turned they would throw him over the edge. He knew it and the men knew it, too.

Someone was fumbling behind him to undo the ties that held his wrists, swearing all the while because they could not see what they were doing. He was free; he flexed his hands, feeling the pain of the blood returning.

"Remember what I told you," she said.

"Thank you, ma'am," Lucas said.

The blindfold fell from his eyes.

It took him a second to adjust to the darkness. There was no moon tonight, and the light of the stars was dim and pale, no more than a glitter on the sea. Lucas looked down and felt a clutch of fear. He was within two feet of the edge of the cliff; a step forward and he would have fallen. He could feel the small stones slipping beneath the soles of his boots. For a second he felt light-headed and nauseous, re-pressing the panicked reaction to scrabble backward for a safer foothold. He forced himself to keep still, slowing his breathing, fixing his gaze on the dark horizon until the world steadied around him.

The whisky smugglers were gone, melting into the shadows as swiftly and silently as they had appeared.

Perhaps they were still watching him. He knew that the only thing he could do was to return to the inn and behave as any other man might do when he had had a narrow escape. That probably meant getting drunk on bad whisky. And remembering to keep his mouth shut about what had happened to him.

He turned his back on the vertiginous drop and started to climb up the cliff face. It was tough going. The rough stems of heather scored his palms. Loose rock slid and slithered beneath his feet where the dry peat soil crumbled. It took him a good ten minutes to reach the path at the top where he turned inland toward the faint light in the distance where the village huddled. He was cold and damp and bruised, but he was damned grateful to be alive. The air seemed sweeter, the light and shadows sharper, the hoot of the owl clearer than ever before. Even the persistent ache in his ribs was welcome as a measure of the fact he was still alive.

It was as he came to the edge of the village, past the kirk sheltering behind its low moss-covered wall, that those instincts that had failed him earlier in the evening blazed into life and told him that he was not alone. He stopped in the shadow of the churchyard yew and waited. His skin prickled, the wind breathing gooseflesh down his spine.

She was here. He could sense it.

A second later he felt the cold caress of the pistol on the side of his throat.

"Remember what I told you. Go back to Edinburgh, city boy. There's nothing for you here." Her whisper was fierce.

Lucas did the one thing he was certain she would not be expecting. He spun to face her, catching her wrist so tightly that she gasped and dropped the pistol with a clatter at his feet. He kicked it aside, pulling her hard against his body, his arms going about her cruelly tight. The shadows were so thick here that he could see nothing of her face, but he could hear the quick catch of her breathing and feel the rise and fall of her breasts against his chest.

It felt astonishing to hold her in his arms, this woman who had saved his life. The blood surged through his veins, bringing with it instant arousal. Everything that had passed between them that evening fused in that moment into a blaze of lust as scorching as a heath fire.

Lucas brought one hand up to push back the hood of her velvet cloak. The material was rough against his palm, the friction delicious. Uncovered, her hair was dark in the faint moonlight, a satin-soft cascade as it tumbled through his fingers. He ran his thumb along the line of her jaw, tipping up her chin so that her mouth met his.

She made a startled sound in her throat that had Lucas's body hardening still further, and then her lips parted beneath the insistent pressure of his. She responded hesitantly at first, then sweetly, passionately, with a lack of artifice that shook him to the core. Her body softened and yielded to his and the kiss spun away into a different realm entirely, a place of heat and need. This was new, and dangerously seductive; Lucas had always had iron control, but now he felt the danger of losing it completely.

Under his fingertips he could feel both delicacy and strength in the exquisite lines of her jaw and neck, and when he dropped his hand to the warm hollow at the base of her throat her pulse beat frantically beneath his touch. It dimly occurred to him that he had no idea what she looked like or even how old she was, nor anything else about her. He could have been kissing a woman old enough to be his grandmother, and in that moment he was not sure he cared. Kissing her was the most explosively pleasurable experience he had ever known.

He pressed his lips to the line of her neck and then the curve of her shoulder, pushing aside her cloak and the flimsy layers of silk he could feel below it so that he could trace the line of her collarbone with his tongue. She gave a little gasp, and he felt her knees weaken so he pulled her down to where the heather made a soft bed beneath them. There he kissed her again, deep, slow kisses this time; kisses that made time stand still. He was aware of nothing but the intimate tangle of her tongue with his, the heat of her body, the smoothness of her skin beneath his fingertips.

Overhead the stars spun in their courses and the moon had risen higher, but it was a mere sliver, too pale to lift the shadows. Lucas did not care that he could not see her. She was the only thing that was real to him, a creature of quicksilver and darkness.

He slid his hand into her bodice and felt the curve of her bare breast warm against his palm. She arched upward, pressing herself into his hand. Her responsiveness had his cock hardening to almost unbearable proportions. He rubbed his thumb across her nipple and heard her gasp. The silk and lace of her bodice felt crisp and expensive, but beneath it her skin felt richer still, soft and sleek to the touch, her body a sensual paradise a man could lose himself in.

The church clock chimed the hour loudly, the ten long strokes vibrating through him and breaking the moment. He felt her go still in his arms, and then she scrambled up, pulling her cloak about her.

"Wait," Lucas said, catching her hand. He could feel her trembling, and the sense of her vulnerability and need made him want to wrench her back into his arms again and finish what they had started. His senses were full of the taste and the touch of her, and he did not want to let her go. "I haven't thanked you for saving my life," he said.

She paused. "I think you have done far more than thank me," she said. Her tone was dry. She had herself back under control now. Her voice betrayed nothing.

"When will I see you again?" Lucas asked.

"You won't." She sounded amused. "Good night, Mr. Ross."

For a second she was a darker shadow against the darkness, and then she was gone. The night was empty and still again. Lucas leaned his back against the churchyard wall and waited for the near-intolerable ache in his body to ease. He had come shockingly close to making love with a woman he did not know and had never seen. The mere thought of it caused his body to harden again. At this rate the walk back to the inn was going to be a long and uncomfortable one, but he could not regret it. It had been quite a night.

Ten minutes later Lucas was back in the village main street and stumbling into the Kilmory Inn. The landlord cast him a curious glance as he pushed open the door of the taproom. Lucas wondered what he must look like with his clothes filthy and torn. There were marks on his wrists, too, where the rope had bitten. The smugglers had not been gentle.

"A drink, sir?" The landlord was smooth but his gaze was sharp. "Get lost on your evening stroll, did you?"

Lucas nodded, sliding onto a hard wooden chair in a corner by the fire. His bruised ribs protested the lack of comfort but he did not think they were broken. He could not risk consulting a doctor, and since he was masquerading as a footman he could not afford one anyway. He was simply going to have to wait for the bruises to fade.

In his pocket was the pistol. Like a rather deadlier version of Cinderella his mystery woman had left it behind when she had run away, which suggested that she had not been as in control of her emotions as she had wanted to appear. That gave Lucas more than a little satisfaction. He decided to have a look at it later in the privacy of his chamber.

He cast a covert glance around the taproom. It was almost full. Three men were playing cribbage in the opposite corner, leaning over the board, wrapped up in the game. No one was watching him—or so it appeared. But word would go around about the smooth fellow from Edinburgh who had come for a job at the castle and had accidentally fallen foul of the local smuggling gang. Small communities like this one were close and loyal. Everyone would know about the whisky distilling.

The landlord pushed a glass toward him across the table. It tasted of smoke and peat, almost strong enough to choke him. Lucas could see the gleam of amusement in the man's eyes. Perhaps he thought him a Sassenach, an English foreigner who could not hold his drink. Or perhaps his accent tagged him as a Lowlander. There was no love lost between the Highlanders and their compatriots to the south. Truth was he was a fusion of races and a mixture of languages. His mother had been an educated woman who had taught him to speak both French and English faultlessly. When he had been thrown out of his stepfather's palace and come to Scotland looking for his inheritance, he had quickly adopted the accent of the streets so that he did not stand out. When he had started to profit in business and made his first fortune, he had shed the streets and readopted the faultless English of his childhood.

He sat quietly, thinking, whilst the noise of the taproom washed over him. The taste of the whisky was mellowing on his tongue and he felt a pleasant lethargy start to slide through him. Contrary to his previous experience, the whisky tasted delicious, warm and deep, once he had got used to the fact that it was strong enough to take the top of his head off. The Kilmory distiller was clearly very talented.

He leaned an elbow on the table, staring into the deep golden liquid. It swirled like magic, like a witch's spell. This was the whisky's skill, he thought; it could make you forget, ease you away from all kinds of raw memories and soothe the pain of the past. But tonight, here in Kilmory, he felt the shadow of the past standing right at his shoulder. It was here that Peter had died. He had stayed with his friends in this very inn, had dined at the castle and had walked on the same cliffs.

Lucas thought about the whisky-smuggling gang. He had heard the men deny any involvement in Peter's death, but he did not believe the word of a bunch of criminal thugs. They would have dispatched *him* swiftly enough had the lady not saved his life, and it was the obvious explanation.

Still, he knew the key to discovering the truth was finding the woman he had met tonight. He would never be able to identify the individual members of the gang, but she was a different matter. He could find her and she would lead him to the others. He could then betray them to Sidmouth.

He thought about what he had learned of her. He thought of her touch, of the rich, sensual rub of her velvet cloak and the scent of her perfume. He thought of her kiss, of the heat and the sweetness of it and the blinding sense of recognition he had felt. The memory of it still disturbed him. If he were a fanciful man, he would have called it love at first sight.

He was not a fanciful man.

It had been lust.

The other stuff, the sense of intimacy, of understanding, was no more than a trick of the senses. He had been fighting for his life and she had helped him. It had been relief and gratitude that had touched him, nothing more.

It seemed that "the lady" was precisely that, an aristocrat. She had spoken with an aristocrat's confidence and authority. Lucas had heard one of the men address her as "my lady" before he had quickly corrected himself. There were not many ladies to the square mile around here. Inescapable logic suggested that she must be related to the Duke of Forres and be a resident at Kilmory Castle.

The landlord brought him his supper at last, a plate of fragrant mutton pie with steaming vegetables, which Lucas fell upon with all the enthusiasm of a man who had just cheated death. As he ate, Lucas thought about what Jack had told him about the duke's female relatives. There was Lady Semple, the wife of the duke's heir. It seemed unlikely that she would be involved with a gang of outlaws but perhaps her daughter might be. He needed to find out more about Lady Allegra. Then there was Lady Christina MacMorlan, the self-effacing spinster who kept house for her father and was eclipsed by her two beautiful younger siblings. The thought of her as the pistol-wielding leader of a band of out-laws was mind-boggling.

On the other hand, there was no better cover for the pistol-wielding leader of a band of outlaws than being the self-effacing daughter of a duke.

But he was getting ahead of himself. There might be other possibilities. The first thing he needed to do was obtain the job at the castle. His lady smug-gler had told him to go back to Edinburgh, but he had absolutely no intention of doing so. Tomorrow he would present himself at Kilmory Castle as a can-didate for the post of footman as though nothing had happened. It would be a test of his acting abilities. He was not good at taking orders, so it would also be a test of his tolerance. He loathed the aristocracy with their opulent lifestyle and their sense of entitle-ment. A position of servitude in a ducal house was the worst possible match for him.

He smiled faintly. It was a small price to pay to find out the truth about his brother. If it also meant that he found his lady smuggler as well, then so much the better. He knew that he would recognize her again. One touch, a hint of her fragrance, would be sufficient.

If she really was the duke's daughter, then he had no sympathy for her. Either she was a spoiled little rich girl playing at being a smuggler for some ex-citement, or she was a cunning, deceitful criminal. Or perhaps she was both. Lucas did not really care about her motives. He could remember what it felt like to steal food in order to survive, to beg and thieve and fight simply to stay alive. He had no time for those who had every privilege and still behaved like delinquents.

In the privacy of his chamber, a tiny little box of a room tucked under the inn's eaves where he was too tall to stand upright beneath the sloping ceiling, he finally took out the pistol and examined it. It was a fine piece of workmanship, expensive, made entirely of brass and beautifully engraved. Lucas suspected it had been made in the late eighteenth century and that it would not look out of place in an aristocrat's collection. He tucked it away at the bottom of his bag, then lay down to sleep. The inn was noisy, but he could sleep anywhere, another legacy of the years he had spent on the streets, seizing rest when and where he could, always half-awake to trouble. Tonight, though, he found it more difficult than usual. He thought he might be haunted by memories of Peter, but instead he slept in snatches of dreams, and always through them there was a woman running away, a woman he yearned for, a woman whose face he could not see.

CHAPTER TWO

CHRISTINA PUSHED OPEN the wooden picket gate that separated the grounds of Kilmory Castle from the road beyond. A path in the shadow of the high estate wall led past the neat row of gardeners' cottages, shadowed by a tall stand of pines whose fallen needles were soft beneath her shoes. On the other side of the pines, a vast expanse of lawn, dotted with cedars, bordered the rose garden and led to a flight of steps up to the terrace. Christina walked slowly, unhurriedly. She had told her family that she was taking a stroll after dinner, and though she had been gone some time, they would not suspect anything. They never did.

Light glowed softly behind the castle windows. She did not particularly want to go back inside. She loved being out at night when the moon was high and the wind blew in the sea fret. She loved it more, perhaps, because ladies were not supposed to wander around alone after dark. She loved doing the unexpected because her days were governed by the expected.

Lucas Ross had been unexpected. She could still taste his kiss. She could still feel the touch of his hands on her body. His scent clung to her, not the cloying pomade and cologne some men wore, but a mixture of fresh air and forest and ocean. It seemed familiar, striking a chord in the region of her heart, making her shiver. Had it been that dangerous sense of recognition that had prompted her to behave with such reckless abandon? She did not know. All she knew was that she had almost made love with Lucas Ross and she could not quite believe what she had done.

Lucas was a servant. A footman, if his story was to be believed, but he had been far more than just a handsome face. He had been forceful, quick-witted and courageous. He had hidden his character well enough before the men and played the ignorant city boy, but she had known. Right from the moment she had first seen him, she had felt that he was different.

She had known that he was dangerous.

She shivered.

"Ma'am?" The door had opened and Galloway, the butler, was peering out, his face lined with worry. He had known where she had gone that night. All the servants knew. So did the entire village. Her involvement in whisky smuggling was the worst-kept secret in Kilmory. The only people who did not know were her own family, and that was because they knew nothing about who she really was and cared less.

"All's well."

The door yawned wider, yellow light spilling out into the night. It was time to become Lady Christina MacMorlan again.

Galloway locked and bolted the door behind her. "Thank goodness you are back, ma'am."

Christina paused to examine her reflection in the hall mirror. She did not look too bad; her hair looked a little windblown perhaps, and she had sand clinging to the hem of her velvet gown, but that was no surprise in this wild place. Her face was flushed and rosy. So was her throat. She remembered the delicious rub of Lucas's stubble against her skin. Fortunately she could pretend that the high color was the result of a cold breeze. It would be more difficult to explain away the stinging pink of her lips and the way they were swollen from Lucas's kisses. She prayed that the shadows in the hall would disguise much of the damage, since she would have a hard time explaining her exploits to her family. They saw her as passionless, almost sexless; efficient Christina who smoothed away all the little details of life that they did not want to trouble themselves with, a glorified housekeeper who kept home, family and clan together with never a word of complaint.

If only they knew.

For a moment she felt the echo of Lucas's kiss through her blood again, his hand at her breast. It was a very long time since she had been kissed, touched. She had not wanted passion in her life. It belonged to the past, to a part of time that she had closed off and sworn never to think about again. Now, though, with the memory of Lucas's touch, she felt restless, sleeping desire awakened again.

She repressed a shiver, turning away from the mirror, stripping off her gloves, removing her cloak.

"Is there a problem, Galloway?" she asked.

"Yes, my lady." The butler was shaking, and Christina was suddenly and forcibly reminded of his increasing age and infirmity. That was why it was essential that they should recruit a quick, intelligent younger man as footman to be Galloway's understudy. But not the man she had met tonight. Lucas Ross would have been ideal—strong, practical, clever—but she could not employ a man who had kissed her to within an inch of her life. Or one that would recognize her as the leader of the whisky gang—it could be disastrous.

"His Grace has lost his latest consignment of books from the Royal Society of Edinburgh," Galloway said. "He has turned the library upside down looking for them and is quite beside himself." A muffled crash from behind the library door gave emphasis to his words.

"I'll find the books," Christina said.

"Lady Semple went down to the kitchens to complain that dinner was burned," Galloway continued, "and now Cook is threatening to leave and you know we cannot get good staff out here in the middle of nowhere—"

"I'll smooth things over with Cook," Christina said. "And I will speak to Lady Semple." Her brother, the Marquess of Semple, and his wife, Gertrude, were the most demanding guests imaginable, always finding fault. They seemed to take pleasure in upsetting as many people as possible. It was the only sport they enjoyed.

"Lady Semple also mentioned that the water was cold again this morning, and Lord Semple complains of an icy draft in his bedroom," Galloway said.

"I draw the line at any involvement in my brother's marital affairs," Christina said. Then, when Galloway looked at her, uncomprehending, "Never mind, Galloway. I suppose the stove went out again?"

"Yes, ma'am," Galloway said. "It always blows out when there is a northwesterly."

Christina gave a sharp sigh. Kilmory was a fourteenth-century castle with a heating system almost as old. It was utterly inadequate to meet the needs of guests like the Semples, who insisted on the best of everything. For the past three years her father, with typical eccentric stubbornness, had insisted on making his home at Kilmory rather than at his main seat at Forres. When she had asked him why, he had muttered something about the wild, west-coast scenery inspiring his academic studies.

"Lord Lachlan—" Here Galloway paused, his mouth creasing into disapproving lines.

"Foxed again?" Christina said sympathetically. "I shall go up and throw a pitcher of water over him, or if that fails I will shoot him."

Galloway gave a thin smile. She was joking, but truth was it was a tempting option. Lachlan's wife, Dulcibella, had left him six months earlier, and he had spent almost the entire time since in an alcoholic stupor. Christina was out of patience with him.

There had been faults on both sides, but Lachlan had done nothing to try to heal the breach with his wife, who sat in her castle at Cardross telling anyone who would listen what a brute her husband had been to her.

Except...except that she couldn't shoot Lachlan, because she had dropped her pistol. She had dropped it when Lucas had kissed her, and until now the memory of that kiss had sent it completely from her mind. She felt a sickening, sinking feeling. Lucas would not have forgotten. She was willing to bet that even now her beautiful engraved brass pistol was in his possession.

It was one more reason to be rid of him. If he dared show his face at Kilmory tomorrow—and somehow she suspected that Lucas Ross would dare a great deal—she would pack him off back to Edinburgh even if she had to put him in a coach herself.

Galloway was waiting, watching her. His eyes looked tired. She wanted to send him to his rooms to rest, but she knew he would refuse. There was always more work to do.

"Any other problems, Galloway?" Christina asked.

"No, ma'am," the butler said gratefully.

Christina nodded. "You are interviewing for the new footman tomorrow," she said. "I have had word that one of the candidates, Mr. Lucas Ross, is...unsuitable. I would ask that you do not offer him the job."

A shade of hauteur came into Galloway's manner. He stood up a little straighter. "Ma'am?"

Christina knew she was trespassing. The running of the servant's hall was entirely the business of Galloway and the housekeeper, Mrs. Parmenter. By interfering she was implying that she thought them incompetent. At this rate Galloway would be the next to resign.

"I want to make sure that any new staff will fit in here at Kilmory," she said carefully. "My father grows ever more eccentric, as you know, and I would not want anyone to upset the balance of his health."

"His Grace need have nothing to do with a new *footman*." Galloway was stiff with outrage at the thought of the duke lowering himself so far. "I am sure that you may trust my judgment in choosing the appropriate candidate, Lady Christina."

"Of course," Christina said, sighing. "I beg your pardon, Galloway." She knew better than to press the matter now, with Galloway already standing on his dignity. Tomorrow she would make the point again and he would listen.

"Mr. Bevan requests a meeting tomorrow morning, ma'am," Galloway said, referring to the duke's land agent. "He says that there are a number of issues he needs to discuss with you."

"I'll see him at eleven o'clock," Christina said. "In the study."

Galloway nodded. The tension had eased from his face. "Thank you, my lady." He took her cloak and gloves. "I will fetch the supper tray."

The clock on the landing chimed ten-thirty with a delicate sweetness. They kept country hours at Kilmory Castle, with dinner at six. The duke preferred it. The ritual of the supper tray had been enshrined in family tradition since Christina's childhood, after which everyone retired early. It gave Christina the perfect opportunity for smuggling business when everyone else was abed.

Christina smoothed the skirts of her velvet gown. She could not go into the drawing room with damp sand on her hem. Gertrude, gimlet eyed and sharp of tongue, would be sure to notice. She should have changed before she went out to meet the gang, but the message had been so urgent that she had not wanted to delay and give the men a chance to do something violent, something they might later regret.

She shuddered. She hated violence, hated the sudden, vicious cruelty of it and the pleasure men seemed to take in it sometimes. All her life she had been caring for people, nurturing them and protecting them, whether it was her younger siblings or the wider family or what was left of the Forres clan. It was the reason she had become involved with the Kilmory smugglers in the first place. She had seen the ruthless exploitation of the revenue officers, imposing exorbitant taxes on families who were already barely scraping a pittance from their lands. Such exploitation infuriated her, and she had been fired with the need to protect them. No one had listened to her conventional protests; she was a woman and women should not meddle in politics and economics, or so she had been told in the politest possible terms when she had written to the government to complain. She had seen that the case was hopeless and only direct action would succeed and so with her usual practicality she had set about organizing the smugglers into a ruthlessly efficient band who could run rings around the excisemen. It was her fault that occasionally these days they could be a little too ruthless.

The drawing room door opened and Gertrude swept out. Small and vigorous, Christina's sister-in-law gave the impression of attacking anything and anyone who had the misfortune to get in her way. Behind her trailed Christina's niece, Lady Allegra MacMorlan. Allegra, at eighteen, had all the MacMorlan good looks but drooped with boredom and lack of purpose. Gertrude spoke of marrying her daughter off during the Edinburgh winter season. Allegra showed as little interest in that ambition as she did in anything else. Christina wondered what it was Allegra did feel a passion for. She was sure there must be something.

"There you are!" Gertrude said disagreeably. "You look as though you have been pulled backward through a hedge." Her sharp gaze traveled over her sister-in-law, itemizing the damage done by the sand, the wind and Lucas's kisses. "In fact, you look quite absurdly wild, considering that you have only been strolling in the gardens. This is why I never allow Allegra to walk anywhere at all. It is very damaging to the complexion."

"Very true," Christina said. "However, I am far too old to pay any consideration to such matters."

"At your age, the damage is already done," Gertrude agreed. "Now, I have a task for you. You need to sack the second housemaid. She has been making eyes at Lachlan and, given the parlous state of his marriage to Dulcibella, I do not doubt that with the least encouragement he will run off with her."

"I'd rather sack Lachlan," Christina said. "He is a great deal less use than Annie is. Where would I find another housemaid? It is difficult enough to get servants out here in the back of beyond."

"You have a most inappropriate sense of humor, Christina," Gertrude said frostily. "I quite despair of you."

"I will speak to Annie," Christina said with a sigh. "But I am sure that you are mistaken, Gertrude."

Gertrude looked contemptuous. "You are as naive as Allegra," she snapped. "You never see what is going on under your nose."

"Apparently not," Christina agreed smoothly. "Would you excuse me, Gertrude? I need to change out of these clothes before supper."

The rattle of the approaching supper tray sent Gertrude back into the drawing room. Allegra slipped away upstairs ahead of Christina, fading into the shadows at the top of the stairs like a wraith. Christina followed her niece more slowly. At the top she paused beside the statue of Hermes that her father had brought back from his Grand Tour. She barely ever noticed it. All the MacMorlan castles were littered with statuary. Her father was a collector in many ways—works of art, academic papers and classical sculpture. Hermes had been a part of the furniture for as long as Christina could remember, and not a part that she particularly admired. She found herself looking at the statue now, though, comparing the cold marble perfection of the high, slanting cheekbones and the sculpted power of the musculature with Lucas Ross's living, breathing masculinity.

She felt heat uncurl low in her belly and turned away hastily, aware that Allegra had paused outside her room and was watching her. She was not sure what was showing on her face; hopefully not an expression that her niece would recognize or understand. As the door closed softly behind Allegra, Christina walked slowly past and into her own bedchamber. It looked as old and familiar as ever, yet she felt different, dissatisfied in a way she could not quite pinpoint, as though she was hankering after something she had forgotten she wanted. Once, a long time ago when she was a young girl, she had been wild. Wanton, Gertrude would have called it. No one had known; no one would even believe it to see the staid creature she had become.

Yet meeting Lucas had stirred those desires to life again, wicked, outrageous, delicious desires, desires she had denied herself because they belonged to a time in her life that had concluded now. For a moment she remembered that time and the way it had ended, and she felt the chill sweep through her and she shuddered. She would not open herself up to pain ever again, because next time that pain could destroy her.

CHAPTER THREE

THE INTERVIEW WAS progressing very much to Lucas's satisfaction. Galloway, the butler, seemed quietly impressed by his excellent references, his willingness to work hard and his respectful manners. Mrs. Parmenter, the housekeeper, seemed to admire his powerful physique. Lucas had caught her staring at his calves and hoped it was only to assess how good he would look in formal livery. He was not sure her interest was impersonal, though. Mrs. Parmenter had a gleam in her eyes that was quite at odds with the respectable image of the traditional housekeeper.

There had been a couple of other candidates for the job, but he was convinced that he had the edge over them. Whether he could do all the work was another matter. He had had no idea that the role of footman was so complex. He had thought that all they did was adorn the back of a carriage, looking pretty, and run off with the lady of the house if they got the opportunity. It seemed he was very much mistaken. Fetching the coal, polishing the silver, cleaning boots and shoes, drawing the curtains, helping to serve the dinner—all those tasks would be a part of his job. It sounded fairly tedious but nothing he could not manage if he rose at five in the morning and retired at midnight.

"Are you experienced in folding a napkin into the shape of a water lily?" Mrs. Parmenter inquired.

"I am afraid not, ma'am," Lucas replied. The sorts of talents he possessed were of absolutely no use to him here. He had a flair for winning at cards, for example, and had made his first fortune at the gaming tables. He had made a second fortune through investment in a shipbuilding company that Jack Rutherford had established. He had other businesses, other investments. He had no skill in folding napkins.

Mrs. Parmenter's face fell. "But you are accustomed to serving dinner?" she pressed. "You are trained in the correct etiquette?"

"Of course, ma'am," Lucas said smoothly, in answer to the second question, at least. His etiquette had been learned in his stepfather's palace, although he had never been the one serving the dinner. In some ways his had been a gilded existence. But the trouble with gilt was that it tended to rub away leaving something ugly beneath.

Galloway shifted in his chair. It seemed that he had heard enough to be satisfied with Lucas's credentials and was moving on to give him some background on the establishment at Kilmory. Lucas listened attentively.

"We are a small establishment here despite being a ducal household," Galloway was saying. "Over the past few years His Grace has preferred to make his home here rather than at his main seat in Forres. It is smaller and also—"

"Cozier," Mrs. Parmenter intervened, shooting the butler a quick glance. "Kilmory is more... comfortable."

Lucas hoped he did not look as incredulous as he felt. If Kilmory was more comfortable than Forres then Forres must be practically uninhabitable. From what he had seen, half of Kilmory Castle was a ruin and the other half was medieval; a squat, ugly edifice that felt as though it had barely changed for centuries. Scotland had many beautiful castles. This was not one of them. Jack had been right about that.

What Jack had not known, though, was how much of a home Kilmory seemed to be. It had a welcoming warmth about it that was more important than superficial elegance. The room in which they were sitting, for example, probably the second-best drawing room, had charm in the slightly rickety chairs with their faded cushions. There was a vase of flowers bright on the mantel and several magazines and papers tossed carelessly on the table. Lucas read them upside down—the *Caledonian Mercury* from three weeks before, the *Lady's Monthly Museum,* the *Edinburgh Review.*

He wondered if it was in fact financial considerations that had led the duke to close Forres Castle. Kilmory would be cheaper to run. But that would be at odds with the reputation of the Duke of Forres as the richest peer in Scotland. Even so, it was worth investigation. A man would often pretend to riches when he lacked them, and it would be useful to know the truth of Forres's financial affairs in case he, too, were involved in the whisky trade.

"It is Lady Christina MacMorlan who runs the estate on behalf of her father," Mrs. Parmenter said. "In practical terms, she is the head of the household."

Lady Christina.

Lucas felt a flicker of elemental awareness along his skin. Christina MacMorlan. Was she the woman he had met the previous night? It was becoming increasingly likely. A woman who was capable of running an estate would have all the skill, efficiency and contacts to operate a whisky-smuggling ring. And if Mrs. Parmenter was right, then Lady Christina might not only run Kilmory but she might also have knowledge of what had happened to Peter. Lucas felt his pulse speed up and schooled his expression to polite indifference.

"It is the land agent who runs the estate," Galloway corrected. "It would not be appropriate for her ladyship to *work*."

Mrs. Parmenter gave a snort, quickly smothered. It was quite clear whom she thought did all the hard work at Kilmory. Lucas's interest in Christina MacMorlan sharpened.

"Speaking of work," Galloway added, with a repressive glance at the housekeeper, "we would require you to turn your hand to almost any task were you to come to work at Kilmory, Mr. Ross. Some footmen have ideas of what is beneath their station." His tone made it clear that such militant modern views were quite distasteful to him. "We are too small a staff here to tolerate such vanity."

"I would be happy to help with any task, Mr. Galloway," Lucas said.

Galloway nodded. He studied the papers lying on the table in front of him, frowning as though something was troubling him. Lucas was puzzled, but he couldn't work out what was holding Galloway back.

"Your testimonials are impeccable." The butler said slowly. "You are entirely suitable for the post."

Lucas inclined his head. Sidmouth's clerks had indeed done a good job in concocting a set of references that were strong and convincing without gushing too much.

"Excuse me," Galloway said abruptly. He gathered up his papers and strode from the room. Lucas caught Mrs. Parmenter's look. She smiled automatically at him, but there was uneasiness in her eyes. They chatted for a while about Edinburgh, where the housekeeper had relatives, but it was clear that she was distracted. After a couple of minutes she, too, excused herself hurriedly and went out.

Left alone, Lucas waited a moment and then stood up and trod cautiously across to the desk. The drawers were packed with account books for Kilmory going back several years. He did not bother to sift through them. He doubted that Lady Christina kept the recipe for distilling the peat-reek handily in her desk, still less anything that might link her and the whisky gang to Peter's death. If he was caught poking around the house at this stage it would look as though he was a thief and he would be thrown out.

He returned to his seat, stretching his long legs out in front of him, sitting back and allowing himself to appreciate the room's warmth and comfort. It felt very unlike the town house he possessed in Edinburgh. That was no more than a set of rooms, expensive rooms, elegant rooms, but with no character or heart. The very untidiness and lived-in quality of Kilmory attracted him, though he felt disconcerted to realize it. He had never in his life wanted somewhere that was more than simply a roof over his head.

Ten minutes passed. A suspicion started to seed itself in Lucas's mind. He was almost certain that Lady Christina MacMorlan was a step ahead of him. She had warned him off the previous night, but he suspected that she had also taken the precaution of warning Galloway not to employ him.

He got up and crossed quietly to the door. Mrs. Parmenter had left it ajar and Lucas pressed his ear to the gap. He could hear the faint sound of voices out in the hall. Galloway was speaking, urgent, agitated.

"Lady Christina, I must protest. There is nothing in Mr. Ross's application to suggest that he would be unsuitable for the job. On the contrary, he seems precisely the man we are looking for. I do not understand your objections, ma'am. You must see that I am in a dilemma—"

"I understand very well the difficulties of attracting suitable staff to Kilmory." Another voice, female, crisp, edged with authority. Lucas tried to work out if this was the woman from the previous night. He strained closer to the open door.

"In this instance I must ask you to accept my assurance, Galloway," he heard Lady Christina say. "I do not want Mr. Ross employed at Kilmory. I am sorry if that poses problems for you. Thomas Wallace will do the job just as well and his family needs the money. We must let Mr. Ross go."

The dust motes stirred, dancing in the shaft of sunlight from the window. Lucas stepped back hastily from the door as someone walked past. He caught a quick flash of damson muslin and a faint breath of perfume. It was the scent of bluebells. Recognition slammed through him and he only just managed not to push open the door and confront her.

By the time that Galloway and Mrs. Parmenter reentered the room, he had resumed his seat and turned a blandly innocent face toward them.

Galloway closed the door with a snap. Color high, he held out a hand to shake Lucas's. "Thank you, Mr. Ross," he said. "That will be all."

"Oh," Lucas said. Then, feigning a note of perplexity, "I was hoping to hear the outcome of my interview immediately..." He broke off. Galloway was looking as stiff as an old soldier. Mrs. Parmenter looked flustered and upset.

"Would you like me to wait for word at the Kilmory Inn?" Lucas asked.

"That won't be necessary, Mr. Ross." Galloway was shepherding him toward the door. "Thank you for your application. We are sorry that you have not been successful and we wish you well in the future." He sounded as though the words were stuck in his throat.

Score two to Lady Christina MacMorlan. Lucas's lips twisted into a rueful smile. She had trounced him last night and now she thought she was rid of him for good. He needed to raise his game.

Galloway escorted him out onto the front steps with the air of a man seeing him safely off the premises. It was a glorious early-summer day, the sky a radiant, cloudless blue, the wind from the sea carrying a hint of salt and with it the soapy scent of gorse. Across Kilmory's beautiful sweep of lawn, Lucas could see three figures standing in the shade of a vast cedar tree. One, gray-haired, slight and leaning heavily on a stick, he thought must be the Duke of Forres himself. He looked small, diminished in some way by his age. Lucas could see why it was his daughter who had a firm hand on the running of the estate.

The other two figures were women, one fair and slender, very young, the other woman older, tall and elegant in a gown of damson muslin. She had seen him and there was an air of sudden stillness about her as though she was holding her breath.

Lucas glanced at Galloway, who was waiting with an attitude of polite impatience to close the door behind him.

Without hesitation he set off across the broad swathe of grass to confront Lady Christina Mac-Morlan. Since he had nothing to lose, he might as well try blackmail.

CHAPTER FOUR

"WHO THE DEVIL is *that?*" Allegra asked.

Christina had been listening vaguely to her father's plans for a twenty-foot-high Italianate fountain in the middle of the lawn whilst simultaneously wondering what she might spare from the dairy to take on her visit to Mrs. McAlpine in the village that afternoon. The poor woman had just given birth to her sixth child—all boys—and her husband had died in a storm that had taken his fishing boat only eight weeks before. When Allegra stopped walking abruptly and stood staring across the grass toward the castle entrance, she practically tripped over her.

"Language, Allegra," Christina said automatically. She had known that having Lachlan around with his blunt conversation would be a bad influence. Gertrude would have the vapors if she heard her daughter speaking like an Edinburgh dandy. And that was another problem; Christina had no idea what she was going to do with Lachlan. He needed a swift kick up the backside to send him back to his wife instead of sulking here at Kilmory.

"Ladies do not use that phrase," she said. "It is shockingly vulgar."

"They use it when they see a sight like that," Allegra said. "Who *is* he?"

Following her niece's pointing finger, another sin against etiquette that Christina simply did not have the energy to correct, she saw the tall figure of a man framed in the castle doorway.

Lucas Ross.

Her heart began to race. Her breath felt tight in her chest. Suddenly the sun was too hot and too bright.

"Damnation," she said involuntarily.

Allegra giggled. "Aunt Christina! How shockingly vulgar."

"Sometimes," Christina said, "ladylike language simply isn't forceful enough to express one's feeling."

And staring at a man might also be improper, she thought, but there were times when it was impossible to resist. No man had the right to be as indecently handsome as Lucas Ross.

In the half-light of the smugglers' cave the night before, Lucas had looked spectacular enough with his strongly marked black brows, his firm cleft chin and tumbled black hair. There was something about him, an air of arrogant distinction that was innate but powerful, setting him apart from most other men. He had height and a broad-shouldered physique that exuded masculinity of the type Christina had never come across in the airless ballrooms or rarefied libraries of Edinburgh's academia. Her sisters' husbands both had something of that charisma and intensity. Christina remembered that she had looked at Lucy and Mairi and felt more than a little jealous of them. But now she thought that such ruthlessness, such uncompromising strength in a man would be too much to handle.

It seemed ludicrous that Lucas Ross was a servant. He was too tough, too in control to be at the beck and call of others. She pictured him more as a soldier, or a sailor, an adventurer, someone who gave orders rather than took them. He was a man born to lead, not follow. But she was being fanciful. A man could not choose his station in life, nor could he necessarily change it.

A shiver skittered down her spine. Lucas had descended the castle steps and was striding across the lawn toward them. He looked very purposeful, and she suddenly felt a desperate urge to run away. It was ridiculous, but even so the panic clogged her throat. He had not followed her instructions from the previous night. That should have told her something about the man he was and she should have thought twice before refusing to allow Galloway to appoint him.

Well, it was done now, and Lucas would simply have to accept it. She *was* the Duke of Forres's daughter and she did not expect to be confronted by a servant or be required to justify her decisions. All the same, as Lucas approached the three of them, the breath caught in her throat and she had to stop herself from pressing a hand against her bodice where her heart was tripping crazily, as though she had run too far, too fast.

Suddenly Lucas was standing directly in front of her. His physical presence was so powerful that

Christina took a step back even though there was nothing remotely threatening in his manner. Their eyes met. His were so brown they were almost black, dark as a winter's night beneath those straight black brows, his expression impossible to read. The rest of his face was equally daunting. There was no warmth or softness in it. It was all hard angles and darkness. He held Christina's gaze; she tried to look away and found that she could not. She was floored by the same physical awareness, fiercely intense, that had possessed her the previous night.

Then it was over, as though it had never been, and he bowed most elegantly.

"Lady Christina?" he said. His tone was deferential, in contradiction to the expression in his eyes, which was anything but respectful. "My name is Lucas Ross. I do not believe we have met, unless you have the advantage of me...." He let the words hang for a moment and Christina's heart gave a wayward thump.

He had recognized her. He knew she was the woman he had kissed the previous night.

She straightened her spine. "No," she said coldly. "I have not had that pleasure, Mr. Ross."

A spark of amusement gleamed in Lucas's eyes as though he was remembering just how pleasurable it had been, how she had melted in his arms, her lips opening beneath his as he had kissed her with heat and skill and passion. She felt a flash of that same sensual heat low in her belly. Damn him. The only thing she could do now was to act the aristocratic lady, disdainful, dismissive—even if cold was the very last thing she was feeling.

"This is very irregular," she said. "In what way may I help you, Mr. Ross?"

Lucas smiled, quick, appreciative. It transformed his whole face, giving it warmth for one brief moment.

"I applied for the footman's post," he said. "Unfortunately my application was not successful. I wondered if you would be good enough as to explain why?"

"The appointment of servants is Mr. Galloway's job, Mr. Ross," Christina said. "You would need to apply to him for an explanation. Now if you will excuse me—"

"But you were the one who refused to offer me the post," Lucas said. "I heard you tell Mr. Galloway not to appoint me."

There was a sharp silence, during which Christina ran through any number of unladylike epithets in her head. She had not realized that they had been overheard.

"I am sorry, Mr. Ross," she said eventually. "I am not in the habit of explaining my decisions to anyone."

The quizzical lift of Lucas's brows was very close to mockery. "I see," he said, and Christina blushed to realize quite how arrogant she had sounded. "But how am I to improve if you will not tell me the areas in which I am lacking?"

Galloway came puffing up at that moment. "Mr.

Ross! How dare you approach Lady Christina in such a ramshackle manner?"

"I meant no disrespect," Lucas Ross said. His gaze had not moved from Christina, and she felt her face heat. "I merely asked to know the reasons why my application was rejected. Do I not deserve that?" He spoke directly to Christina so that only she could see the hidden amusement in his eyes. She felt trapped, flustered. Lucas knew perfectly well why she had rejected him and she had a disturbing feeling that unless she changed her mind he would be quite prepared to share the reason with everyone. Allegra was looking from one to the other with speculation. Even the duke was looking mildly interested. As for Galloway, he was avid to know her reasons since she had refused to give him any.

She was not sure which was worse, the fact that Lucas could expose her as a whisky smuggler or the fact that he could disclose that the previous night he had tumbled her in the heather. The first might land her in jail and the second would ruin her reputation.

She was trapped.

"I expect," Allegra drawled, unexpectedly coming to her rescue, "that Aunt Christina rejected your application because you are too handsome, Mr. Ross." Her blue MacMorlan gaze was drifting over Lucas with undisguised appreciation. "My poor aunt has to consider the smooth running of the household, you know. Your looks would cause havoc below stairs and scandal above."

"Allegra!" Christina snapped, torn between relief and embarrassment at her niece's intervention.

"What?" There was a hint of childish petulance in the way that Allegra shrugged one slender shoulder. "You know it's true."

Lucas smiled easily. He addressed Christina rather than Allegra. "It has always been a terrible disadvantage to me to look like this, I confess."

Christina was almost tempted into an answering smile by his dry tone. "I am sure that your plight garners a great deal of sympathy, Mr. Ross," she said, equally drily. "It must be a terrible burden to be cursed with such good looks."

Appreciation sparked in Lucas's eyes. "Oh, it is. But I scarcely think that is the reason you dismissed me, Lady Christina. Do tell us your real explanation or I shall be obliged to speculate."

Christina took a deep breath. That was a clear threat and she was not going to be intimidated. Lucas Ross needed to understand that he could not expect to blackmail her into giving him a job.

"I think that would be a mistake, Mr. Ross," she said. "Think carefully before you say something you might regret."

Lucas's eyes danced, daring her to call his bluff. "Are you *afraid* of the truth, Lady Christina? Do you not want it to come out?"

The man was a scoundrel. He deserved all that was coming to him.

"Well," Christina said, injecting what she hoped was sincere regret into her tone, "I was thinking only of protecting *your* reputation, Mr. Ross, but as you are so monstrous persistent I can see that nothing but the truth will suffice." She took a deep breath. "I am afraid that there was a problem with one of your references."

She could see that Lucas had not been expecting this. A shade of wariness had come into his expression. Good. He was far too sure of himself.

"I was hoping not to have to raise this," Christina said, warming to her theme. "I imagine it is an uncomfortable topic for you, Mr. Ross...." She risked another glance at Lucas and saw that he was watching her with so much wicked amusement in those dark eyes now that she almost forgot what she was saying.

"On the contrary, Lady Christina," he murmured, "you find me positively agog to hear what you have to say."

"I am a little acquainted with one of your previous employers, Sir Geoffrey MacIntyre," Christina said. "Your reference from him was most generous— positively glowing. However—" she gave Lucas a look of limpid innocence "—I understood from him when we met last winter in Edinburgh that he had in fact sacked his footman for gross impropriety. I am therefore obliged to doubt the veracity of your references, Mr. Ross."

For a second Lucas looked completely taken aback and it gave her the most immense satisfaction. Then his lips twitched. "I do believe you are accusing me of faking my testimonials," he said.

"I would do nothing so crude as to accuse you of fraud," Christina corrected. "I merely point out that this raised some concerns in my mind."

"What sort of impropriety?" Allegra piped up. She was looking enthralled. "Did you run off with Lady MacIntyre, Mr. Ross? How wicked of you!"

"I am sure that Lady Christina will tell us precisely what impropriety I have committed," Lucas murmured. His gaze challenged her. "Well, Lady Christina?"

"I am afraid it was financial impropriety," Christina said solemnly. "I am sorry, Mr. Ross—" She flicked him a sympathetic look. "I imagine this is very difficult for you."

"It is not what I expected, certainly," Lucas said. "However I am afraid there has been a misunderstanding. I have never been accused of financial impropriety in my life. Perhaps you have confused me with another of Sir Geoffrey's footmen?"

"I doubt I could ever confuse you with anyone, Mr. Ross," Christina said, with perfect truth. "You have made sure of that."

Again she saw that flash of amusement in his eyes. "I am flattered to think so," he said.

"You should not be flattered," Christina said. "I hope you will understand, however, that no amount of…persuasion…will convince me to change my mind."

Their eyes met, cool blue and unreadable black. Christina could feel her heart racing. Then Lucas inclined his head. "I apologize," he said. "It was a misjudgment on my part." His tone had changed. It was respectful, practical. "I can offer other testimonials. The Duchess of Strathspey will vouch for me. She knows me well and will assure you of my honesty."

Christina raised her brows. "Are you giving *me* orders now, Mr. Ross?"

Lucas smiled again. It was difficult to resist that smile. It was so wicked it made her feel quite hot all over.

"Merely a suggestion," he murmured.

Then, unexpectedly, the duke spoke. Christina had almost forgotten that he was there. He had been staring vacantly out across the gardens as though his mind had been fixed on his latest academic project or ridiculous architectural design, but now his pale blue gaze swung back to focus on her. He smiled benignly.

"Hemmings and Grant need help in the gardens, my dear. Some sort of assistant, an under gardener, what?" He turned to Lucas. "You'd be ideal, young fellow. Since my daughter don't seem to want you in the house, you'd be better off outside."

"Papa!" Christina was mortified, torn between fury that her father was undermining her and embarrassment that he made Lucas sound of no more account than the horses in the stables.

"Thank you, Your Grace." Lucas accepted swiftly, undermining her further. "I would be delighted to accept."

"Good, good," the duke said absentmindedly.

"You'll find Hemmings in the hothouses. He'll tell you what to do."

"Papa," Christina said again. "You cannot simply appoint Mr. Ross as under gardener on a whim!"

The duke turned his pale blue myopic eyes on her. "Why not? It's my garden." He sounded like a spoiled child.

Christina repressed another sharp retort. It was only her father's estate when he decided on impulse that he wanted to do something. The rest of the time, when he was closeted with his academic papers, it was very much her responsibility.

"I know that both Mr. Hemmings and Mr. Grant are elderly and need some assistance in the gardens," she said carefully. "But Mr. Ross applied for a job as a footman. He is not qualified—"

"He looks qualified to me," the duke said irritably. "How difficult can it be?"

"I am most grateful, Your Grace," Lucas said, ignoring Christina's fierce frown. "I am very eager to acquire a job at Kilmory and am happy to take whatever is on offer."

"Splendid, splendid," the duke said, beaming again. He slapped Lucas on the shoulder and strolled off toward the house.

Christina shut her mouth with a snap. She could see Lucas's lips twitching as he tried not to laugh. She was neatly outmaneuvered.

"Well, then," she said, masking her irritation. "As the duke quite rightly said, you will find Mr.

Hemmings in the glasshouse, Mr. Ross. He will give you instructions on your work and find you a place to live. The outdoor servants have accommodation in the stables cottages, but they take their meals in the servants' hall." She waved a dismissive hand. "Mr. Galloway can advise you on anything else you need to know. Galloway—" she turned to the butler "—pray send to Strathspey Castle to request a reference for Mr. Ross from the Duchess of Strathspey."

"Ma'am." The butler bowed, stiff and proper again. His tightly pursed expression suggested that he absolutely deplored this turn of events. Christina shared his feelings but she knew there was no point in objecting. The duke liked to think that he was head of the household and could be very stubborn when contradicted.

"Thank you, my lady," Lucas said. "Mr. Galloway."

"How diverting this has been," Allegra said. "Welcome to Kilmory, Mr. Ross."

"Allegra," Christina said, her patience hanging by the thinnest thread, "is it not time for your pianoforte practice? Mr. Ross—" she turned to Lucas "—a word, if you please."

Allegra gave an exaggerated sigh and strolled off across the grass with one last, provocative glance over her shoulder at Lucas, who ignored her. His gaze was fixed firmly on Christina. She had never in her life been the focus of so much masculine attention. It unnerved her; her mouth dried.

"More mutual blackmail, Lady Christina?" Lucas asked lazily, when everyone was safely out of earshot. His voice was low and intimate. "Financial irregularities…most imaginative. I do congratulate you."

"Let me offer you some advice, Mr. Ross," Christina said briskly. "Last night I gave advice and you chose to ignore it. This time I suggest you think very carefully before you do the same. If you do not wish your time at Kilmory to be cut short, I counsel you not to put a foot wrong. You will behave with absolute decorum. Is that clear?"

"As crystal," Lucas said.

"You will not speak of last night," Christina continued.

"What aspect of last night?" Lucas queried.

"Any aspect of it," Christina said shortly. "We will never mention it again. And," she added, "I would like my pistol back, if you please."

"Of course, ma'am," Lucas said.

"Thank you," Christina said. "Good day to you, Mr. Ross."

She did not look back as she walked across the lawn to the house but she was certain that Lucas was watching her.

Trouble, trouble, trouble.

She did not need a crystal ball to see that Lucas Ross was very bad news indeed. She was not entirely sure what he was—other than dangerous—but she had a bad feeling that she was going to find out.

LUCAS RELEASED THE breath he had been holding in a long, silent sigh.

So that was what his lady smuggler looked like. He had known from the moment she had walked past him in the castle that she was the woman he had met the previous night. As soon as he was close to her, the recognition, the awareness between them, snapped into life.

He watched Christina walk away across the lawn. She did not look back. Lucas grinned. Of course she did not, although he was willing to wager that she burned to turn around and check if *he* was watching *her*.

He was. He could not take his eyes off her. He watched her all the way to the house. She did not hurry, but she did tilt her parasol back to block his view of her face. He would swear that was deliberate and nothing to do with the angle of the sun. The parasol was made of spotted damson muslin and trimmed with lace to match her gown. It looked frivolous but she was not a frivolous woman. Everything about her, from her height to her authoritative manner spoke of cool, calm competence.

He estimated that she was about a half dozen years older than he, not a grandmother, but not a debutante, either. He could see now why people might overlook her, because most people judged on appearance and Christina MacMorlan did nothing to enhance hers. Her hair was shades of brown, coiled into a no-nonsense bun in the nape of her neck. She dressed plainly. A man could make the mistake of thinking her features were unremarkable. Yet Lucas could see they were not. Her skin was flawless, pale cream and pink rose, a true Scottish complexion, scattered with endearing freckles. Her blue eyes had a sleepy gaze that was both misleading and sensual. When she had looked him in the eyes he had felt the impact like a punch through his whole body. But it was her mouth that was so potent, full and lush, reminding Lucas of her kisses. He shifted slightly. He found Christina MacMorlan ridiculously seductive and he was quite at a loss as to why that should be the case. But it might be useful. Christina's was quite evidently the hand that steered the Kilmory estate whilst her father dabbled in whatever outlandish project took his fancy on any particular day. She was also the leader of the whisky smugglers, and he was convinced now that they had had a direct involvement in Peter's death.

Over to the west, beyond the clipped hedges of the parterre, he could see the Duke of Forres wandering through the rose garden. He appeared to be talking to the plants, which was a curious thing to do. Lucas watched as the duke strolled over to the sundial in the middle of the garden and leaned over to check the time. It was quite clear that the man was an eccentric, in a world of his own. Lucas thought it unlikely that the duke was aware of anything that went on in his household, let alone that his eldest daughter ran a smuggling gang.

He had been lucky that the duke had offered him the job. Lady Christina certainly would not have yielded to his blackmail. The minute he had applied a little pressure she had come back with plenty more of her own. It was an unfortunate coincidence that Sidmouth's clerk had given him Sir Geoffrey MacIntyre as a reference when Lady Christina was acquainted with the man. But actually he doubted everything that Christina had said and suspected she had made up the entire tale of financial impropriety simply to be rid of him.

His lips twisted in wry appreciation. It would not do to underestimate Lady Christina MacMorlan. She was strong, determined and clever, more than a match for him.

She would be entirely capable of covering up a murder.

He had to remember that and not let the fierce attraction he had to Christina MacMorlan cloud his judgment.

He watched the front door close behind her. He was forgotten. A small smile touched his lips at the lordly way in which the duke's daughter had dismissed him. It would be useful if she considered him beneath her notice. Servants were meant to be invisible; he could go about his investigation whilst remaining unobserved.

Beyond the tall pine trees that bordered the terrace he could see the corner of a building and the glitter of the sun on long glass windows. That must be the hothouse where he would find Hemmings, the head gardener. Being outside, laboring in a physical job was far preferable to him than being

CHAPTER FIVE

Damnation.

Christina loved her father, but there were times when she could happily wring his neck, and this was one of them. She closed the door of her private parlor behind her with exaggerated calm and sank down into her favorite armchair. For a moment she closed her eyes and breathed deeply, inhaling the scents of wax polish and roses mingled with the faint smell of dust and the ashes in the grate. It was quiet, reassuring. For a little while she felt soothed, comfort flowing through her and easing her tense muscles. Then she remembered Lucas's smile—and the fact that he was now a member of the staff at Kilmory Castle, which was precisely the outcome she had not wanted.

She opened her eyes and blinked, rubbing her forehead where the beginnings of a headache stirred. She told herself that it did not matter; Lucas was clearly very keen to have a job at Kilmory. He would do nothing to put that at risk.

She was a fool to think he'd risk his future by kissing her again. Lucas Ross was a great deal younger than she was and sinfully handsome. Of course he would not be attracted to an old maid. Their passionate encounter the night before had been driven by a wild relief and the vivid excitement of being alive. Now, in the cold light of day, everything was different, and she should welcome that because lust, passion, held no place in her life.

There were no mirrors in her parlor. In fact, when they had moved to Kilmory Castle, she had removed several of the ancient speckled pier glasses from the walls because she did not want to see her reflection forever staring back at her. She knew what she looked like: a thirty-three-year-old spinster in elegant but not particularly modish gowns whose hair was neither auburn nor brown nor blond but some sort of mixture of all three, whose eyes were pale blue and fanned by fine lines that grew less fine and more deep as the years passed, whose complexion had lost its youthful sparkle and whose chin was already showing signs of sagging. In fact, everything was showing signs of sagging, as it did with age. She had no illusions, and before the previous night she had had no desire to look any different. Her appearance had been almost irrelevant to her. Her sisters were the beautiful ones.

Now, though, Lucas's youth and vitality made her keenly aware of the passing years. She felt old and faded, and ashamed of feeling so fierce an attraction to him. She knew that her late mother's dearest friend, Lady Kenton, would laugh at her for such scruples. Lady Kenton firmly believed that a view was there to be admired. But Christina did not want to feel anything for Lucas. She did not want to feel anything for any man. It was too risky. She, who took risks with her life and her personal safety every day when it came to outwitting the revenue officers, was too scared to risk her heart again.

A politely deferential knock at the door roused her. It must be Mr. Bevan, the land agent, early for their meeting. But before Christina could call him in, the door opened and Galloway poked his head in.

"I beg your pardon, ma'am, but Mr. Eyre is here to see you."

Christina felt a sharp stab of alarm. Mr. Eyre was the exciseman, the government's tax collector, who hounded the local families mercilessly for every last penny they owed. Possessed of a zealous desire to drain every drop of revenue from Kilmory's farmers and villagers, he had threatened to arrest the illegal whisky distillers and see them hang.

"Please tell Mr. Eyre that I have an appointment in ten minutes and cannot spare him the time—" she began, only for Eyre to shoulder his way past Galloway and barge into the room.

"This won't take long, Lady Christina." He was a big man, florid, with small gray eyes in a fleshy face. His gaze darted about the room as though checking to see that she had not concealed an illegal whisky still beneath the table. "Still consorting with criminals and smugglers, I hear."

"I *beg* your pardon?" Christina's voice dripped ice.

Eyre, however, was not a man to be intimidated.

He thrust his hands into his pockets and rocked back on his heels, smiling. "I saw you entering Mrs. Keen's cottage yesterday. Her son was arrested for illegal distilling back last year—"

"Which is one of the reasons why I visit her." Christina did not trouble to hide her dislike. "She is an elderly woman, in poor health, alone in the world, who has little income and who has been persecuted unforgivably by the authorities."

Eyre snapped his fingers. "She should not have harbored a known criminal, then."

Christina could feel her temper rising. She knew that Eyre deliberately set out to anger her; he had been an enemy ever since she had written to Lord Sidmouth to complain about his methods and his corruption. It was always a struggle not to rise to his provocation.

"Was there a point to your visit, Mr. Eyre?" she inquired politely.

"Indeed." The excise officer's eyes gleamed. "I am here to introduce my nephew, Richard Bryson, my sister's boy, who has come to help me hunt down the malefactors who plague our area. I am confident that with his help and the other resources granted to me by Lord Sidmouth, we shall soon have the Kilmory Gang behind bars."

"How gratifying for you," Christina said. She had not seen the younger man who was hovering in his uncle's shadow, but now he came forward into the room and made a bow.

"At your service, Lady Christina."

This was a very different man from his uncle. He was young, surely no more than twenty, slight and fair, with dreamy brown eyes and the hands of a musician. His bow was elegant; he could have stepped from an Edinburgh drawing room. His uncle was looking at him with ill-concealed contempt. Christina wondered how on earth the two of them could possibly work together and why a man like Richard Bryson would want to take on the dirty task of the excise officers. But perhaps he had no choice. She thought of Lucas Ross again and how inappropriate it was that he was a servant. A man had to earn a living, no matter how incongruous it might seem or how ill suited to it he might be.

"I wish you success in your career, Mr. Bryson," she said. She gave his uncle a cool smile. "If you will excuse me…"

As Galloway ushered the gentlemen out, she wondered at Eyre. There was not a courteous bone in his body. His visit had been for quite another purpose, to warn her, perhaps, of his intent to increase his efforts at trapping the whisky smugglers. He suspected her of more than sympathy toward the smuggling gang.

Christina shivered. His visit had been a threat. Of that there was no doubt. She was going to have to be very careful indeed.

THE SUMMER LIGHT was fading as Lucas left the servants' hall to stroll back to his tiny cottage in the castle grounds. Dinner had been delicious, a rich lamb stew with dumplings that had been just what he had needed after working up an appetite digging over the flower beds. He had been at Kilmory for three days and already he was settling in to the routine of his work. It was physically hard but not challenging in other ways; he simply had to keep his head down, watch, listen and not put a foot out of line.

The servants were wary of him. A stranger who looked and sounded as though he should be serving tea in an Edinburgh drawing room rather than digging up root crops in the Highlands was bound to be treated carefully. Word had gone round of his failure to obtain the footman's post—a boy called Thomas Wallace looking shiny and scrubbed in his new livery was proudly sitting in the footman's chair. There was a whiff of uncertainty about Lucas's background that he chose not explain, though the reference from the Duchess of Strathspey that had arrived that afternoon had helped to soothe any concerns. Galloway at least was now treating him as though he was less likely to steal the silver.

Lucas was quite happy for people to think him dour and uncommunicative, though he had stayed to share the pot of tea after dinner when jackets were loosened and conversation warmed up a little. From this he had learned something of the family, which, whilst not directly useful to his work, was still interesting. Angus, the heir to the dukedom, was generally disliked as a bully. His wife, Gertrude, was actively hated for her interfering ways. Everyone shook their heads when Lachlan's name was mentioned. He had a problem with drink, Lucas heard, and also with his wife, a she-devil called Dulcibella who held the purse strings and was shriller than a Glasgow costermonger. Mention of the duke made them smile with exasperation. But Christina was loved. Their affection for her was simple and powerful and it took Lucas aback. As he strolled back through the castle grounds he wondered what Christina had done to earn their loyalty.

When he reached the relative privacy of the gardeners' cottages he took from his pocket the letter that Galloway had passed to him after dinner.

"From the Duchess of Strathspey herself," Galloway had said, with a mixture of respect and disapproval, as though Lucas should have been far too lowly for a duchess to take notice of him.

Lucas let himself inside and unfolded the letter to read. He did not light a lamp; instead, he tilted it to catch the last flare of twilight.

"Lucas," his aunt had written in her forthright manner.

What on earth is going on? I have written you a glowing reference—naturally—but would appreciate some sort of explanation of your new interest in horticulture. Have you lost all your money? Are you really working as an under gardener to the Duke of Forres? Could you not do better than that? Please try to remember you are my nephew—and a prince, for that matter—and aim a little higher.

She had signed off with her usual strong black flourish.

Lucas grinned. He had known that his aunt would not let him down. He knew she was no snob, either. And he did owe her an explanation.

He took out a pencil from his pocket and scrawled back:

Thank you, ma'am. I am in your debt, as always. Business brings me to Kilmory, but I find it more useful for the time being to keep that business a secret, hence the role of gardener. I can only hope that I do not inadvertently kill off the entire ducal flower garden in the process.

He signed it and placed it under the chipped enamel jug on the dresser. Tomorrow he would contrive an errand to Kilmory Village and find a carter to take it to Strathspey. He did not want to send it from the castle. That was too dangerous.

He went through to the inner of the cottage's two rooms and threw himself down on the narrow iron bedstead. His aunt was no fool; she had known of Peter's death and she would work out quickly enough what he was doing at Kilmory. She would not approve. He doubted she would give him away, but no doubt like Jack Rutherford she would also think it a fool's errand, that because of his grief he was unable to accept Peter's death and let the matter go.

The duchess would laugh to see him now, he thought as he stared up at the pallor of the whitewashed ceiling. His surroundings were neither princely nor palatial, two rooms, this one with a wooden chest and a heather-stuffed mattress and the other with a table, two chairs, a dresser and a few other sticks of furniture. Outside there was a stone sink for washing. It was a far cry indeed from his grandfather's palace. Still, it was clean and dry. Someone had made nice curtains and matching patchwork cushions that sat rather daintily on the upright chairs. There were a couple of rag rugs on the flagstone floor. Lucas wondered who had gone to the trouble of furnishing the place, making it appear as though they cared enough for their servants to see them comfortable.

He thought of Christina MacMorlan. He had promised Jack that he would not involve her in this business but that was before he had learned that she was already involved up to her neck. And she had something he needed. Information.

He felt no stirring of conscience. Conscience was something that rarely troubled him. In general he was comfortable with the decisions he made and this was no exception.

It would not hurt to take advantage of Lady Christina's attraction to him. She had been all that was starchy and proper on the surface, but even so she had not been quite able to hide the fact that she was drawn to him. That was good; he would exploit that attraction to learn what he could. He would use her.

He slept well that night.

CHAPTER SIX

"I SAY," LADY Allegra MacMorlan drawled, propping herself against the stone window embrasure in the parlor and gazing out at the garden, "what an absolutely splendid view."

"Kilmory always looks beautiful on a summer morning," Christina agreed, without looking up from the letters she was reading. Breakfast was over; there had only been four of them present. The duke had not yet risen for the day and Gertrude preferred to take breakfast in bed.

Angus and Lachlan had already gone out to the stables with some plan of taking an early-morning ride. Christina hoped Lachlan would be able to stay in the saddle. He had drunk himself into a stupor the night before and had been bleary-eyed and unshaven at breakfast. His valet had resigned the previous week when Lachlan had thrown a jug of water at him, and since then there had been no one to attend him. Christina hated to see the way Lachlan was spiraling into despair, perennially angry, short of money, unhappy, but she did not know how to help him.

"I'm not talking about the view of the sea," Allegra said, half turning toward her and pointing a languid hand in the direction of the lilac walk. "I'm talking about *this* view."

With a sigh Christina laid the letters down in the breakfast crumbs and went to join her niece at the window. It was another crystal clear morning. The sky was a deep, cloudless blue, the distant sea a darker ribbon on the horizon. Following Allegra's inclination of the head, Christina's gaze drifted across the tall pines beyond the terrace, skipped over the obelisk sundial and came to rest on the naked torso of Lucas Ross as he reached up to prune the lilacs. His back, broad and muscular, was turned to them. The sun gleamed on his black hair.

Christina gave a little gasp. "Oh, my goodness!"

She watched the way Lucas reached up to cut the fading flowers away, wielding his shears, the muscles rippling in his wide shoulders. A pair of tattered trews clung to his lean hips. Below that his calves were bare, his feet thrust into worn boots.

"Allegra!" She came to her senses, not before time. "Avert your gaze!"

"Oh, I am averting it, Aunt Christina," Allegra said demurely. She ran her fingers over the edge of the window embrasure whilst taking another peek at Lucas from beneath her eyelashes. "Mr. Ross is certainly a fine figure of a man."

"He should not be flaunting himself about the place," Christina said crossly. She turned away and made an elaborate business of picking up her half-empty cup from the table and refilling it.

"Perhaps you should make him tend the garden in full Forres livery," Allegra said, giggling. She was as sweet and pink in the face as a full-blown rose. Christina felt a vicious wave of envy for her niece's youth and prettiness, and a second later a pang of shame for her envy.

"Suddenly the idea of running off with one of the servants takes on some appeal," Allegra said. "Wouldn't *that* annoy Mama? It is almost worth doing for that reason alone, although I confess Mr. Ross's luscious looks are a tremendous incentive, as well."

"I doubt you would enjoy living on a gardener's salary of twelve shillings a week," Christina said shortly. She had not spoken to Allegra about her flirtatious banter with Lucas on the day he had arrived, hoping that her niece's butterfly mind would have moved on to something else.

"Romance so seldom survives the hard realism of economics," Christina said. "You should think about that."

Allegra looked baffled. "Twelve shillings a week? I spent more than that on my last bonnet."

"Then you would bankrupt your husband before the ink was dry on your marriage lines," Christina said. "Democracy in love may seem very appealing when it looks like that—" she nodded at Lucas's figure "—but it would soon lose its gloss."

"You have not a drop of romance in your soul, Aunt Christina," Allegra said. Her mouth drooped sulkily.

"I'm a pragmatist," Christina said. She stifled a smile. Allegra, her parents' only child, had been spoiled and her every whim indulged. If she saw something she wanted, she saw no need to deny herself, and forbidding her something simply made her more obstinate. Pointing out the hard financial facts of a situation succeeded far better.

"Well." Allegra brightened. "At least the view is free. I shall take a walk in the gardens. It will be good for my health." She whisked out of the room.

Sighing, Christina went to fetch her parasol and shawl. Someone had to go out and tell Lucas to put some clothes on. It was indecorous for him to be seen in such a state of undress. With good fortune she should be able to find Mr. Hemmings and ask him to instruct his assistant in proper behavior. That way she would not need to go near a seminaked Lucas herself.

Luck, however, was not on her side. Mr. Hemmings was not to be found in the hothouses or the potting sheds. Scanning the gardens, Christina could not see him along any of the walks. She was going to have to tackle Lucas Ross's indecent appearance entirely on her own.

Lucas had his back turned and did not appear to hear her footsteps on the gravel. He was humming beneath his breath as he worked, a folk song with a lilting cadence that did not sound Scottish. In his deep baritone it was very attractive. Christina paused for a moment, listening to the music, watching the grace and economy with which he worked and the sheen of the sun on his skin. When she realized that she had been staring for far longer than was appropriate, she cleared her throat. Lucas did not turn. He seemed lost in thought so she put out a hand and tentatively touched his bare arm. It felt warm and smooth. Her fingers seemed to tingle from the contact.

Lucas spun around. "Lady Christina."

The front view, Christina thought, was even more spectacular than the back. His chest was broad and deep. His scruffy trews rode low on his hips, and a line of silky black hair led down from his navel. Christina's throat turned dry. All manner of inappropriate images flashed through her head. She wanted to press her lips to the hot skin of his stomach, to trace the line of those hip bones down...

Lucas sketched a bow and reached with what seemed unnecessary slowness for his shirt, shrugging it over his head.

"I apologize that you found me shirtless," he said. "It is already a hot day."

"I am glad that you realize that it is inappropriate for you to flaunt yourself in such a state of undress, Mr. Ross," Christina said. She knew she sounded ridiculously pompous, but it was the only defense she could muster. "And I did not find you like this by accident. I saw you from the parlor window."

Lucas raised one dark brow. "So you saw me undressed and came especially to find me," he murmured.

"Yes," Christina said. "No! My niece—" She

broke off, feeling flustered. Already he was provoking her, twisting her meaning, making her say things she did not intend.

"You appear to have very little idea of proper behavior, Mr. Ross," she said. "It is most unseemly for you to remove your shirt even on a hot day. We have standards here at Kilmory and we expect our servants to adhere to them." She stopped. Lucas had reached for the stone bottle that was standing on the wall beside him. Keeping his eyes on her face, he tilted it to his lips. Christina watched his throat move as he took a long swallow.

"It is also unseemly," Christina said, "to drink whilst I am speaking to you!"

"I beg your pardon." There was a spark of amusement in Lucas's eyes now. "I should, of course, have offered it to you first." He wiped the top of the bottle and held it out to her.

"No, thank you," Christina said, putting her hands behind her back.

"You do not care for ale? It is very refreshing on a hot day."

Christina was feeling hot, too. Prickles of annoyance and awareness were running up and down her spine.

"Mr. Ross," she said. "I do believe you deliberately misunderstand me. Must I spell it out? It is not appropriate for you to go around half-naked. Nor is it appropriate for you to drink ale whilst I am addressing you. Or, indeed, any beverage," she added hastily. "Finally, it is not your place to offer me a drink."

"Under no circumstances?" Lucas queried.

"None!" Christina said.

"Even if you were dying from thirst?"

"The situation would not arise," Christina snapped. "Mr. Ross, you are being deliberately provocative."

"I suppose that is forbidden, too," Lucas said. He was holding the bottle loosely between his long brown fingers, watching her. She knew that her haughty manner amused him and also that it did not overawe him in the least. There was nothing deferential in the way he was looking at her. On the contrary, there was something so bold and challenging that she found she was trembling a little.

"What are you waiting for?" she demanded, thoroughly ruffled.

"I am waiting for you to dismiss me back to my work," Lucas said. "I assumed that was the correct behavior."

"You are dismissed," Christina said. Then, remembering that she had a question for him, "Oh, Mr. Ross—"

Lucas had already picked up the shears and was resuming his work. The wind caught the voluminous folds of his shirt, plastering them against his chest. The effect was no less unsettling that the sight of his naked torso had been.

"Lady Christina?" He stopped and looked at her quizzically. "How may I serve you?"

"Where is Mr. Hemmings?" Christina asked, ignoring the way he had deliberately phrased the question to goad her. "I expected to find him in the hothouse. The fruit espaliers are his pride and joy."

"Mr. Hemmings has the gout," Lucas said. "He is confined to his bed today."

"Poor man," Christina said. She wondered why Mrs. Parmenter had not told her about the gardener's worsening condition. She had not seen the house-keeper that morning but no doubt she would give her a full update later when they met to discuss the day's menus.

"I will take him some ice to relieve the swelling and some crocus extract," she said.

"Crocus?" Lucas cocked an eyebrow. "Mr. Hemmings will have a relapse if you dig up his bulbs."

Christina laughed. "The autumn crocus is sovereign against the gout. Thank you, Mr. Ross." She turned to leave.

"My lady—" Lucas touched her arm lightly, and she paused, very aware of him and the brand of his fingers against her skin.

"I wonder if you might show me the plans for the duke's grotto," Lucas said. "Mr. Hemmings asked me to do some work on it, but he is unable to show me exactly what needs to be done. If you would be so kind…"

Christina had no intention of being kind. There was no possible way she was going to be trapped in the drawing office with Lucas Ross. It was too small and he was too intimidating. She felt panicked at the mere thought.

"You need to speak to my father," Christina said. "Or perhaps Mr. Bevan, the land agent—"

"Neither gentleman can see me until later in the day," Lucas said. His voice fell. "Please, Lady Christina. I appreciate that you are busy. I need only five minutes of your time...."

"I..." Christina was looking for words of refusal but they seemed strangely elusive.

"Please." Lucas smiled again, warm and engaging. Christina felt hot and confused.

"Oh, very well," she said reluctantly, reflecting that Lucas seemed able to persuade her to almost anything. "But I can only spare a moment, and I know very little about the plans."

A disquieting gleam came into Lucas's eyes, and immediately she regretted agreeing. "Thank you, ma'am," he said.

He followed her along the path. Roses, weighed down with overnight rain, bowed across the gravel. Lucas held them aside for her with exemplary courtesy. She could not fault his manners now, and it felt strangely enjoyable to be treated with such care. Normally everyone assumed she could look after herself and so they never troubled to hold doors for her or give her their hand over stony ground. And, of course, she *was* eminently capable of taking care of herself but, oh, it was lovely for once to feel that someone was taking care of *her*. In fact, it was dangerously seductive, but she let the illusion wrap her about just this once.

The drawing office was in a corner of the old

courtyard. Here the original stables stood gaunt with roofs open to the sky and the timber beams exposed. Only the southern range had been repaired; it housed the carriage horses and Lachlan's and Angus's stallions.

"Do you ride, ma'am?" Lucas inquired, pausing to stroke the nose of Lachlan's bay as it stuck its head inquisitively over the door.

"No," Christina said. "I have no aptitude for riding. The estate is only small. I walk or take the pony trap." She watched Lucas run a hand down the stallion's neck. "You seem comfortable with horses, Mr. Ross. Have you worked with them?"

"I rode as a child, ma'am," Lucas said. His tone was short. His eyes were blank like a slammed door. Christina felt the unspoken rejection. He did not want to discuss his past. Well, that was fine. There was no reason why he should. Lucas's hand fell to his side. In silence they crossed the yard, their footsteps loud on the cobbles. He held the door of the drawing office open for her to enter. The room smelled stale and airless, of dust and old books. The dim light, after the brightness outside, made Christina's head swim a little. On the table a series of plans and maps of the gardens were pinned down beneath a long wooden ruler. Their edges fluttered gently in the breeze from the open door.

"Mr. Bevan, the land agent, has a larger office inside the castle," Christina said, "but he keeps all the current drawings here so that anyone working on the estate can consult them." She left the door open so that the sunshine spilled over the flagstones. "You are welcome to come here anytime, Mr. Ross, to view my father's designs for his Gothic garden."

"This is the plan for the grotto," Lucas said. He was resting one hand on the table, leaning forward, studying the pencil drawings on the top of the pile.

"Yes," Christina said. She sighed. "My father has fanciful ideas for creating a series of interconnecting chambers with a cascade and fountain. The interior is to be lined with shells and decorated with statuary and the exterior will be draped with ivy."

"You don't approve of his plans?" Lucas half turned to look at her.

"It's an expensive indulgence," Christina said.

To her surprise, Lucas smiled. "You don't approve of extravagance, Lady Christina? Do you think self-indulgence is a sin?"

He spoke quietly, with some emphasis on the word *sin*. The word sent a riot of sensual images galloping through Christina's mind, awakening all the lustful thoughts she had successfully repressed. She could feel her body turning hot again. She fought the sensation, thinking instead of Scottish winters and ice dripping down her neck, an image sufficiently uncomfortable to banish the most persistent of wanton dreams.

"There are a lot of demands on the ducal purse here at Kilmory." She could hear the stiffness in her tone. "Many families on the estate and in the village are desperately poor. Under the circumstances, fulfilling my father's fantasies is not a priority to me."

"But surely there can be a time and place to indulge a fantasy?" Lucas's soft words sent a shiver over her skin. In a second the image of pure, cold snow was overlaid with another, a great deal more heated, of bare, tangled limbs and smooth sheets and breathless lust.

Pushing aside the wayward thought, she ignored Lucas's comment and went up to the table. "You will see here that there is already a spring on the site," she said briskly. "The water needs to be channeled into a cascade, which forms a pool." She pointed to the plan and noticed that her hand was shaking a little. "The pool is already built, but the cascade is not."

"I can't imagine Mr. Hemmings having the strength to construct this," Lucas said. He had leaned in for a closer look, and a lock of black hair fell across his brow. As he raised a hand to push it back his sleeve brushed Christina's breast. She caught her breath. She could not help it. It was a tiny noise, but Lucas heard it. He straightened slowly. Suddenly there was no sound in the office but the thunder of her heartbeat in her ears and the sound of Lucas's breathing. She was acutely conscious of his nearness, the lean hardness of his body a mere hand's breadth from hers, his dark gaze narrowing on her face as a spark of something hot came into his eyes. In a flash she remembered the touch of his palm against her breast and the skillful stroke of his thumb over her nipple. She felt heat curl and twist in her stomach.

How long they stared at each other she had no idea. With a huge effort of will she broke the contact and looked down at the pencil drawings. They seemed to dance before her eyes, making no sense at all.

"A man from the village was employed to do the construction work." Her voice sounded husky. She cleared her throat, pressed on as though nothing had happened. "Unfortunately he was…arrested a few months ago and no work has been done on the grotto since. But now the weather has improved, perhaps you could begin again."

"What was his crime?" Lucas asked.

"Whisky smuggling." Christina met his eyes very straight. His gaze was dark, unreadable. "He was arrested by the excise officers," she said. "It was most inconvenient."

That wicked smile came into Lucas's eyes, making her feel even more as though she was trapped and could not breathe. "It must be an occupational hazard," he murmured. "Do you never fear the same fate yourself?"

He took a step toward her. Christina took one backward and felt the corner of the table press painfully into her hip.

"No," she said. "They will never catch me at the whisky still, and that is the only way I could be arrested. They cannot even *find* the whisky still, for that matter." She took a breath. "Mr. Ross, I do hope you are not still thinking about your experience the night you came to Kilmory. We agreed you should forget it—for the sake of your health, if nothing else."

Lucas was silent for a moment, his expression dark. "Those men were dangerous," he said.

"Which is precisely why you should forget it ever happened," Christina said. Her heart was suddenly banging hard against her ribs.

"Have they ever killed anyone?" Lucas asked.

"No," Christina said shortly. "When it comes to it, they are all kilt and no balls beneath." It was mostly true; the gang got restive sometimes, but she found it easy enough to talk sense into them under normal circumstances.

She saw Lucas's eyes light with amusement. "A descriptive phrase," he said, "but it didn't feel like that to me." His hand went to his side and Christina remembered the kicks to the ribs. She pulled a face. "I am sorry about that," she said. "Sometimes they do get a little carried away."

"Whereas you detest violence," Lucas said slowly, "which makes it all the more surprising that you should be mixed up in something like the smuggling."

Christina felt a pang of shock. He was too perceptive. It was disconcerting. "I don't know how you could possibly know that—" she began, before stopping and biting her lip. She barely knew this man, but it felt as though he could see right through her to all the secrets she kept hidden, all her deepest thoughts and feelings.

"I felt it," Lucas said. He had drawn closer to her. She had never felt more aware of anyone in her entire life. "That first night," he said. He did not take his gaze from her face. "When they were hurting me, you hated it. I sensed that in you, that absolute revulsion you had for violence."

Christina half turned away from him. She could not look at him. Her feelings felt too exposed. "I do hate it," she admitted. "I hate the way men turn to brutality sometimes to achieve what they want. I hate bloodlust and cruelty." She gave a little shiver. This felt dangerously personal and she had sworn to keep this man at arm's length. "Mr. Ross—as I said, it is best to forget it."

"All of it?" Lucas said. His tone brought her gaze back up to his and she felt another twist of heat and awareness flare inside her. She knew he was not talking about the smugglers now but of their encounter later by the churchyard.

"Yes," she said, ignoring the hot pulse of response deep inside her. "Try."

She waited a moment and saw a rueful smile touch Lucas's lips.

"I suppose my memory can be adaptable," he said.

"Good," Christina said. "Then adapt it. Excuse me, Mr. Ross," she added. "I am meeting with Mr. Bevan shortly."

Lucas nodded. "Of course. Thank you for sparing me the time, Lady Christina. I will start work on the grotto at once."

"Should you require anything else, I am sure that Mr. Bevan will be able to help you," Christina said. "As Mr. Hemmings is unable to supervise your work at present, I shall ask Mr. Bevan to—"

"Keep an eye on me?" Lucas cocked a brow. "In case I abscond with the shells and the statuary?"

"Be available to help you," Christina corrected. Her voice was so starchy it positively crackled. She could see that he found her stiffness amusing, but she did not dare be any other way with him. She was afraid she was already transparent to him, her attraction to him all too obvious.

"I had not imagined that you would supervise my work yourself," Lucas said drily.

"It is Mr. Bevan's job to oversee all aspects of the work of the estate," Christina said, "and besides, I would not expect—" She stopped abruptly.

"You would not expect to show any interest in a humble gardener," Lucas finished. "Quite so."

Christina was stung by the unfairness of that when her father did not give a damn and it was her efforts that kept the estate together. "I hope I take an equal interest in the work and welfare of everyone at Kilmory," she said coldly.

"I am sure that you do," Lucas said. His tone was only a shade short of disrespect.

Christina's control snapped. "Really, Mr. Ross, you are insolent! You are fortunate to have a job at Kilmory at all. I did not want you here, and it was only through my father's interference that you were able to stay—" She broke off, horrified at having been provoked into the indiscretion of criticizing the duke in front of Lucas Ross.

"I am aware that you did not want me here," Lucas said. He shifted slightly. "And I wonder why—apart from the awkwardness of my knowing that you are a whisky smuggler—you want to be rid of me."

His gaze captured hers again, and the hot flicker in his eyes seemed to steal her breath. It was impossible to admit that there was a part of her—a very large part—that had wanted him gone for her own peace of mind. Damn the whisky smuggling; she wanted rid of him because of the way he was looking at her now and the way that made her feel. She could not be attracted to a servant over a half dozen years her junior. It was outrageous. It was *wrong*. She did not want it.

She took a breath to steady her erratic pulse. "I am not in the habit of giving my servants grounds to blackmail me, Mr. Ross," she said coldly. "And since that was precisely what you tried to do to gain a job, is it any wonder I don't trust you?"

Lucas smiled, his teeth a flash of white in his tanned face. "When you put it like that," he said, "I can see your point."

"Thank you," Christina said shortly.

"But you can trust me." Lucas had turned aside. She could not see his face. "I work for Kilmory now."

"I'm gratified to hear it," Christina said drily. "If you try to blackmail me again I will sack you. And damn the consequences."

This time he did look at her. There was admiration in his eyes and something else that for a second looked oddly like regret. The silence rippled between them. "If I make the same mistake twice," Lucas said softly, "I will deserve it."

A clatter of hooves in the courtyard outside reminded Christina that they could be interrupted at any moment. It was time she ended this before it went any further.

"Good day, Mr. Ross," she said. She spun on her heel to leave and in doing so her shawl caught on a loose nail sticking out from the wall. There was an unpleasant ripping sound.

"Wait a moment." Lucas had moved quickly to her side, reaching to free the delicate material before she could damage it further. "You're trapped."

For a second she felt so overwhelmed by his physical proximity that she almost tore the shawl from the nail simply to escape. With the greatest effort of will she squashed the feeling down and stood still whilst Lucas's dexterous fingers worked to slide the delicate material free. There was something disturbing about watching his hands, strong and brown; she felt another wave of heat engulf her and fixed her gaze on his chest instead.

It seemed to take forever to unhook the shawl. Christina's heart beat a fierce tattoo in her chest. The atmosphere in the tight confines of the room had thickened further and felt as oppressive as a thundery day. She did not dare look up into Lucas's intent dark eyes.

"Thank you," she said, and it came out as a whisper.

He stood back. "My pleasure, ma'am." His voice was very smooth. It seemed to vibrate deep inside her.

Christina pulled the shawl tight about her even

though it was a warm day, and she almost ran through the doorway into the courtyard. Once in the fresh air she turned her face up to the sun and took several long, deep steadying breaths. She felt as though she had run a mile. She was shaking. And yet nothing had happened.

LUCAS STOOD IN the doorway of the drawing office and watched Christina walk away. She moved with an innate dignity and elegance, unhurried, as though those long, turbulent moments between them had never occurred. Yet he knew how much it had shaken her. He had seen the pulse drum its frantic beat in the hollow of her throat. He had seen her hands tremble. He had felt the same irresistible pull of attraction that she had.

It was disconcerting to be so drawn to a woman whilst simultaneously suspecting her of involvement in his brother's murder. The most disconcerting thing about it was that his intuition told him she was innocent. Since he was a man who operated on evidence, not emotion, this was more irritating than reassuring. He had no reason to exonerate her and every reason to mistrust her. Her professed hatred of violence fascinated him. She had saved his life but he wondered if she had failed to save Peter's and that was why she was now revolted by brutality. He did not know, but he was going to find out.

He waited until she was out of sight, then turned back into the drawing office, closing the door behind him, searching quickly and neatly through the drawers and cupboards. He found endless drawings and designs that paid tribute to the duke's extravagant plans and wild flights of imagination, but nothing that related either to Peter or to the whisky smuggling. He had not expected it, but he was starting to feel frustrated by his lack of progress. In the past week he had caught not a whisper about Peter's murder. Later that evening he planned to search for the sea cave where the smugglers had held him on the first night. It was dangerous, but he would be a great deal more careful this time.

Lachlan and Angus MacMorlan were handing their horses over to one of the grooms as Lucas closed the door of the drawing office behind him and started to walk across the yard. It was the first time Lucas had seen Lachlan, who rumor had it was usually so addled with drink that he seldom got out of bed before the afternoon. Lachlan possessed the good looks that were such a distinct feature of the MacMorlan family, but his eyes were bloodshot and his gait unsteady. Angus was a big, fleshy man with an air of superiority and a long nose that seemed perfectly engineered to look down. Neither man thanked the groom nor acknowledged Lucas's presence with a single word or look. The groom caught Lucas's glance and rolled his eyes meaningfully. Lucas grinned.

It was as the two men were disappearing through the archway that Lachlan turned and looked back. For a moment it seemed to Lucas as though Lachlan's gaze shed its blurred drunkenness and focused on

CHAPTER SEVEN

ALLEGRA HEARD THE music as she came down the path toward the bay. It was the high, thin sound of the fiddle, snatched on the breeze and tossed away out to sea. She hurried, the sand and pebbles slipping beneath the thin soles of her shoes. As she half ran, half stumbled down onto the beach the music stopped abruptly and strong arms seized her, pulling her behind a tumble of rocks.

They wasted no time on words. She was in his arms and he was kissing her like a man half starved. He tugged the ribbons of her bonnet and threw it aside. The wind had already whipped her hair into tangled strands and he gave a groan as he plunged one hand into the shining gold. She kissed him back eagerly, trembling helplessly, feeling as though her heart was bursting with relief and love and pleasure. When he held her she could forget all the barriers they faced. Nothing mattered other than that they were together again.

"You came for me," she whispered when he released her for a moment.

"Did you doubt me?" He sounded amused, but his brown eyes were dark with passion. He kissed her again and her knees weakened. She clutched at his jacket and they sank down onto the sand. It was warm in the sun, and sheltered between the rocks, but when he slid the gown from her shoulders she still shivered at the nip of the sea air. The rock felt hot against her bare back, and the sunlight beat against her closed lids. She kept her eyes shut because although he had seen her naked before, she was still very shy. She liked the wickedness of it, the chill of the breeze and the warmth of the sun and his mouth now at her breast, but she was not ready to admit it yet. It was too new to her, each new intimacy as shocking as it was delicious.

She opened her eyes a sliver and looked down at his head at her breast. His hair, a rich chestnut in the sunlight, brushed the sensitive skin there, and she shivered in deep pleasure. His lips and his fingers worked magic on her. Her body was heating, melting. There was such a sweet ache in her belly. It made her moan. He licked her nipple, tasting her, and her entire body jerked in uninhibited response. Her eyes flew open. It was one of the things she loved about him, that he looked so cool, that he seemed so controlled, and yet beneath it he was all fire and he could make her burn, too. She was lost in the sensation, dizzy with it, disbelieving and enchanted.

"Take me."

She was naturally autocratic, and now the wickedness pushed her past her inhibitions. She was pulling up her skirts as she spoke, parting her thighs, loving the cold press of the air on her skin. She wore no drawers, and she heard the harsh catch of his breath as he saw her.

"Allegra…" He sounded shaken. It was gratifying. He had always been the one in control when they made love. It made it all the more exciting now to shock him, thrill him.

He was fumbling with the fastening of his trousers now, kneeling between her thighs. Impatience gripped her, and fierce hunger. She felt the tip of his cock at her opening and then he was inside her and she gasped, arching back against the stone as he drove into her with such desperate need, almost out of control. She matched his desperation stroke for stroke, driven on by the ever-tightening spiral of excitement and desire. Blinding pleasure caught her hard and fast, and she cried aloud, the sound mingling with the relentless crash of the waves on the beach and the wild calls of the birds wheeling overhead.

Afterward he drew her into the curve of his shoulder. He was breathing hard, one arm shaded across his eyes.

She waited for him to say something sweet, something loving.

"You have to tell your mother," he said. He sat up, gripped her wrists. "Allegra, you have to tell your mother we are married."

She tried to pull away from him, feeling obscurely hurt and upset. She knew that he was right; she might be carrying his child. She had no idea how she would explain that. Yet her mind spun away from the thought of telling her family the truth. They would be angry with her, and for one terrible moment she was not sure if her love for Richard was strong enough to withstand that.

She freed herself, straightened her gown, drew her knees up and hugged them like a little girl, hunched, protective.

"It's too soon, Richard."

He shook her, but gently. "No. It is not. We have been wed for a month now and the longer we go on like this the more difficult it will be."

There was silence. The pounding of the sea had dulled to a murmur. The high, plaintive call of the seabirds had faded. After a moment, Richard sighed.

"Perhaps your father—"

"No." Allegra was adamant. Of all the people likely to help her, her father was last on the list. Generally he had no interest in her at all, but he would be very interested to discover that she, the heir to all the unentailed Forres fortune and estates, had thrown herself away on a penniless government official with no connections and no prospects. Interested, outraged, furious. She shuddered.

"Then tell your aunt Christina." Richard sounded patient, coaxing. "I met her today. She seems very nice. I am sure she could help us."

Allegra considered it, watching the birds sail high and fast against the deep blue of the sky. She liked Christina best of all her aunts and uncles. Christina was ancient, of course, and she could have no idea what it felt like to be desperately, hopelessly in love, or to do anything wild and mad and passionate. But Allegra knew that she cared about people and tried to help them. She had seen Christina's kindness toward her father's tenants and those who were sick or poor, lonely or desperate. Christina was a loving person where her own parents were cold and empty of humanity.

She considered telling Christina what she had done, and that felt safe enough. She could do that. But the thought of going with Christina to tell her mother made her tremble. Cold fear gnawed her gut.

Richard was talking. "Now that I have this job as riding officer I have more to offer you. Perhaps if I make a success of this commission to capture the Kilmory Gang, Sidmouth will reward me and your family will be more inclined to accept me—"

He broke off as though he had sensed just how pointless his words were. They both knew that nothing short of him inheriting a dukedom would make a difference to Allegra's parents.

Allegra jumped to her feet. Her gown was crumpled and stained. Suddenly she felt grubby and ashamed and close to despair. She had not meant for it to be like this. She had met Richard and wanted him very much, and so she had run off and married him in secret. No one knew. It had all seemed simple then. "I must go," she said.

Richard swore under his breath. His hands were as clumsy fastening his trousers as they had been in unfastening them. The sight shot her through with love and misery and she had no idea why. She had not thought love would hurt so much.

"I'll tell them," she said in a rush, wanting to make it better, wanting to make him happy. "I promise." She went to him, touched his arm. For a brief second his hand covered hers.

They both knew she was lying.

Christina closed the door of the bothy softly behind her and leaned back against it, feeling the wood rough against her palms. Here, in the warm, whisky-laden darkness, she finally felt some of the peace she had been seeking all day. She had worked her fingers to the bone for the past twelve hours, blocking out thoughts of Lucas.

She knew that attraction was no respecter of age or rank or status. Still, it disturbed her that she was so drawn to a man who was her junior by at least half a dozen years and was unsuitable in every way there was. She did not like it, she did not understand it and she did not want it. Yet part of her liked Lucas well enough; the part that she had been denying for years, the part that wanted to indulge her fantasies.

Madness. It could not happen. It would not happen.

She closed her eyes and inhaled the scent of the distilling whisky, letting it fill her senses, letting go of her thoughts. The air smelled heavy and rich, the whisky spirit mingled with the smoke of the peat fire. It was hot and heady, and Christina felt as though she could get drunk on the whisky fumes alone.

"Evening ma'am." Seumas Mor MacFarlane came in with water from the stream outside. It slopped over the side of the bucket and splashed onto the earthen floor. His was the task of keeping the fire burning and keeping the whisky distilling at precisely the right temperature. His brother, Niall, had the task of stirring the fermenting barley, another part of the process that required skill and delicacy. Each member of the gang had his role, whether it was in producing the spirit itself or shipping it out safely under the noses of the riding officers.

"I've distilled it four times," Seumas said. "It should be ready."

Christina nodded. Each batch of Kilmory peat-reek was normally distilled four times for the best flavor and purity. Known as the *Uisge bea' ba'ol,* it commanded a high price. Some they distributed locally, some was taken by boat from the cove to customers farther afield.

Seumas already had a new batch of the peat-reek distilling. She took the flask he proffered and poured some of the *Uisge bea' ba'ol* into a glass. His face was watchful as she held the liquid up to the light. The lamplight lit it with a deep glow, the color of old gold. She sniffed it; nodded. The flavor burst on her tongue, fierce and strong. The heat and power of it went to her head, making it swim. Suddenly her limbs felt weak and she wanted to drink the peat-reek down and lose herself in it.

"It's perfect," she said, and saw Seumas Mor's expression relax into pleasure. He was a man of few words, rough around the edges, yet with such a feel for the whisky, his trade learned from his father and grandfather before him.

"Thank you," she said. "That is ready to be put in the barrels and moved out. You got the last consignment away successfully?"

Seumas Mor's expression darkened. "Just. The excisemen were sniffing around."

"When are they not?" Christina said tiredly.

Seumas Mor shook his head. "This time it's bad, ma'am, worse than before. Mr. Eyre caught Niall down on the beach with his boy just after the boat had gone. Niall told him they were fishing but Eyre didn't believe him. They took them both to Fort William to the jail."

Christina's head jerked up. Horror closed her throat. "They took Callum, as well? But he's only eight years old!"

Seumas Mor shrugged. "Nothing you can do, ma'am. Nothing any of us can do. They went straight to Niall's cottage and burned it down."

Christina rubbed her eyes against the sting of tears. She felt wretched. She knew that Niall would not talk and that Callum knew nothing about the smuggling, but that was not the point. She thought of the boy locked up in a dark, dank cell, probably separated from his father, alone and afraid. She thought of their home destroyed and their possessions trampled. Eyre was a monster who would use anyone and anything to break the gang. He had no scruples.

Each time a man was taken, Christina thought

about giving up the distilling, but stubborn determination always made her fight back. If they gave in to Eyre, the fierce pride the Highlanders had taken in brewing their peat-reek, the rights they had held in defiance of London laws and the money they had made to ward off the crippling poverty of their existence would all be destroyed. But this was too much. If Eyre started to wage war on women and children then she had no choice.

She filled the glass again and raised the peat-reek to her lips, draining half of it in one gulp. At this rate she would rival Lachlan as a drunkard, but she needed it. She was so tired of having to stand up alone for the people of Kilmory. No one else gave a damn—her father, her brother, both out for what they could get from the land and the people rather than what they could give.

"I'll speak to Eyre," she said. "They cannot ride roughshod over people's lives like this."

Seumas shook his head. "You're the one Eyre wants, ma'am," he said roughly. "He'll go through any number of us to get to you."

A cold shard of shock and fear pierced Christina. She had known for a while that Eyre suspected she might be protecting the smugglers. But she had no notion that he believed her to be a part of the gang, and still less that he would seek to arrest her for it.

"Why on earth would they want me—" she began, but then she saw it so clearly she felt naive. Eyre was ambitious and he cared nothing for ingratiating himself with the nobility. In fact, he hated the life of privilege that she had been born into. He hated her even more since she had complained of him to Sidmouth. It would be the greatest coup of his career to bring down the Kilmory Gang with her as its leader.

She drained the rest of the glass and set it down softly. Already the spirit, so strong, was starting to take the edge off her thoughts. She felt warm and a little dizzy. She would think about Eyre and the problem he posed in the morning. She nodded to Seumas, who was watching her dourly. "I'll do what I can," she said.

"Aye, ma'am." He dipped his head. "We know you will." He passed Christina a small stone bottle of the peat-reek. She knew it was to be left as a traditional gift for her father, the laird who turned a blind eye to the smugglers' activities. For once she felt bitter about it. The duke did nothing to help the smugglers. He turned a blind eye because he was utterly indifferent to their activities. He deserved no thanks.

Outside it was a mild night, starry, warm. The wind rifled the pines and played through the heather. The bothy was set along the edge of Loch Gyle, tucked away in the lee of a rise in the land where there was a running stream and where the smoke from the fires would not be seen. Christina carefully traced her path along the edge of the loch, its waters shining silver in the moonlight, and took the path down the valley to the castle. Along the way she took the stopper from the bottle of peat-reek and took a long swallow. Whisky was not really her sort of drink; apart from the tasting, she never normally touched it. Tonight, though, she rather thought she could get a craving for it. It took the edge off the pain of Niall and Callum's capture, but beneath the dulling taste of the drink her heart ached.

She met no one on the walk home. She let herself into the castle grounds and wandered across the gravel to the door at the base of the west tower. Here she always hid a key for those occasions when she went out at night and the castle was locked up. She did not always like to ask Galloway to leave a door open or to wait up for her.

She bent down to search for the key amongst the tumble of stones at the base of the tower. It was a mistake. Her head swam suddenly from the combination of tiredness and drink. She put out a hand to steady herself and her fingertips grazed the rough stone of the wall. She fell over with as little grace as a collapsing balloon, and the whisky flagon rolled away from her across the gravel.

"Damnation!" She made a grab for it and missed, sitting down hard on the ground, her skirts billowing around her.

There was a sound behind her, a step. A shadow fell across her.

"Dear me." It was Lucas's voice, low, cool and amused. "Can I be of any assistance, Lady Christina?"

SHE WAS DRUNK.

Lady Christina MacMorlan was indisputably foxed on contraband whisky. Of all the people in the world that Lucas would have suspected of sampling the peat-reek as well as brewing it, Christina would have been at the bottom of his list. Her starchy, proper manner evidently concealed a very improper soul.

And now she was as drunk as a lord and sitting on the gravel drive outside her own door looking ruffled and confused and strangely appealing. Her skirts were tumbled about her knees, showing a froth of virginal-white petticoats, a tempting curve of thigh and a frankly naughty scarlet garter, another sign that she was very far from the staid and respectable old maid she pretended to be.

Lucas smothered a smile and courteously offered her a hand to help her rise.

"Mr. Ross," Christina said. "What a surprise!"

"Isn't it?" Lucas agreed. In fact, he had been waiting, night after night, for Christina to leave the castle on smuggling business. Tonight he had followed her. He now knew the precise location of the whisky still, which was the most valuable piece of information he could pass on to Lord Sidmouth.

She took his hand and propelled herself to her feet with rather more enthusiasm than finesse. Lucas found his arms full of her, warm, yielding, soft. The scent of peat smoke clung faintly to her clothes, almost lost beneath the stronger scent of the fresh sea air. She turned her face up to his and the urge to smile died in him, crushed beneath a lust so strong it felt like a physical blow. Her eyes were shining, her lips parted. He wanted to kiss the life out of her.

Peter.

The memory of his brother was sufficient to break the spell. This woman might be Peter's murderer; he could not afford to feel anything for her. Already the blazing attraction between them, which he had thought to use against her, was working against him, too. It had even made him forget for a brief moment that she represented everything he disliked and distrusted, a world of inequality and privilege that had treated him so viciously.

He put Christina gently away from him and bent to pick up the bottle of peat-reek, handing it to her. She took it from him, but when her fingers closed over his, she did not let go. Startled, he met her gaze and saw that she was nowhere near as drunk as he had imagined her to be. Or if she was, she was still wary, still suspicious. He needed to tread carefully.

"What are you doing here?" she said.

"I saw you when I was on my way back from the Kilmory Inn and thought you looked as though you could do with some help," Lucas said. The lie came less easily than he had wanted. Somehow, with her hand still resting in his, it felt difficult to deceive her. Her gaze, her touch, demanded honesty from him. He cleared his throat.

"You should be more discreet, Lady Christina," he said. "If you wish to avoid detection, I suggest that you delay your activities until after closing time at the inn. The revenue officers drink there, too."

There was a moment of silence whilst she weighed his words, and then her hand fell to her side and she nodded. "That's good advice," she said. "I am surprised, though. I would not think any revenue officer welcome at the inn."

"Their money is," Lucas said, "and Eyre cares nothing for a cold welcome. His nephew is a different man, but he was not there tonight."

Her gaze searched his face again, as though trying to assess his honesty. Lucas could feel his heart thudding. She should have looked ridiculous trying to assume some dignity and authority when she was so disheveled, and yet there was something very endearing about her. In the moonlight, her eyes looked huge and dark. There was something so innocent and vulnerable about her expression, and he was all too aware of the soft, feminine curves beneath her practical black cloak. He felt desire stir again and repressed it ruthlessly.

"Can I do anything else to help you, ma'am?" he asked.

"I should be grateful if you could find the key," Christina said. She waved the bottle of peat-reek in the vague direction of a pile of stones. "I hid it over there."

It didn't take Lucas long to find it. The key fitted neatly into the door and the door itself swung open on recently oiled hinges. He would have expected nothing less of her. She was always efficient; at least she was when she was sober. Tonight she was warm and vibrant in his arms, wriggling a little as he tried to bundle her up the worn spiral stair, a lantern in one hand, Christina in the other. Her body felt delicious against his, the silk of her gown slippery and smooth. Lucas gritted his teeth.

"Why are you drunk?" he asked.

"Peat-reek." Her breath whispered across his skin. Her lips brushed his jaw. His skin shivered. It was all he could do not to turn his head and sample that lush mouth so close to his. She would taste of whisky and sweetness and he wanted to kiss her very much but again he fought back the impulse. He needed to use tonight to gain information and to build her trust in him.

"I guessed that," he said. "I did not realize that you drank the peat-reek as well as brewed it. What I meant was, why did you feel the need to get drunk?"

"I don't drink whisky usually." A faint hint of hauteur had come into her voice. "Only tonight…" Her shoulders slumped suddenly. The light and warmth and happiness went out of her like a candle blown out.

"They took a child," she said softly. "Eyre arrested the son of one of my men. He is eight years old."

Lucas could hear the pain clear in her voice. It was sharp and unmistakably sincere. Lady Christina MacMorlan cared. She cared about what happened to the people of her clan. Anything that hurt them also hurt her. She was no privileged aristocrat playing at smuggling because she was bored or spoiled. It was not as simple as that.

"Eyre is so vicious," she said. Lucas felt her shiver. "He takes pleasure in brutality. He is one of the most violent and dangerous men I know."

Lucas had not met the riding officer yet, though he had heard plenty about him. Sidmouth had told him that Eyre would be in touch with him and would help him, but so far Eyre had completely ignored him. Lucas was not sure if Eyre resented his presence on his patch, but it would be in character with his self-importance and pride to want to keep his information to himself. There was always an undertone of complaint at the inn about the man's methods and the way he would pursue the villagers for the last penny they owed, searching houses, raiding barns, trampling crops, scaring livestock, careless of their lives and their livelihood.

"Smuggling is a harsh business, Lady Christina," he said. "It's not a game."

"I know that." Her tone was sharp now, and yet Lucas sensed beneath that sharpness a vulnerability that she was doing her best to hide. She did not want him to know how much she cared. She did not want her emotions stripped bare in front of him.

The light from the lantern fell on her face. There were lines of tiredness and grief etched in her countenance, and Lucas felt something stir inside him.

"You blame yourself, don't you," he said abruptly. "You blame yourself for what happens to the child."

He felt another shudder rack her. "Of course," she said. She tipped the flask to her lips again. "It's my duty to protect the people of Kilmory," she said, "not to put them in harm's way."

"What will you do?" Lucas asked.

"Go to Eyre, I suppose," Christina said. She was

slurring her words slightly now. "Beg him to release Callum MacFarlane. I suspect he will enjoy seeing me beg."

They had reached the top of the stairs. Christina stood up on tiptoe to take a key from the lintel above the door. For a second she swayed against Lucas, her hair brushing his shoulder, her breast pressing against his arm. She smelled of bluebells and the earthiness of peat and the faintest hint of whisky. His body tightened and he shoved his hands in his pockets to keep from touching her.

She fumbled with the key in the lock for so long that Lucas stepped forward and took it from her, sliding it into the lock and turning it. The door swung open, silently again, to reveal a small dressing room furnished with two deep, comfortable armchairs and a thick carpet on the floor. Beyond that an open door showed the corner of a big tester bed and a grate where a fire burned low. The room had the same shabby coziness that characterized the rest of the castle. Lucas felt again that unfamiliar sense of warmth and welcome drawing him in. He, who had never had a proper family home and had never wanted to create one, felt its appeal.

"Thank you for your help, Mr. Ross," Christina said. She was sliding the cloak from her shoulders, draping it over the back of one of the chairs. Her gown was a little lopsided, dipping down to reveal the curve of her left shoulder. Lucas stared, fascinated. Her skin was creamy, pale and scattered with freckles, the faintest shadow cast by the delicate line of her collarbone. He wanted to press his lips to the elegant curve where her neck met her shoulder. He wanted to see if the rest of her body had that tempting dusting of freckles, too. He badly wanted to know.

"You may go, Mr. Ross," Christina said, interrupting his thoughts. "Please lock the door on your way out and hide the key." She looked him straight in the eyes, or at least she tried to. Her gaze seemed slightly out of focus. "I hope that I can trust you not to tell anyone about this."

"You can trust me," Lucas said.

Another lie.

He was disturbed to feel a jolt of guilt. There was something about this woman that seemed to demand honesty, and he could not give her that. He did not even understand why he felt the need to. All he knew was that she was intoxicated and vulnerable and that for some reason that made him feel protective of her.

He forced himself to think about Peter. Like Callum MacFarlane, Peter had been someone's child, someone's brother, scarcely more than a boy himself. He wondered if Christina had cared about that.

"Answer me one thing before I leave," he said. "You owe me that."

Her eyes opened wide. She blinked. "I don't owe you anything, Mr. Ross." She was making an attempt to sound crisp, reminding him of his place, comically dignified given her tousled state.

"I think you owe me plenty for my help tonight," Lucas said.

"And I think you presume a lot," Christina said.

Lucas smiled. "That's true, I do." He paused. "What if I ask nicely?"

She sighed. "What do you want to know?"

"I do not understand how a woman like you comes to be involved in something like this," Lucas said. He looked around the room. "You don't need the money," he said slowly, "and after what you have said tonight I would swear you do not do it for the excitement. So why *do* you do it?"

She was silent. After a moment she sat down in one of the armchairs, half turned away from him. He watched the play of firelight and shadow across her face. She was just drunk enough to be indiscreet, he thought, whilst sober enough to be coherent. It could be interesting.

"I'm good at it," she said after a moment. Her chin came up. She looked defiant. "I am the taster, the only one with the ability to judge when the whisky is ready to be distilled. It's important…a skilled job."

"I'm skilled at picking pockets," Lucas said. "It doesn't mean I should do it."

"Are you?" For a moment she sounded intrigued. "What an extraordinary talent to possess! How did you develop it?"

"I had a misspent youth on the streets," Lucas said. He had not meant to talk about himself, but with Christina it was all too easy to let down his guard and forget. He could see her looking at him curiously; it was not pity he could see in her eyes but compassion. "I was an orphan," he said. His voice was harsh. He had never told anyone but Jack about his childhood. He was astonished to hear himself telling her now. "I had to learn any number of tricks to survive."

"I'm sorry." Her voice was soft. "Your parents—"

"I don't speak of them." He slammed the door shut before he could betray himself entirely.

"What you do is different," he said, as much to remind himself as to provoke her.

"Of course." A defensive note had crept into her voice. "I do not have to fight for survival. But, equally, I don't act for personal gain. The rest of the gang divides up the profits. They need the money. I don't." She rushed on, her words tumbling out far quicker than normal in her hurry to justify herself. "You've seen the poverty in the village, Mr. Ross. Many of the young men have left to join the Highland regiments, or taken their families overseas. There is no work, nothing to keep people here ever since my grandfather put up the rents sixty years ago and offered his tenancies to the highest bidder. He drove people from the land."

Lucas had recognized the poverty in Kilmory Village within the first day of being there. What Christina said was true; there was little work on the land now, few ways to give any man a job and a living wage. And with that loss of work went a loss of self-respect. He understood that; he knew how fiercely a man's pride and his independence were tied up in his ability to provide for his family. Christina's grandfather had destroyed the traditional bonds between the laird and his people, and it seemed that her father had done nothing to try to improve their welfare, even though he was reputedly a rich man.

"Is it too late to reverse that process of decline now?" he asked.

Christina shrugged. "I do not know. But Papa..." For a second she faltered as though considering the disloyalty of speaking out against the duke. "Well, he has no interest in the land, no interest in anything other than his studies. By the time he inherited his estates, the damage was done, and he handed his lands over to be administered by those who could make him the greatest profit."

"It sounds as though your father is not really concerned with the future of his people," Lucas said, "whilst you work to limit the harm he can do by feeding them and keeping a roof over their heads."

"Oh..." She sounded embarrassed. "I would not have you think that Papa cares nothing for people. Truth is, he does not really notice. He is a scholar, caught up in matters of more academic importance..." Her voice faded away unhappily.

Fiddling whilst Rome burned, Lucas thought. It seemed to him that the Duke of Forres was like a great big overgrown child who indulged his whims without thought for the consequences or the toll it took on others. It was not sufficient to ascribe his neglect to eccentricity or scholarly absorption. He was draining his lands of their money and his people of their livelihoods for personal gain.

"So it is left to you to give the people of Kilmory

back their self-respect," Lucas said. "I imagine you do the same at Forres, and all the duke's other estates."

"I don't run smuggling gangs there," Christina said, "but I do try to help the people make a living."

"A dishonest one, in Kilmory's case," Lucas said.

Her lips twitched into an enchanting smile. "Do I infer that you disapprove of me, Mr. Ross? I had no idea that you were so incorruptible."

"Smuggling is illegal," Lucas said.

She raised a brow at his blunt tone. "Well, theoretically, yes—"

"There's no such thing as a theoretical criminal," Lucas said. "You either are or you aren't."

She shrugged. "Bad laws make for bad men." She gave him the glimmer of a smile. "And women." She tipped the flask to her lips again. "My dream would be to run a distillery of my own," she said after a moment. "I think I would be very good at it."

"A splendid idea," Lucas said. He removed the bottle from her grasp and placed it on a high shelf next to a dusty pile of books. "In the meantime, though, you have had quite sufficient whisky to drink."

She pouted. "I give the orders around here," she said. "Give it back."

Lucas laughed. "No," he said. "You are going to have a dreadful headache in the morning. It may taste nice now, but whisky is the worst drink for making you feel bad later. Drink lots of water," he added, "and try to eat something in the morning even if you don't feel like it."

She raised her eyebrows in faint mockery. "Food advice now," she said. "How do you know these things, Mr. Ross?"

"My misspent youth again," Lucas said. "There were plenty of mornings when I woke up feeling much the worse for drink."

She smiled faintly. "How fascinating. You must tell me more about that misspent youth sometime." She picked up her cloak and folded it over her arm. In the candlelight something sparkled silver—a jeweled clasp on the collar of the cloak. Lucas had not noticed it before because the light had been too dim, but he recognized it now. The last time he had seen it had been on the velvet collar of Peter's coat as his brother had stood on his doorstep in Edinburgh.

All the breath seemed to leave his body. The light spun as though he was the one who was drunk. He put out a hand automatically to steady himself on the back of the chair.

"That's a very unusual clasp." His voice did not sound quite right in his ears. He realized that he was shaking.

He saw Christina glance down and smile as she ran her fingers over the silver surface. "Isn't it beautiful?" There was uncomplicated pleasure in her voice. "Papa gave it to me for my birthday a couple of months back. He said the stones came from India. They have fine amethysts there."

They might well have, Lucas thought, but these

amethysts had come from the mines of Siberia and had been mounted in a silver clasp that had belonged to his grandfather. It was engraved with his family's crest and motto.

He felt tightness in his chest. One of the items that had been stolen from Peter's body was right here in Kilmory Castle, a gift, Christina had said, from the duke.

Could the Duke of Forres be involved in Peter's murder? It seemed impossible. Yet was it any more likely that Christina, who seemed so honest and had spoken so passionately about the need to protect her clan, was a liar and a murderer? His instinct told him she was not, that she would never be mixed up in so vile a crime. Yet instinct could be an unreliable guide.

"Good night, Mr. Ross." Christina had come up to him. "Thank you for your help tonight." She stood on tiptoe to kiss his cheek. She really was tipsy, Lucas thought. She would be mortified in the morning to remember how familiar she had been with him when normally she was so careful to be starchy and proper. He took her hands to steady her and she looked up, her blue eyes meeting his. Something shifted inside him, an emotion he did not recognize; an unaccustomed sense of vulnerability swept through him and he tightened his grip on her hands.

He saw the expression in her eyes change. He could see confusion in their depths and the compassion she had shown him earlier when he had made the mistake of talking about his childhood. Suddenly he needed her desperately. He bent his head and kissed her and she responded sweetly, openly, without reservation. Heat sliced through him. Lust slammed into him, so hot and hard and fast that it stunned him. Beneath the lust was the same blinding sense of recognition that he had experienced on the first night they had met, fierce and devastatingly right. Something about Christina MacMorlan could reach inside him and awaken emotions he thought long dead. He could not understand it, could not explain it, but in that moment he did not want to. He only wanted her.

When he let her go they were both breathing hard and he was shaking, shocked by his reaction to her and emotions it had unleashed. He saw his astonishment mirrored in her eyes. She touched her lips lightly with her fingertips, and the gesture sent another spike of desire straight through him.

"That was a mistake," she whispered.

"Yes," Lucas said grimly. The lit room beyond the doorway seemed to beckon him with its wide, deep bed and intimate firelight. He swallowed. His mouth was as dry as dust.

"I should go," he said.

"Yes." For a moment she looked desolate and he wanted to reach out to her and draw her back into his arms. He clenched his fists at his sides. It felt right but it was wrong, impossible. The light glittered on the silver clasp, taunting him, reminding him who she was and of her possible guilt.

CHAPTER EIGHT

"WHAT DO YOU THINK, my dear?" The Duke of Forres, his face bright with childish pleasure, turned to Christina. "This fellow has done a damned fine job, hasn't he?" He slapped Lucas on the back. "Damned fine," he repeated. "Eh, Christina?"

"It looks beautiful, Papa," Christina said obediently. They were standing in the duke's garden grotto. The light was dim and the air cool. Outside the rain beat down with an unrelenting heaviness. It seemed to echo through Christina's head. Lucas had not been wrong; she had the devil of a headache this morning.

The grotto was far from finished, but Lucas had certainly made good progress. The pool had been hollowed out and lined with the stone that her father had had imported specially from Italy. A cascade of water now splashed down into it from the spring that rose in the bank above them.

Christina turned to admire the way the light played across the rippling cascade. Her father was still talking, but she let his words flow over her. Instead she watched Lucas in the reflection on the dancing water. It felt strange, intimate. She was so self-conscious that she could not look directly at him. In the enclosed space of the grotto, she was almost unbearably aware of him standing next to her, of his arm brushing hers, of his gaze on her face. She had woken late with snatches of memory from the previous night drifting through her mind. She wished she had not been able to recall any of it, but unfortunately her memory was not that obliging. She remembered all too clearly that Lucas had had to pick her up off the gravel when she had fallen over, that he had helped her up the stairs, that she had drunkenly confided in him her reasons for smuggling the whisky, that he had kissed her with a fierce passion and that she would have been quite happy if he had carried her off to her bed there and then. Despite the chill of the day, she felt hot color mantle her cheeks.

As a debutante, she'd had a reckless, dangerous affair with the man to whom she had been betrothed, Lord McGill. At the time, she had been hopelessly infatuated. The snatched meetings and illicit passion had pandered to her romantic nature, and she had not seen the danger because she had assumed that nothing could spoil her happiness. She had learned that lesson fast enough; learned that nothing in life was certain or safe. Her mother had died and the bottom had dropped out of her world. She had lost almost everything; mother, lover, the promise of the future.

The attraction she felt for Lucas was at least as strong as her girlish passion for McGill had been, though she was not stupid enough to tumble thoughtlessly into love with any man these days. It did not matter how powerful that dangerous illusory sense of connection was that she shared with Lucas. She knew that the only relationship she could have with him would be as mistress and lover, and there were too many reasons why that could never happen, so there was nothing for them; she knew it.

"My statues will look splendid in the wall niches." The duke was twirling around with excitement like a small child at the circus. "And with the shells on the ceiling reflecting the light…" He waved his arms about enthusiastically. "Oh, yes, I can see it now!"

"I have drawn up some detail for the decoration, Your Grace," Lucas was saying, laying out a sheet on the stone ledge that ran around the edge of the pool. "I thought to have a fresco with dolphins and putti, and perhaps a motto etched in the stone…."

Christina was intrigued that Lucas knew about Renaissance design. She wondered if he had gotten the ideas from talking to Bevan. She leaned over to look at the neat pencil sketches. The duke was shortsighted without his glasses. He was nodding and smiling, but Christina was not sure he could see the drawing in detail, least of all the lettering around the fresco. He was bound to ask her to describe it later.

"'Vincere vel mori,'" she read. "To conquer or die." It was the motto from her silver clasp. She looked up at Lucas in surprise. "Did you choose that yourself?" she asked. "Why those words?"

Lucas did not look at her. He was watching the duke. "I thought they were your family motto," he said. He glanced at her, and for a moment she saw some emotion in his dark eyes that chilled her, it was so remote and cold. She wondered if she had misread his expression in the pale light of the grotto, but then her father claimed her attention. The duke seemed agitated, running a hand through his hair, shaking his head violently.

"No, my dear fellow, that simply won't do!" he exclaimed. "No cherubs, no dolphins and certainly no motto!"

"I'm afraid you have made a mistake," Christina said to Lucas. "The Forres motto is Constant and Faithful."

Lucas smiled at her. "That seems more appropriate," he said, "to you."

Christina blushed at the compliment but her father did not appear to notice. He was rolling up Lucas's plans and his hands were shaking slightly.

"I don't want a motto on it," he said querulously. "Statues of nymphs and river gods! That's what I want!"

Lucas took the sketches from him. "Very well, Your Grace," he said. "I shall go back to the drawing board."

Christina frowned at her father, who had the grace to look a little abashed. "Good job all the same, old chap," he muttered. "I will see you get paid extra for all your hard work. Bevan will see to it." He nodded to Lucas, smiled agreeably at Christina and wandered off out into the rain.

Christina was about to follow him when she saw

the expression on Lucas's face. He was staring after her father and he looked angry.

"He did not mean to insult you with the offer of the extra money," she said quickly, putting a hand on his arm. "He thought only to reward you for what you had done."

"He doesn't even remember my name," Lucas said. "And I don't need the money." He turned away and Christina dropped her hand. She was dismayed—and taken aback. Nothing about Lucas's demeanor suggested that he was rich enough to turn down extra wages, and she was surprised he was so sensitive about it. This morning he looked as threadbare as ever in an old shirt, patched trews and a battered pair of boots.

"I'm sorry if we have offended you in some way—" she started to say uncertainly.

He turned back to her so quickly that she caught her breath. The light was behind him and she could not see his face, but she had the impression that he was smiling, and it made her feel quite hot.

"*You* have not offended me," he assured her. His voice was intimately low.

"You cannot expect Papa to know everyone by name," Christina said.

"Why not?" Lucas said. "You do." He stepped aside to allow her to precede him down the small tunnel that led out into the gardens. "It doesn't matter," he said. "How is your head this morning?"

"It hurts," Christina admitted. She fidgeted with the braiding on her sleeve. The sensible thing to do would be to drop the subject, but that felt a little churlish after the help he had given her.

"Thank you for rescuing me last night," she said. She looked up into his eyes. The amusement she saw there made her heart beat hard.

"It was a pleasure, ma'am," Lucas said.

"I am afraid I was rather drunk," Christina continued.

His lips twitched. She knew that he was trying not to laugh. "I had noticed," he said.

"I probably said some things that I should not," Christina said.

"I imagine you certainly said some things you regret," Lucas said. He slanted her a look. "Assuming you actually remember?"

"Unfortunately, I do," Christina said.

This time he did laugh. "Do not give it another thought," he said. "We have all been the worse for drink at times."

"Not me," Christina said.

"I can well believe that," Lucas said. "You are normally so restrained in your behavior, Lady Christina."

There had been nothing restrained in the way she had kissed him the previous night. The thought made hot color sting her cheeks even more brightly. She knew she should broach the matter and explain that it was a mistake that had only occurred because her judgment had been blunted by drink and grief and tiredness. That morning the tiredness had gone, but the grief remained. She had already written a stiff note to Eyre asking for an interview so that she could plead for Callum MacFarlane's release. Next she was going to the village to see what could be salvaged from the pitiful remains of Niall's burned cottage. But whilst she might use the peat-reek as an excuse for her behavior, it was not the real reason. She had confided in Lucas because she had needed him. She had turned to him for more than comfort, and it was dishonest to pretend that it had meant nothing to her.

"I do apologize for my behavior last night," she said in a rush. "Especially when I... When we..." She waved her hands about in embarrassed description.

Lucas laughed again. "I think the phrase you are looking for is 'when we kissed,'" he said. He gave her a slight, mocking bow. "I am at your disposal, Lady Christina, in that as in everything else."

"Really, Mr. Ross," Christina said. She had never felt so ruffled, so breathless. "I am trying to apologize and you are not making matters easy for me."

"You are apologizing because you are a lady," Lucas said, "but I never pretended to be a gentleman."

"Clearly," Christina said. She was not quite sure how a simple apology and thank-you could have become so complex, but it was evidently time to end the conversation. "Well, I am glad that we got that sorted out," she said briskly. "Good day to you, Mr. Ross."

She unfurled her umbrella and stepped out into the dripping gardens, scurrying up the path toward the shelter of the castle. Evidently the kiss had meant nothing to Lucas other than some meaningless dalliance with the mistress of the house. Her face burned. She knew she should be glad that he had dismissed it so casually. His attitude was a perfect match for her thoughts. There could be no relationship between them other than the formal one of lady and servant. It had only been her feminine pride that had made her want the kiss to mean more to Lucas than it had.

THE KILMORY INN was half-empty that night. Word had gone around about Callum MacFarlane's arrest and it seemed no one had the stomach for a drink. Lucas slid into a seat in the corner and the landlord brought him a glass of peat-reek without a word. The room was warm, dark and thick with the scent of the peat fire and pipe smoke. Lucas took a set of cards out of his pocket and idly dealt a hand.

The peat-reek was as good as ever. It tasted of smoke and heather and honey. Lucas thought about Christina; it was true that she had a remarkable talent for distilling, though he wondered if she would still have a taste for whisky after the previous night.

That morning he had laid a trap for her along with her father. The duke's reaction to the motto had been revealing. He had seemed very agitated that Lucas had chosen to use those words. Which must mean that he knew they were on the silver clasp and did not want to draw attention to them. It was a clear sign that he was culpable in some way.

Christina, on the other hand, had seemed merely puzzled. She had shown no signs of guilt, only confusion. Either she was an exceptionally fine actress, far better at dissembling than her father was, or she was innocent. Lucas knew that his attraction to her predisposed him to want her to be blameless. He had to be careful. Already his feelings for her were blunting his judgment.

The door banged open and Eyre came in. It was typical of the man to make a grand entrance, Lucas thought. Eyre was taunting the villagers of Kilmory with his presence—and his money. It was no wonder they hated him. He slapped down some coin on the table and called loudly for a pint of ale. Lucas saw the glint of gold.

Conversation sank to a menacing murmur and then to silence. Eyre swaggered across the room and sat down with a grunt across the table from Lucas. Lucas ignored him and continued to deal the cards.

"What's your game?" Eyre said.

"Speculation," Lucas said. He saw Eyre's lips twitch into a sour smile.

"Do you want to play for money?" The riding officer asked.

"I don't have much." Lucas fumbled in the pocket of his jacket and put a few pennies on the table.

"Not what I heard, Mr. Ross," Eyre said.

"This isn't the time or place," Lucas said with a quick glance around the room.

"There's nothing like hiding in plain sight," Eyre said. He leaned back in the chair and took a long draught of the ale. The conversation had resumed around them, but they were getting some dagger-sharp glances. "Beat me at cards," Eyre continued, "and every last man of them will thank you for humiliating me."

"That's true," Lucas said. He dealt three cards each, then put the pack down and turned up the top card.

"The jack of diamonds," he said.

Eyre smiled again. "Sidmouth tells me you're here to find out who killed the Russian boy," he said softly, allowing the clink of glass and the murmur of conversation around them to hide his words from prying ears.

"That's right," Lucas said. He kept his eyes on the cards.

"Who are you really?" Eyre asked. "Sidmouth didn't say."

"You don't need to know," Lucas said.

He could feel Eyre watching him, enmity and calculation in his narrowed gray eyes. He did not care what Eyre was thinking or whether he liked him or not. That was immaterial. What he needed was Eyre's help.

"I don't want you queering my pitch with the smugglers," Eyre said, suddenly vicious. "I've been working this patch a long time. Those arrests are mine."

"I'm not interested in the smuggling," Lucas said. "Only in murder."

Eyre stared at him, pale eyes unblinking. "Sidmouth thinks the smugglers did it," he said. "I'm not so sure."

"That's what I'm here to find out," Lucas said.

He thought that Eyre was probably right, based on his findings the previous night. However there was a lot he still did not know, and until he could find further proof of the duke's involvement he was not prepared to rule anything out.

"You'll tell me anything useful you find." Eyre was curt. "I don't care who you are—I need to know. The location of the whisky still, where they hide the barrels…" He slapped a card down.

Lucas already knew the location of the whisky still, but he had no intention of telling Eyre. Not yet. He needed to search the bothy. The last thing he wanted was Eyre and his men charging in there, destroying the evidence and arresting the smugglers or worse, making a hash of it and sending the gang to ground. That way he would find out nothing useful at all.

"I'll pass on anything I can," he said.

Eyre nodded, seemingly satisfied. "I'll get them in the end," he said venomously. "And that stuck-up little bitch, Lady Christina MacMorlan, who protects them."

Lucas's head came up. His skin prickled to hear Christina referred to in such disrespectful terms. It was all he could do to keep his fists at his sides and not smash them into Eyre's face. He dropped his eyes to the cards again, dealing another hand, shuffling the deck.

"Lady Christina does her best to protect the whole village," he said carelessly, after a moment. "It should not surprise you that she disapproves of the way you work."

Eyre gave a bark of laughter. "Don't tell me you're sweet on her, too, Mr. Ross? Everyone seems to think she is some sort of saint."

Lucas shrugged. "I don't have much time for aristocrats," he said truthfully, "but I admire hard work when I see it."

"Well, you won't see it at the castle," Eyre said. His mouth twisted into a sneer. "Lazy bunch of bastards." He slapped down his glass and looked around to summon the landlord for another pint. The landlord ignored him.

"Another one asking for trouble," Eyre groused. "I'll shut him down. I'll shut down the whole village for their sneaking, law-breaking ways." He nodded toward Lucas's empty glass. "Was that the peat-reek you were drinking?"

"I've no idea," Lucas said. "I didn't ask."

Eyre's lips twisted into a mirthless smile. His eyes were very cold. "You're a slippery customer, aren't you, Mr. Ross? I'm not sure I trust you."

Lucas shrugged. "Please yourself. But I do have a favor to ask you."

Eyre grunted, which was not exactly encouragement.

"Release the child, Callum MacFarlane," Lucas said quietly.

Eyre jumped, knocking over his empty glass. "What do you know of that?" he snarled. A number of men turned to look at them.

"Softly," Lucas said. He raised his voice. "Sorry to take your money, Mr. Eyre," he said with a cocky smile, "but you can afford it better than I." He took Eyre's pile of coins and slid them over to his side of the table.

"I hear that if you don't let him go, the smugglers will shut down their operation," he said quietly. "If that happens, you will never capture them and I will not find out what I need to know."

"Where did you hear that?" This time Eyre kept his voice discreetly low.

"People talk," Lucas said evasively.

"Not to me," Eyre said.

"Well," Lucas said, "that's hardly surprising."

"I tried to turn a few," Eyre said. "No one was interested. Not even for money. Tight as clams."

"They're loyal," Lucas said, "and they don't like the government and they don't like the English."

Eyre stared at him. "You sound English yourself, Mr. Ross, if it comes to that."

"I don't belong anywhere," Lucas said. He leaned forward. "Will you do it?"

Eyre was silent for a long time, and then he nodded abruptly. "I'll see what I can do." His eyes narrowed on Lucas again. "If you're sure that's the real reason?"

Lucas thought of Callum MacFarlane in the jail in Fort William, alone in the dark with the rats, the walls running with damp, a child used as a bargaining chip to make a man spill his secrets. Callum was younger than Lucas had been when he had had to struggle to survive on the cold streets of Edinburgh. The boy might be from tough stock, but he would never have been without his father's protection before. Lucas had failed to protect his brother. He would do what he could for another man's child.

He met Eyre's gaze very straight. "What other reason would there be?" he asked. "I'm not a sentimental man, Mr. Eyre."

Eyre laughed. "All right. I'll do it. What do I get in return?"

Lucas paused for a moment, drawing rings on the tabletop with the base of his glass. He did not want to give Eyre any advantage that might endanger Christina. Despite the doubts he still harbored toward her, his stubborn instinct was determined to keep her out of this. He could not tell Eyre the location of the whisky still. Which left only one option.

"I can show you the sea cave where the smugglers have been storing the peat-reek," he said. He had searched it the day before and found nothing. The smugglers were long gone from there, and he doubted it would benefit Eyre. Even so, it felt oddly as though he had betrayed Christina, and he felt a pang of guilt. He swore under his breath.

"I've searched the entire coastline for that," Eyre said. "How did you find it?"

"You don't need to know how," Lucas said. "Take it or leave it."

"I'll take it." Eyre stood up, still eyeing him suspiciously. "Tomorrow night. Meet me by the church.

And I'll keep my side of the bargain and let the boy go home to his mother."

"He doesn't have a home left," Lucas said. "You burned it down, remember?" He put the ace of diamonds down on the table. "I believe I win again."

Eyre peered at the cards, gave a grunt and slapped down another handful of pennies. "What were you before you were a gardener, Mr. Ross?" he said. "A card sharp?"

"Something of the sort," Lucas said. He pocketed the money and raised his empty glass of peat-reek in mocking salute. "Your good health, Mr. Eyre."

There were jeers as Eyre left the pub. Lucas left the money on the table to buy a round of drinks, and let himself out into the night. Across the road the blackened spars of Niall MacFarlane's house stood out stark against the night sky. There was a scent of wet wood and burning in the air.

Lucas resolved to write to Lord Sidmouth as soon as he was sure that the smugglers were not involved in Peter's death. He wanted to be free of any association with Eyre. The man might be enforcing the law, but his methods were illegal in themselves. He worked through terror and destruction, and Lucas wanted no part in that.

A light rain was still falling, and his jacket was soaked through by the time he reached the castle. He let himself into his cottage and lit the lamp on the table. Immediately the room sprang into brightness, the warm colors of the rug and the cushions mocking the coldness of the empty grate and the chill air.

Someone had put a pile of coin on the table, a pile that gleamed silver in the lamplight. Beside it was a vase of flowers with a note propped against it. Lucas unfolded it, assuming it was from Bevan, accompanying his tip from the duke. However, it was from Christina.

"Please take the money, Mr. Ross," she had written. "You have earned it. Thank you."

Lucas sighed. He let the note drift down to lie on the table. The money was not a problem. He could always give it away. But the flowers were a different matter. They were so vivid, a flash of warmth in the dullness of a room he had refused to make his own. He knew Christina must have chosen them and brought them here. She had done it because she cared. She had seen his discomfort when the duke had offered to pay him and had misinterpreted it as pride, so she had tried to soften the gesture with a gift.

Anger possessed him suddenly, a fierce rage that he was not what she thought him. At each turn he suspected her and at each turn she repaid that suspicion with generosity of spirit. He did not want her kindness. He did not want her to care. Whatever she thought, he did not belong at Kilmory. He belonged nowhere and he did not want to. He had always been solitary. It was the best way, the only way to avoid hurt, to avoid loss. He had learned that lesson at twelve years old and he would never forget it.

He put the money in his wallet and he put the flowers outside in the rain, and then he shut the door on them. In the morning they were still lying there, rain washed, wilted, their colors fading as he set out to work.

CHAPTER NINE

ALLEGRA WAS LYING in a blissful tumble, half asleep, half awake, cradled in Richard's arms. They were in her chamber at Kilmory in the luxury of a deep four-poster bed with sheets that felt smooth and silken against her skin. It had been another boring day of rain and pianoforte lessons and no visitors at tea except for the doctor's wife and her colorless daughter, but tonight more than made up for the tedium of the day. Allegra had taken her maid into her confidence. It had been the only way to smuggle Richard inside the castle. The girl had thought the situation impossibly romantic but Allegra did not trust her to keep quiet even though she had paid her. Sooner or later she knew that word would get out, and then she would have to face the truth—and her parents. She wondered if she was starting to take deliberate risks. It felt to her as though she would rather be caught than confess.

"We're making progress in our investigation into the whisky smugglers." Richard was stroking her hair gently away from her face. "We're closing in on the leader of the gang."

Allegra smothered a sigh. She did not want to talk,

least of all about Richard's work, which she considered tedious in the extreme. On the other hand, Richard had sounded very pleased with himself so she made a noise that indicated how clever she thought he was and snuggled deeper into his embrace, turning her face into his throat and pressing her lips against the warm, damp skin there. His arms tightened about her. She thought there was nothing nicer than this intimacy, unless it was making love itself. She loved the slide of Richard's body against hers and the feel of him inside her. And she thought she was probably quite good at sex. It was pleasing to find something that interested her so much; all her previous attempts at activities such as needlework or playing the piano had been such a bore.

"We found the cave where the smugglers have been hiding their contraband," Richard said. He was stroking her hair absentmindedly, and Allegra could tell that his thoughts were on his work and not on her. "It was empty of the peat-reek," Richard said, "but we caught someone there. They come from here—from the castle."

Allegra half sat up out of his arms and blinked at him. "Here?" The thought disturbed her. She was not sure why. She knew that whisky smugglers were very active in the neighborhood. Everyone knew that. But it had never occurred to her that they might have connections to Kilmory Castle itself. "Who was it?" she said. "Is he a member of the smuggling gang?"

"I can't tell you that," Richard said. He sounded so smug Allegra wanted to slap him. "But they gave us some useful information and they are going to spy for us."

Allegra's feeling of disquiet increased. She had no loyalty to the smugglers, but she disliked the thought of someone from the castle acting as informer. It felt deceitful, dangerous and wrong.

"I expect the leader of the gang is Uncle Lachlan," she said, yawning, sliding down under the covers again. "He drinks so much whisky he probably needs to make it himself."

"Lachlan MacMorlan is nowhere near the drunkard everyone imagines him," Richard said drily. "Even so, we're looking for a cooler head than his." He stretched. "If we stamp out this plague of smugglers, the home secretary himself will commend my work. Your parents must accept me then—"

He stopped. Allegra had not been able to stifle her sigh. "They will," she said soothingly to forestall his next comment. "They just need time to get used to the idea of you as a son-in-law—"

"You still haven't told them," Richard said flatly. "You promised me you had. I thought, tonight…"

"You thought I was bringing you in secretly through the servants' quarters because they knew we were married and wanted to meet you?" Allegra sighed. "Oh, Richard! Anyway—" she ran a hand over his chest "—I *will* tell them. And it is more romantic like this, more exciting."

Richard, however, evidently did not think so. He had sat up and was starting to pull on his clothes. Allegra shot upright. "Where are you going?"

"I have to leave."

"But why?" Allegra remembered at the last minute to keep her voice from becoming a wail. "It is barely past midnight. We have the whole night—" She let the covers fall artistically to expose her breasts. Richard stopped, stared for a moment and then picked up his boots, turning away. In the faint twilight Allegra could see his profile and the mutinous line of his mouth. Her heart sank. This was not about him making a discreet exit unseen. It was about punishing her for keeping him a secret.

He partially turned to face her. "I'm not your lover, Allegra," he said. "I'm your husband." His voice was hard. "If you do not tell them within the week, I will do it myself."

"Very well," Allegra said. She knew when to sound meek. A lifetime with her mother had taught her that. "I promise," she said. She slid across the bed to sit beside him, placing a hand on his bare shoulder. "You do not have to go."

He glanced sideways at her. She loved the way that his hair fell across his brow, so tousled, like a poet, and the lean curve of his cheek and the sensuality of those lips. She kissed him and felt the resistance in him falter, so she experimented by exerting a little pressure against his chest and was gratified when he lay back with a sigh. It did not take her long to unfasten his trousers. She had been practicing. He made a sound of acquiescence when she took his staff in her hand and stroked it, and a strangled cry when she leaned over to take him in her mouth.

"Allegra—" He tried to sit up, but she gently pushed him back. "You must not..."

"Hush." She ran her tongue over him, tasting. It was so strange and yet so delicious. She had been right; she definitely *was* a wanton.

"How did you know..." His voice was faint.

"I read about it." She felt pleased with herself. She paused, licked the tip and enjoyed his groan. "You can find everything you need in grandfather's library."

THE DUKE'S DISSATISFACTION with his grotto had a very beneficial effect; it enabled Lucas to get into the castle. Mr. Bevan called him into the drawing office on the morning after his meeting with Eyre. The land agent was a pleasant man, spare and sandy and dry in manner. Lucas liked him.

"In strictest confidence, Ross, I think this project of His Grace's is a waste of time, money and resources," Bevan said, pushing the hair back from his forehead with a tired gesture. The lines bit deep around his eyes and mouth as he frowned. "Lady Christina and I agree that there are many more parts of the estate in more urgent need of attention. However—" he sighed "—His Grace is adamant that this should be a priority and he will not be gainsaid. So..." He shrugged with a mixture of resignation and good humor. "I should be obliged if you could take the matter in hand. Go into the library and consult these books His Grace mentions." He passed over a list written in the duke's extravagant scrawl. "Good luck, Ross."

It was more than Lucas could have hoped for. The library was an excellent place to search for a key to Peter's death.

It was Thomas Wallace who let him in at the front door, proud in his footman's livery, his round, freckled face polished and scrubbed.

"I can read and write myself, you know," he confided, when Lucas told him his errand. "I went to the school in the village, the one Lady Christina's mother set up."

It was the first time that Lucas had heard anyone mention the late Duchess of Forres. He vaguely remembered Jack once saying that she had died many years before and that it was Christina who had raised her younger siblings. He wondered if Christina derived her nurturing spirit from her mother, and how she had felt to give up her own future to care for her brothers and sisters. She never spoke of it, of course. Lucas knew it was not something she would broach with her servants, but he felt a curiosity to ask her.

As he went into the library he saw that he was not alone. Christina was at the other end of the room, standing on a rickety-looking ladder as she attempted to replace a book on a high shelf. As she stretched upward the ladder wobbled alarmingly. She reversed hastily down the steps, so hastily that she ended up cannoning into Lucas as he came forward to help her.

Once again, Lucas found his arms full of warm woman. She smelled clean and fresh with the faintest hint of summer grass. She was pressed tightly against him, held fast in his arms. Now he was so close Lucas could see how thick and dark her eyelashes were, a striking contrast to the very deep blue of her eyes. She gave a startled gasp and her lips, right beneath his, parted, and the urge to kiss her roared through him. His body's response to her was so fast and so fierce there was nothing he could do to hide it.

She felt it. His erection was so hard she could scarcely have missed it. He felt the shock rip through her, saw her eyes widen farther, and she looked at him so accusingly he almost laughed.

"Mr. Ross! For shame! In the library!"

Lucas placed her very gently away from him. "I'm afraid that the male anatomy is fairly indiscriminate about location, my lady, though if you prefer we could go elsewhere."

Christina gave an exasperated huff and fussed about straightening her clothes. She very deliberately avoided his gaze. Lucas was fascinated by her reaction. She had certainly been taken aback by the very obvious response he had to her, but she had not indulged in outraged vapors. He remembered the uninhibited way in which she had responded to his kisses. Her behavior suggested that she was not a virgin. Either that or her education had been quite appallingly broad, which, knowing the Duke of Forres's unconventional academic interests, was not impossible.

"If I were a gentleman I would apologize," Lucas

said. "However, we have previously established that I am not. I am delighted that I was there to catch you, Lady Christina."

Christina's eyes flashed with irritation. Her lips thinned as she looked at him with absolute contempt. "Just when I think you could not possibly be more inappropriate, Mr. Ross," she said icily, "you surprise me by reaching a new low."

"I may have surprised you but I don't think I have shocked you unbearably," Lucas said. "You are… ah…accustomed to the male anatomy, are you not, Lady Christina?"

The color swamped her face. She might be experienced, but she was not in the least brazen. Lucas suddenly wished he had not embarrassed her. There was something gallant and touching in the way she raised her chin and glared at him.

"That," she said, "is *absolutely* none of your concern, Mr. Ross."

Well, that was true. Even so, Lucas wondered. Convention demanded that the unmarried daughter of a duke should save herself for her husband on her wedding night. Perhaps Christina, believing she might never wed, had wanted to know what she was missing. The thought did nothing to douse his lust for her. From the start he had found her extraordinarily alluring; he had not even needed to see her to want her. Now everything about her, from the rounded curve of her cheek to the sweet tilt of her lips, made him want to kiss her.

"What are you doing indoors, Mr. Ross?" Christina said. "In the library of all places?"

"I can read," Lucas said mildly. "And I am house-trained and so may be safely allowed indoors."

"I don't doubt it," Christina said. "However, what I meant was why does your work bring you inside the castle?"

"Mr. Bevan has asked me to take a look at the books of Gothic architecture that have inspired the duke's plans," Lucas said. "As you know, my work does not currently live up to his expectations."

Christina gave an exaggerated sigh. "No one's work ever does, Mr. Ross. So far Papa has created an ornamental lake, two bridges, a summerhouse, an arbor and a lime avenue. The Gothic grotto is merely his latest fancy and none of them seem to please him when they are transferred from his imagination to mortar and stone."

"It must be very disappointing for him," Lucas said, "to fail to translate his dreams into reality."

"It is never Papa who fails," Christina said drily, "only the rest of us who fail to live up to his standards." Then, as though she realized that she had criticized her father to a servant, she blushed. "Excuse me, Mr. Ross," she said. "I have a great deal to do."

"If I could trouble you to show me where the duke's books on architecture are to be found..." Lucas said.

Christina nodded. She led him down the long room past rank upon rank of high bookcases and took a left turn. Here there was a desk in a stone bay window. The sun, slanting in through the high colored glass at the top, patterned the floor and made the dust motes dance in the light.

"More dust." Christina sounded distracted. "Poor Annie. There is nothing so hopeless as trying to keep a castle like this clean." She waved a hand over a scatter of books on the leather top of the desk. "Here you have them, Mr. Ross. I hope they will give you an idea of what my father has in mind." Her gaze fell on the top book and she bit her lip, recoiling slightly. "Oh, my goodness! I assume papa does not intend his statues to be *quite* so overendowed."

"I now have a mental image of the garden grotto as a woodland glade in which satyrs ravish innocent maidens," Lucas said, enjoying her discomfiture. He was sure that for a moment her gaze had flickered to his groin as though comparing him to the preposterously huge naked men in the book.

"Pray remove that image from your mind," Christina said sharply. "We do not require you to use your imagination, Mr. Ross. Not at all. Here…" She riffled through the book, her fingers trembling slightly. "These are the vases and urns and statues that would look most appropriate in the grotto, and this is the archway that Papa admires. There is no need to include the seminaked goddess," she added quickly.

There was a wanton-looking woman sitting astride the point of the arch in a most suggestive fashion. Her gown was slipping down to her waist and there was a dreamy smile on her face.

"Ah," Lucas said. "Yes. Far more respectable to ignore a goddess pleasuring herself." He smiled. "What a very fascinating collection of books your father possesses, Lady Christina."

"It is literature," Christina said. She cleared her throat. "Literature and art."

"That is one description for it," Lucas said. "I begin to see what a wide education you have had, Lady Christina."

Christina looked so ruffled and confused, as though the experience earlier, his proximity, his obvious desire for her, had completely overwhelmed her usual cool competence. Her blue gaze touched his and slid away. "I shall leave you to…ah…research in peace," she said. "I hope you do not find it too disturbing an experience."

"On the contrary," Lucas said. "I—"

He stopped. Christina had bent to pick up a flower basket from the floor. Evidently before the contretemps with the book, she had been arranging the peonies that glowed a soft pink in the vase on the desk. The sun was burnishing the auburn of her hair, picking out threads of gold and copper and rich brown. It also struck the jewel-bright colors on a painting on the shelves to the left of her, a painting showing the baby Jesus clasped in his mother's arms. It was no bigger than the size of a book and it stood in a recessed alcove, half-hidden by the books around it. Lucas felt a chill rush through his body like icy water. Very slowly he walked forward to stand in front of it.

"This is unusual," he said. His voice was steady, surprising him.

"Pretty, isn't it?" Christina had come back down the aisle to join him. Her head was bent as she traced the line of Mary's face with one finger. "What a serene expression she has. It looks very old and…" She paused. "I don't remember seeing it in here before. It's Russian, I think. I believe Papa has some other ones in his collection. He must have decided to exhibit them."

"Where did it come from?" Lucas asked. He knew the answer; it had been Peter's and before that their mother's. It was an icon, a Russian religious picture. He remembered it from his childhood. He had loved it for its delicate beauty. His mother had told him it was ancient and very precious. The sunlight seemed to dance in front of his eyes, the colors blurring.

Christina was shaking her head. "I am not sure." A shade of uncertainty entered her voice. "As I say, I believe that Papa has a number of them. He bought them when he was on his Grand Tour."

She was frowning, and the look she gave Lucas was edged with doubt. "Why do you ask, Mr. Ross?"

"No reason," Lucas said. "I thought it pretty, that is all." His mind was racing. Once again the Duke of Forres was implicated in Peter's death. Yet was so slight and frail a man really capable of murder? It seemed unlikely, if not impossible. Perhaps the duke had been the unknowing dupe of the real murderer who had sought to capitalize on his crime by selling off those items he had stolen.

He fell into step beside Christina. "I think I will bring the plans from the drawing office so that I can compare them with the designs in the book," he said. He wanted to talk to her, to find out more about her father's collection and about Peter's visit to Kilmory but he did not want to keep Christina standing in the library lest it aroused her suspicions. He opened the heavy oak library door for her and stood back to let her pass.

"May I escort you anywhere?" he asked.

"Oh…" She seemed taken aback at his offer. "I was going to return my basket to the hothouses and then check on Mr. Hemmings's gout. I know it still pains him." She glanced up at Lucas's face. "But there is no need to walk with me, Mr. Ross."

"It's no trouble," Lucas said. "We are heading in the same direction."

It did not look as though his answer pleased her, but short of dismissing him directly there was little she could do. Lucas knew she had been avoiding him and did not particularly want his company. She was attracted to him and she did not want to be. In her eyes he was a servant, a man younger than she was and so far beneath her socially that he barely registered on the scale at all. It was an improper attraction in so many ways and she was sensible to try to ignore it. Lucas knew that he should do the same. He was certain now that Lady Christina MacMorlan was innocent of Peter's murder. Her response to the icon had been the same as it had to the silver clasp; she had no knowledge of their true origins. If he were not to deceive her further, if he were not to hurt her as he had promised Jack he would not, he needed to keep out of her way and continue his investigation without her involvement.

He glanced down at her. She looked very neat this morning in a prim yellow gown, her hair in a no-nonsense chignon. Yet he knew what it was like to feel the silkiness of that hair between his fingers as he kissed her. He knew the curve of her breast beneath that prim bodice and the crisp shift underneath. And he really should not be thinking such thoughts since they did nothing to ease his arousal.

Galloway was in the hall. His long face lengthened even further when he saw Lucas.

"Mr. Ross! Should you be inside the house?"

Lucas gritted his teeth but it was Christina who answered. "Papa has asked Mr. Ross to do some additional work on the plans for the grotto," she said. "He is to be permitted to come and go as he pleases so that he may use the library."

That was even more helpful to Lucas's search than he had hoped. He shot her a grateful look. "Thank you, ma'am."

They went outside and walked side by side down the uneven path toward the hothouses. Tall cedars shaded the path, but even so it was bright, the sunlight startling after the shade inside. Lucas could not focus on the day. All he could see was the tiny icon that had belonged to his brother. Unlike him, Peter had been brought up in a religious tradition all his life. He had loved the little icon and had told Lucas that it would protect him on his travels. It seemed it had failed him.

He squared his shoulders. Now, more than ever, it seemed that something had happened to Peter at Kilmory Castle. He could ask the duke directly how Peter's icon came to be in his collection, but the danger was that if Forres really were implicated, his inquiries would do nothing other than cause suspicion. He needed to tread carefully.

He looked at Christina. She had not stopped to collect a bonnet and so his view of her face was unimpeded. She looked preoccupied, a little distant, as though she was thinking about something that troubled her.

"Wasn't there a Russian lad met with an accident around here a few months ago?" Lucas asked. Then, catching Christina's upward glance, "I read about it in the Edinburgh newspapers."

He thought she relaxed very slightly. "I see," she said. "Yes, there was a young man, scarcely more than a boy, really. He was attacked and robbed whilst out walking on the cliffs near here. It was terrible." Her voice had softened into regret. "I felt so sorry for his tutor having to take his family such terrible news."

"Had you met him?" Lucas said. His heart pounded as he waited for her reply.

"He dined at the castle," Christina said. The stiffness was back in her voice, as though she did not want to talk about it. "They all did, all four of them. They were young men on a tour of Europe who had wanted to see something of the west coast because it has such a wild and romantic reputation."

A cloud covered the sun for a moment. Lucas thought he saw her shiver.

"What was he like?" he asked.

A sudden smile lit her eyes. "Oh, he was charming! Funny and sweet and eager for the experience of travel and so young…" Her smile vanished. "It was a dreadful tragedy," she said. "We were all very upset." She spread her hands. "I tried to help…afterward. The tutor wanted to return to Edinburgh as quickly as possible. He was a superstitious man. I think he was afraid something might happen to another of his charges."

"Probably afraid for his job," Lucas said. He could only imagine what his stepfather might have done by way of retribution to the man who had failed to protect his only son and heir.

Christina slanted a look up at him. "You are a cynic, Mr. Ross."

"On the contrary," Lucas said. "I am a realist."

Christina sighed. "The authorities investigated. They sent men from London but they could not find the culprits. They think he fell foul of some ruffians who make a living from highway robbery and theft. It is unusual these days, but not unheard of." There was vivid regret in her expression. "I am only sorry he was so unlucky to fall in with such a band near Kilmory."

To Lucas's mind there had been nothing of bad luck about it. He wondered if robbery alone would have been sufficient motive for murder. It seemed unlikely. Peter had been rich and his possessions valuable, but there had been no need to kill him for them.

"The papers were full of the lurid details of the case," he said. "It was a sensation."

"Really?" Christina's expression showed her distaste. "Well, scandal sheets will print anything if they think it will sell more copies. How unpleasant to make profit from it, when it was such a tragedy. That must have hurt his relatives even more." She fell silent for a moment. "He spoke of his family, you know," she said. "His father, his brother…" A frown touched her eyes. "There had been some estrangement, I believe. He was so happy to find his brother again. He hero-worshipped him, as young men are so inclined to do. I often wonder—" She hesitated. "How his brother must have felt when he heard the news."

He felt angry, cheated, despairing…

Lucas felt an echo of that anger ripple through him. Of course she could not know of his connection to Peter, but it hurt to hear her speak of him; it felt like an open wound. It was even worse that she spoke with such compassion when it could have been the jackals in her smuggling gang who had stabbed his brother and taken the signet ring from his finger and the clothes from his back and had sold his belongings.

He cleared his throat. "You are always worrying about the feelings of others," he said. "What makes you grieve for his brother when you do not even know him?" The words came out more harshly than he had intended, but she did not seem surprised.

"I know what it is to lose someone dear to me," she said quietly. Her blue gaze was clouded. "My mother died when I was young. My life changed completely." She looked away across the sweep of the park. "One is so unprepared for loss," she said, half to herself, "and yet one's whole future can change in an instant. I think it better not to love than to lay oneself open to that pain."

"You have too much of a loving spirit to do that," Lucas said roughly.

Don't become like me, he thought. It was too late for him—he had cut himself off from love many years before when his stepfather had cast him out. Christina was different, though. She cared too much for people to deny the love that was in her.

"I am sorry you lost your mother at a young age," he said. "I imagine that must have been very hard for you. But it does not mean that you should never risk loving someone again."

Something flickered in her eyes, like a door closing. Lucas had the strangest sensation that she was deliberately shutting down the memory. "I imagine you must have found it difficult, too." Her gaze appraised him. "You mentioned that you were an orphan."

"My mother died when I was twelve years old," Lucas admitted. "Yes, it was hard."

"And your father?"

"I never knew him. I was illegitimate, a bastard."

He heard her catch her breath at the bitterness of his tone. He had not intended to show his feelings quite so openly. It was completely unfamiliar to him, uncomfortable, strange. Yet her gaze on him was steady and sure, with no pity, only compassion in it and the same understanding she had shown that night in the tower when he had admitted he was orphaned.

"It is hard for a boy to grow up fatherless," she said. "I imagine you had to learn very quickly how to survive."

"Yes," Lucas said. "I begged, I stole food, I picked pockets, I was cold, always hungry. There were plenty like me in the back streets of Edinburgh." He shrugged. "As I grew older, I got work sometimes. I didn't want to be a thief all my life."

"How did you come to train as a servant?" There was a spark of interest in her voice that was not feigned. "It must have been difficult to persuade anyone to give you that chance."

"By a very roundabout route," Lucas said truthfully. He did not want to lie to her. In fact, the urge to tell her everything was dangerously strong. He did not understand why. "We were speaking of you," he said. "Do not think that I had not noticed that you turned the subject."

She laughed. "Oh, I am a very dull topic."

"I don't believe that," Lucas said. "I heard that after your mother died you gave up your own future to raise your younger brothers and sisters."

Again he saw that flicker of expression in her

eyes, a flash of pain, but her voice when she answered was quite steady.

"Who told you that?"

"Servants talk," Lucas said. He was not even sure why he was pushing her on it except that it interested him. He wanted to know more about Lady Christina MacMorlan.

"Of course they do." She sounded weary. "Well, there was not a great deal of future to give up."

"I heard there was a betrothal," Lucas said. "A marriage of your own."

"It was hard for them." She swept aside her own loss with a dismissive wave of the hand. It was as though it simply did not count—or was too painful to remember. "My little sisters were so young when mama died. And Papa… He could not cope on his own. He needed me."

"You worked very hard to keep your family together," Lucas said. "You still do. The whole village is your family now." She had put everyone else first for years, he thought. She had taken the love that might otherwise have been lavished on a family of her own and had given it freely to those about her. It was generous, it was endearing, but it was also maddening that she had so little thought for her own needs and desires. He wondered what those desires had been before the Duke of Forres's selfish whim had set them aside.

"Family is important." She spoke simply. "People are important. We all need to belong."

"I don't agree," Lucas said. He thought of the

Black Strath, the estate his father had left him, another place where he did not belong. "I have no real home," he said, "or family, and I am happy enough."

"Are you?" Suddenly the look in her blue eyes was keen and far too perceptive. It felt as though she could see right through him: see the hopes he had cherished of building a relationship with his brother and the pain of loss; see the fierceness with which he rejected all ties that could bind him, hurt him. He had a rule to keep himself apart. He had broken it for Peter and had suffered for it. He would never take that risk again.

"Well..." She brushed the matter away as though she had realized that this was not the sort of conversation she should be having with the gardener. "I do not suppose we should be discussing such personal matters," she said. A hint of color came into her face. "I am not sure why I talk to you so much, Mr. Ross. It is quite inexplicable."

Lucas smiled at her. "Perhaps you view me as a confessor figure," he suggested. "Like a priest."

She gave a snort of laughter, quickly repressed. "Anyone less like a priest..." she said.

The cedar walk opened out into a broad expanse of parkland. Christina paused, her gaze fixed on the distant boundary where the bank and ditch of the ha-ha separated the park from the bracken-and-heather-clad hillside beyond.

"Did you go to see Eyre?" Lucas asked. He wondered if the riding officer had kept his word.

Christina's gaze came back to fix on his face.

"No," she said. "There was no need." She frowned slightly. "Word came this morning that he had released Callum MacFarlane. Perhaps he has some humanity in him after all."

"I wouldn't bank on it," Lucas said. "You heard that he burned a barn over at Kilcoy when he was hunting for the peat-reek? Unfortunately he did not trouble to check first whether anyone was inside."

He felt a shudder rack her. She turned to look at him, face pale, eyes frightened. "What happened?"

"Some children almost died," Lucas said harshly. "They had been playing and hid in fear when they saw the riding officers coming. They breathed in the smoke."

He heard her catch her own breath. "Will they live?"

"No one knows," Lucas said.

There was silence but for the soft crunch of the path beneath their feet, then she sighed. "I heard that you yourself met Mr. Eyre a few nights ago," she said. "At the Kilmory Inn."

"Your spies are very good," Lucas said, amused. It was a sharp reminder that he needed to be very careful. "We played a game of cards," he said. "I beat him."

"I don't suppose anyone else is prepared to play with him," Christina said.

Lucas shrugged. "I'll play cards with any man for money and a drink."

"Yes," Christina said. The look she gave him was opaque. He could not read it at all. "That reminds me of something I wished to discuss with you, Mr. Ross."

"Oh?" Lucas said.

She did not speak immediately and he could not see her face as she was half turned away from him. The sleeve of her spencer brushed his arm. He heard her give a little sigh, and then she stopped and squared her shoulders, tilting her face up to his.

"We need to talk about your drinking habits, Mr. Ross," she said. "It has come to my attention that you spend almost all your spare time and most of your pay in the Kilmory Inn." She frowned a little, wrinkling her nose up. "I hope that you do not have a problem with alcohol?"

"That is quite a question," Lucas said, "from a woman who took refuge in the peat-reek to escape her guilt and her grief."

"Mr. Ross!" Christina's eyes flashed. "You are—"

"Presumptuous," Lucas said. "Insolent. I know. In general, it is not a good idea to use drink as an escape."

She had turned away from him, her lips set tightly, anger in every elegant line and curve of her body. "That was different," she said. "You know it was. Whereas you... I hear you visit the inn almost every night."

Lucas sighed. He could hardly tell her that he only frequented the Kilmory Inn in order to pick up clues about his brother's death. And something about Christina's resolve to tackle a difficult subject touched him. She thought he might have a problem. She wanted to help.

"Lady Christina." He softened his tone. "I do not know what you have heard, but I assure you that I am not reliant on drink."

A frown still marred the smooth skin between Christina's brows. "You may think so, Mr. Ross, but I assure you that it is all too easy to become dependent without realizing. My brother—" She stopped abruptly.

Lucas put his hand on her arm. "I am sorry about Lord Lachlan," he said. The entire castle, the entire village and probably all of Scotland knew that Lachlan MacMorlan's life was slowly unraveling.

Christina shook her head and Lucas knew she was rejecting his comfort. It was not appropriate for him to offer it; no servant should presume so far.

"I am merely perturbed that if you drink too much you will not be able to work effectively," Christina said abruptly. Lucas saw her fingers clench on the handle of the basket. "My concern is entirely practical and in the interests of the estate."

"I am in no danger of putting a garden fork through my foot," Lucas said. He did not bother to call her on the lie. They both knew her concern for him had been personal, and she betrayed herself again a moment later when she said hesitantly, "If you have spent all your wages and are in financial difficulty I could give you an advance on the next week."

This time Lucas caught her elbow and pulled her

to a halt. "Your concern for me is very sweet," he said softly, "but quite unnecessary."

Confusion flickered in her eyes. "I am concerned for the smooth running of the establishment at Kilmory," she corrected. "I spoke only out of duty."

"Not quite," Lucas said pleasantly. "You care about people, not just their ability to work." He saw her take a breath to contradict him and continued, "You are concerned that no one starves in the village and that your father's tenants have their grievances addressed justly and that you look after all your relatives and dependents. Duty is cold. You are not cold."

Her color deepened but she did not correct him. He could feel the resistance in her, though, the need to break away from him and restore the fragile barriers she had erected between them. He was not inclined to let her destroy that intimacy. Suddenly he wanted to make her see, make her understand that there were times when she should put herself first. He gave her arm a little shake so that she looked up at him again.

"What about you," he said a little roughly. "Who takes care of you, Lady Christina?"

The confusion in her eyes deepened. Seeing the vulnerability there, Lucas was ambushed by a fierce desire to kiss her. Exasperation and frustration warred in him. Here was a woman who spent so much time caring for others that she did not even understand his question. She did not consider her own needs and neither did anyone else. For some reason that made him furious.

It also disturbed him. He did not like the warmth and protectiveness that possessed him whenever he saw Christina. Warmth, affection, belonging—none of these had any place in his life. They were emotions that weakened a man and made his judgment falter. He did not want to feel. He did not want to *care*.

She was still looking at him, her chin tilted up slightly, the sunlight on her face, that lush, sensual mouth. Lucas felt his body harden again, his blood running hot.

Hell and the devil.

He stepped back, sketching a bow. "Excuse me, Lady Christina," he said a little abruptly. "I will leave you here and go to the drawing office. Good day to you."

She looked nonplussed for a moment—could she really not see how attracted he was to her?—and then nodded. "Good day, Mr. Ross." She sounded as cool and collected as ever.

Lucas watched her walk away, a neat, precise figure in her summery yellow gown and spencer. She carried the wicker basket over one arm and looked as unpretentious as any country lady. He smiled wryly as he watched her pass the laundry and pause for a word with the maid hanging out the washing before knocking at the door of Hemmings's cottage and disappearing inside. Lady Christina MacMorlan, her life's work to care for others. He was damned if he knew why her happiness mattered to him, but it did.

CHAPTER TEN

CHRISTINA PUT DOWN the sheaf of papers she was holding, took off the glasses that were pinching her nose and rubbed her eyes. They felt dry and gritty. She felt tired after hours of wading through the household expenditure. She had forgotten that that evening they were due to dine with the minister and his family, and, even though it was a short journey, she should have gone upstairs to get ready so much sooner.

She opened a drawer and shoved the account books inside, noticing as she did so the set of references for Lucas Ross that the Duchess of Strathspey had provided, the references that had made Christina feel slightly uncomfortable.

"Mr. Ross comes from a good family and I have known him for many years," the duchess had written. "You will find him entirely reliable, diligent and trustworthy and able to turn his hand to any task you require."

It was in all ways completely satisfactory, and Christina was at a loss as to why she felt so uneasy about it, but uneasy she was. There was no hint of impropriety in the duchess's relationship with Lucas, no suggestion of anything other than a long and respected association, and Christina felt guilty for even imagining it. She wondered whether Lucas had in fact been a protégé of the Strathspeys. Perhaps they had been the ones to find him on the streets of Edinburgh and give him a chance of a better life. They might even have paid for him to go to school. Certainly Lucas's speech and other aspects of his behavior suggested that he had been educated far above his current station. But in that case, Lucas would have risen equally far above the role of either footman or gardener. He would have become a clerk and would have hired servants himself.

It was a puzzle, but she could not write back to ask the duchess for more detail without betraying a most unladylike interest in her new gardener. She had already betrayed that interest to Lucas far too much. He let slip so little information about himself. She imagined his solitary nature had been forged all those years ago when he had had to fend for himself as a child, but it hurt her that now, as a man, he still fiercely rejected any sense of belonging. Her family, her clan, was everything to her.

She shoved the reference back into the drawer and closed it with a snap, standing up, frowning as she noticed the ink that had stained her fingers and left a blot on her gown. She would have to ask Alice Parmenter if she had any remedies to remove the stain. The previous housekeeper had been a positive mine of useful information but Alice was less helpful; there was something surly in her manner these days. If the duke had not insisted that she be given the job at Kilmory, Christina would have had no hesitation in sacking her.

Promptly at five the carriage drew up on the gravel sweep outside Kilmory Castle's main door. Christina gathered the family all together: her father, still scribbling distractedly on a piece of paper as she coaxed him into his jacket; Lachlan, who had not bothered to shave and looked like a brigand; Gertrude, proud in olive silk and a matching turban; and Allegra, whose eyes were bright with the excitement of different company.

"I am hoping to see MacPherson's collection of first editions of Drayton's poetry tonight," the duke said, pushing his papers haphazardly into his pockets with ink-stained fingers. The minister was a friend and academic colleague of his. They had been at Oxford together. "I hope he has brought them back with him from Edinburgh."

"You may have to make do with conversation tonight, Papa," Christina warned. "The MacPhersons have visitors from Edinburgh and the minister may be too preoccupied to spare time for poetry."

"MacPherson always introduces the most stimulating topics at the dinner table." The duke's face was alight with childlike pleasure. "Last time I believe we spoke on Tillotson's principles of benevolence."

"This is precisely the sort of society we should mixing with," Gertrude agreed as she allowed Galloway to help her on with her cloak. "It is far preferable to your indigent spinsters and charity cases, Christina. They cannot possibly do us any good. Although Mr. and Mrs. MacPherson are without title, they are well connected and are worth cultivating. When Angus and I are in charge of the Forres estates, there will be no hobnobbing with the local peasantry."

Allegra rolled her eyes. Christina tried not to smile to see it. Gertrude was still talking as she herded Allegra ahead of her down the steps.

"It simply isn't good enough having only the one carriage," she was saying. "Angus and Lachlan are obliged to ride because there is not enough room for us all. The Duke of Forres arriving with only one carriage! I could sink with the embarrassment of it."

"Try to bear it, Gertrude," Christina said drily. "When *you* are Duchess of Forres, you may of course keep as many carriages as you please, but for now it is not financially worthwhile for us to run more than one."

Gertrude made a huffing sound. "As though you need to penny pinch! Why, everyone knows that the duke is the richest man in Scotland and that you yourself will have an independent fortune within a couple of years!" Malice tinged her voice. "It will be some small recompense, I suppose, for being an old spinster, long on the shelf."

Christina felt her stomach drop in sickening fashion. She was used to Gertrude's spiteful digs, but they were still painful to bear. She knew her sister-in-law deliberately tried to provoke her. She was doing it again now because Christina had refused to rise to her previous comment.

"What was the name of that fellow you were betrothed to?" Gertrude was musing. "McMahon? McGregor?"

"McGill," Christina said expressionlessly.

"McGill!" Gertrude said with glee. "He went off to London and married a grocer's daughter! One chance to secure a husband, Christina, and you fail because Lord McGill preferred the daughter of a cit!"

Christina gritted her teeth. Sometimes it seemed, looking back, that her life had been a house of cards, and the tiniest breath of wind had sent them tumbling. She had thought her life was built on rock, but there had been nothing but shifting sand.

She became aware of a tall figure standing by the carriage steps waiting to help them ascend. It was Lucas. The Forres livery of black and scarlet suited his tall, broad-shouldered physique. Christina realized she was staring and shut her mouth with a snap just as Gertrude let out a crow of delight.

"Ah! There you are, Ross! Galloway did find a uniform to fit you, then. That's excellent. It was quite unacceptable for that other footman to escort us tonight. He was far too unprepossessing." She gave Lucas a comprehensive glance. "A pity you do not have a twin. You would have looked very pretty together on the back of the carriage."

"Gertrude!" Christina was simultaneously appalled at her sister-in-law's high-handed dismissal of Thomas Wallace and the way she spoke to and about Lucas as though he were no more than an ornament. "You cannot simply tell Thomas that he is not to accompany us. It is part of his job! Imagine how that must make him feel. I suppose—" she allowed her disgust to color her tone "—you told him he was too ugly to be seen on the back of a carriage?"

Gertrude looked blank. "Of course I did not offer an explanation. What an odd idea. I merely told him that his services were not required tonight."

Christina was so furious she stormed up the carriage steps, ignoring the hand Lucas held out to help her and equally ignoring the fact that Gertrude, always so keen on asserting her precedence, wanted to take the best seat. The journey to the manse passed in an uncomfortable simmering silence.

Gertrude's taunting words seemed to ring in Christina's ears. *An old spinster, long on the shelf...*

It was true. That was precisely what she was and perhaps that was why it hurt so much. What made it worse, though, was that Lucas had heard. That was humiliating. Of course, Lucas knew her situation. Yet she did not want Lucas to pity her. She did not need sympathy. She had chosen this life.

Having got into the carriage first, Christina was the last down the steps when they finally arrived. This time Gertrude made sure to sweep out with a great fuss and swish of skirts, her back still rigid with outrage.

Lucas was again waiting to help, but Christina felt reluctant to take his hand even though she needed it this time, as there was quite a drop to the ground. Gritting her teeth and telling herself not to be so stupid, she put her hand in his. Immediately Lucas's fingers closed about hers, long and strong. It was such a small thing, only a touch, and it should have been impersonal but it was not. Christina felt the sensation shimmer through her down to her toes, and she stopped dead on the top step.

Immediately Lucas stepped forward and Christina knew he was about to scoop her up in his arms. "There is no need to carry me, Mr. Ross," she said quickly. "I am not an infant."

"I beg your pardon, ma'am." Lucas's voice was low and amused, his lips so close to her ear that she felt her hair stir with his breath. "I thought that after your experience in the library you might have developed a fear of heights."

"As usual, you exceed your duties," Christina said.

Lucas gave her a smile. "Ma'am."

"That was not a compliment," Christina said.

Lucas's smile disappeared. "Ma'am."

"I believe we also owe you an apology, Mr. Ross," Christina said stiffly. "It was inappropriate for Lady Semple to ask you to do Thomas's job this evening, and even more so for her to comment on your appearance."

"Yes, ma'am," Lucas said. "Thank you."

Christina was unsure whether he was agreeing with her or simply acknowledging the point. Servants were not supposed to have opinions. Not that Lucas Ross had ever behaved as he was supposed to do.

"It was equally inappropriate," she said, "to rehearse our family's tedious personal affairs in front of you. I apologize for that, too."

"I wouldn't call them tedious," Lucas said. "And forgive me, ma'am, but Lady Semple's conclusions were quite mistaken." His voice had changed, hardened. Christina could have sworn there was a thread of anger in it now. "I do not know who this McGill was, ma'am," he said, "but he sounds like a complete fool."

Christina felt a pang of shock. "Thank you," she said, "but—"

"Any number of men would be happy to marry you, ma'am," Lucas continued, "and they would be fortunate to do so."

"Because I am an heiress," Christina said. She felt a flash of bitterness.

"No, ma'am," Lucas said. He dropped his voice so that no one could overhear. "Because you are generous and kind and you kiss like an angel."

"Mr. Ross!" Christina's face flamed and her heart beat so hard she thought he would surely hear it. "I am not sure there has ever been so improper a servant as you are," she said. "You take the most appalling liberties."

"You did ask, ma'am," Lucas said, with a smile that was entirely disrespectful.

"It strikes me, Mr. Ross," Christina said, ignoring the flare of heat that look engendered, "that you are in completely the wrong job. You need to be employed in something where you can exercise your initiative and express your opinions freely since you do that anyway." She shook her head. "Did I not tell you right at the start that flirting with a member of the family was improper?"

"I thought it might be," Lucas said. "Except I was not flirting. I was telling the truth."

"Enough," Christina said. "Are you trying to incite me to sack you, Mr. Ross? Think about what I said. If you wish to study or apply for more challenging work, I would be happy to sponsor you."

Even though it was getting dark, she saw the sudden flare of astonishment in Lucas's eyes. Perhaps he had not believed her sincere. Perhaps he was accustomed to people making empty offers. His background and upbringing as an orphan on the streets of Edinburgh could not have made him the most trusting of men.

"That is extremely generous of you, ma'am," he said after a moment, "but I do not require such charity."

Christina stiffened. She could not help herself—she felt offended at the rebuff. She should have realized. Lucas Ross needed no one. She had lost count of the number of times he had spurned her attempts to help him. He was utterly self-contained, utterly cold. She thought of the flowers she had left him, which the following day she had found wilting on the compost heap behind the potting sheds and had felt a strange sense of desolation sweep through her.

"My lady—" Lucas said, and she realized that her feelings must have shown and now he did pity her. She shook her head and walked away up the path to the door. She could see Mr. and Mrs. MacPherson in the brightly lit hall, waiting to greet her, and Gertrude's cross face peering back at her through the dark.

"Christina!" Her sister-in-law's tone cut like glass. "What on earth are you doing out there? You are taking *hours!*"

"Nothing," Christina said, with a sigh. "I'm doing nothing at all."

LUCAS HELPED THE groom and coachman stable the horses, for which they were properly grateful, though they gave him some banter about dirtying his smart uniform. Acting as footman was a complication he had not seen coming. Annie, the second housemaid, had asked him to coach Thomas Wallace in his duties because poor Thomas was hopeless and Galloway was becoming increasingly exasperated with him. Lucas had been on the terrace giving Thomas some practical advice when Lady Semple had come across them and had promptly decreed that Lucas would accompany them that night in Thomas's place.

"We are condescending to visit a relatively modest household," she had said. Her cold gaze had slid over Thomas, itemizing his flushed, freckled face, untidy hair and untucked shirt. "We need to show them how to do things properly. You will not do, Wallace. Not at all."

Thomas had slipped away, looking mightily relieved, and Lady Semple had sent Lucas off to be sized up for a footman's livery, much to Galloway's disgust.

"Don't go getting ideas, lad," he had said to Lucas as he'd unearthed an ancient and slightly moth-eaten uniform. "Currying favor with her ladyship is all very well, but your place is in the garden, not the drawing room."

"Of course, Mr. Galloway," Lucas had said. He'd been tempted to remind the butler that at his interview, Galloway had told him he might need to turn his hand to anything at Kilmory. However, he did not think that would help. It was an irony, since he could not bear Lady Semple and had absolutely no desire at all to curry favor with her, as Galloway put it.

Gertrude, as Lucas had already realized, was inclined to ride roughshod over anything and anyone in her way. She and her husband were precisely the sort of aristocrat that Lucas abhorred: arrogant, self-obsessed and full of that sense of entitlement that he deplored. They did nothing useful, but expected to be rewarded handsomely simply for existing. More heinous was the way in which they both treated Christina. Gertrude's casual contempt for her sister-in-law made Lucas seethe, whilst her husband's bullying ways made him want to punch the man. He knew it should not matter to him one way or the other, but it did. It mattered to him a great deal, and there was nothing he could do about that.

The horses had picked up on his tension and were watching him with dark, intelligent eyes, ears pricked as though anticipating trouble. Lucas deliberately banked down his anger and frustration in order not to spook them. Working with horses was something he enjoyed. He had learned to ride as a child on his grandfather's estates, and later, when his stepfather had thrown him out and he had gone to Scotland, he had eventually found work driving the dray horses that delivered goods around the streets of Edinburgh.

He remembered Christina asking him if he had worked with horses. He had rebuffed her question as he generally did if anyone asked him something too personal or got too close. He had done the same thing tonight when she had offered to sponsor him in finding a new job or studying to better himself. Her open generosity completely devastated him; he did not know how to deal with it. So he pushed her away—and now he felt bad about it because he had upset her. Christina was too kind, he thought as he closed the stable door softly behind him. Several times now she had tried to help him, reaching out to him, only to be rejected. Christina cared, and as a result she laid herself open to hurt.

He swore softly under his breath. He did not want to hurt Christina.

A housemaid was at his shoulder. "You're to take dinner in the servants' hall," she said, gesturing toward the steps that led down to the basement. "Keep your head down—Cook has burned the pheasants and Mr. Dixon, the steward, is on the warpath. Proper bad mood he's in tonight."

Lucas nodded, repressing a smile. "Thank you," he said.

The girl nodded and withdrew and Lucas strolled

across the yard and down the basement steps to the servants' hall. It was brightly lit, rich with the smells of roasting meat and busy with the bustle of a working household.

A harassed steward strode past, saw Lucas's livery and paused. "What's your name?" he demanded.

"Lucas, sir."

The steward nodded. "Well, Lucas, I have a house full of guests and no footman working with me as he was foolish enough to sprain his wrist yesterday. You can help serve dinner."

"Yes, sir," Lucas said. He hoped he could remember his etiquette. He was more than a little out of practice.

It was the worst dinner Christina had had to endure for a very long time. The food was delicious, the wine was very fine, conversation sparkled and she sat frozen like a pillar of salt to the chair. It was Lucas's fault, of course. When she saw him come into the dining room and realized that he was to help serve dinner she felt a very peculiar nervousness, as though she was a debutante at her first formal meal, terrified of dropping her wineglass or using the wrong fork. Her appetite vanished. For a moment it felt as though her mouth was filled with sawdust and she could not swallow.

She found her gaze riveted to Lucas's hands as he served her. The sight of a footman handling vegetables had never previously caused her to blush, but she was so on edge now that she was practically dancing on her chair. She saw Mrs. MacPherson give her a curious glance and felt even more self-conscious.

She knew she could not really blame Lucas for her discomfiture. It was not his fault that she could not behave naturally in his presence, and she admired his coolness in stepping up to the job when clearly he had been drafted in at the last minute to help Mr. and Mrs. MacPherson's very harassed steward. His service was immaculate, deferential and smooth; although he did not look at her once, Christina felt as though she was on display. It was very uncomfortable.

Eventually the ladies withdrew to leave the gentlemen to their port, and she found herself drawn into conversation with Mrs. MacPherson and her cousin, Lady Bellingham, as they sat together on a wide rose brocade sofa. She had met Lord and Lady Bellingham on their previous visit to Kilmory and liked them a great deal. She the impression that Mrs. MacPherson had deliberately sought her out and made sure that Gertrude could not join them. Her sister-in-law sat glowering at them from a deep armchair across the room.

"I hear that you have been fixed in Kilmory for some considerable time, Lady Christina," Lady Bellingham said, looking thoughtfully at Christina with her bright brown eyes. "How do you find it? Not too dull, I hope."

"Oh, there is plenty to keep me busy," Christina said lightly. It was her standard reply when anyone asked her how she felt. "Papa prefers Kilmory to Forres for his studies."

"But what about you?" Lady Bellingham persisted gently. "Is there much society for you here? Running the estate is all very well—" She smiled when Christina made a slight gesture of protest. "My dear Lady Christina, everyone knows that you are the one who *really* takes care of the people of Kilmory. You are laird in all but name. It was the first thing I heard when I came here."

Christina, aware of Gertrude's deepening frown, blushed. "I merely keep the household running, ma'am…."

"And only that until Angus comes into his inheritance," Gertrude said, adding with a false sweetness that set Christina's teeth on edge, "Then dear Christina may take a very hard-earned break from her housekeeping duties."

"Well," Lady Bellingham said, a chip of ice entering her voice, "let us not hurry the duke to his demise quite yet!" She smiled at Christina, pointedly excluding Gertrude. "My dear, I should be so delighted if you wished to visit me in Edinburgh sometime. Do say you will! I insist on it." Then, as Gertrude opened her mouth, presumably to invite herself, too, Lady Bellingham said, "I would invite you, too, Lady Semple, but as the future chatelaine of Kilmory you must be so occupied with family and other commitments that I would not dream of adding to your burdens with another invitation."

Gertrude's mouth closed with a snap and she looked chagrined.

Mrs. MacPherson leaned closer to Christina, dropping her voice a little. "I must apologize that we commandeered your footman so shamelessly to serve dinner tonight," she said. "It was very bad of us but he rose to the occasion with aplomb."

"Oh, Ross is excellent in every way," Gertrude said, seizing the opportunity to enter the conversation again. She shot Christina a triumphant glance. "I was the one who recognized his potential. Dear Christina had him laboring in the garden!"

"Actually, it was Papa who appointed Mr. Ross as under gardener," Christina said stiffly. She felt a prickle of annoyance to hear Gertrude speak so possessively of Lucas.

"When we return to Castle Semple, I am thinking of taking him with me," Gertrude continued as though Christina had not spoken. "He is wasted at Kilmory. I will offer him promotion and more money."

"I beg you to do no such thing, Gertrude," Christina said sharply. "It is already difficult enough to get good servants here, and with Mr. Hemmings so sick the gardens are already neglected. Besides—" she got a grip on herself, realizing that her tone had betrayed perhaps more than a professional interest in Lucas "—Mr. Ross himself might surely have some say in the matter."

Gertrude looked blank. "Gracious, what a notion! I do not require *opinions* from my servants."

"Then you will be sadly disappointed in Mr. Ross," Christina snapped. "He has plenty of opinions and is not slow to share them!"

She was aware of astonishment on the faces of Gertrude and Mrs. MacPherson, and a lively spark of speculation in Lady Bellingham's eyes. Yes, decidedly, she had betrayed too much.

There was an awkward silence, broken only when Mrs. MacPherson glanced at the clock. "Excuse me. I must go and see about a fresh pot of tea for when the gentlemen join us."

Lady Bellingham went to talk to Allegra, and as Christina had no desire to be left alone with Gertrude, who would no doubt be harping on about how different everything would be when she was mistress of Kilmory, she, too, excused herself to the ladies' withdrawing room. She tidied her hair, smoothed her dress and took several deep breaths in an attempt to steady herself.

The house was hot and stuffy, too, perhaps because the MacPhersons were worried that their guests might be cold, even in a Scottish summer. Christina's head was aching, though, from the heat and the tension. She pulled back the heavy velvet drapes that cloaked the window and with a sigh of relief, drew up the window sash to let in a breath of fresh air.

It was a clear night but a windy one. A gust rattled the branches of a tree against the glass. Glancing out, Christina saw a tall shadow crossing the courtyard. From the way he moved she knew at once that it was

Lucas and her heart did a strange little skip. It was odd that she recognized him so quickly, so instinctively, and yet she had no doubts.

A second later the breath caught in her throat as another figure stepped out of the shadows. It was one of the maids, a pert, dark-haired girl who had taken Christina's cloak on arrival with a respectful dip of the head. She had then almost dropped Christina's cloak when she had caught sight of Lucas. Christina had noticed it at the time and thought it amusing, but she did not find it quite so entertaining now as the girl put a hand on Lucas's arm to arrest his progress, stood on tiptoe and their shadows merged.

A pain wedged like a knife between Christina's ribs. It was fiercer than she could have imagined. She had not realized until now quite how much she had liked Lucas.

Fool.

So now she was jealous of a housemaid for kissing a handsome footman, which was what housemaids had done since time immemorial. And of course Lucas would kiss her back. He was young and good-looking and the housemaid was extremely pretty. Christina felt hot and envious and mortified to be feeling anything at all.

She pressed her burning forehead to the cold pane of the glass. What a stupid little fool she had been to conceive such a *tendre* for Lucas Ross and to imagine for a moment that he might admire her, as well. He had only been playing with her. He was probably laughing at her. No doubt it was a game he had played many times before and she, the sad, elderly spinster aunt had allowed it, indulged him, even though she knew she should not, because it had flattered her and excited her and made life so much more vibrant and bright.

She let the curtain fall back into place. Automatically she tidied her hair and smoothed her gown for a second time, taking comfort from the repeated movements, the habit of tidying herself and presenting a calm facade to the world. The mirror reflected a wan face, though, and she sighed to see it. Gertrude would be sure to notice and tell her she looked sallow.

As she came out into the passageway, Lucas was coming through the green baize door leading from the servants' quarters carrying a tray with a silver teapot. When he saw her he smiled, and she could not help herself—her heart gave its customary little tumble of excitement and pleasure.

Fool.

CHAPTER ELEVEN

WHEN THE KNOCK came at the door of his cottage the following evening, Lucas was in no mood for company. It had been a long, hard, hot day and he had spent it hauling stone for the grotto and digging out the rest of the watercourse. He ached in muscles he could swear he did not possess and all he wanted was a hot bath and to sleep. The former was impossible—his cottage possessed nothing more luxurious than a stone trough fed with cold water from the pump outside—and the latter was unlikely since his mattress was old and lumpy and the blankets coarse.

The door had opened without his invitation. A woman stood there, cloaked, her hood up. For a moment Lucas's heart leaped at the thought it might be Christina. He had not seen her since the previous night. She had thanked him politely for his services when they had returned to Kilmory Castle, but he had sensed a chill in her, a sense of withdrawal that he was at a loss to explain. He was not sure why he needed to explain it, why it disturbed him, but it did.

The figure stepped into the room and Lucas's heart steadied. This woman was too short and too slight to be Christina. Besides, Christina would not visit him here. She was far too proper.

"I brought you food." Alice Parmenter was placing a cloth-covered wicker basket on the wooden table. "You missed supper."

Lucas gave a grunt of acknowledgment. He tried hard to ensure that he took his meals in the servants' hall since his fellow servants were an indispensable source of information but on this occasion he was bone weary.

Alice had come into the cottage now and was looking around her with a critical eye. Lucas supposed that his housekeeping was not up to her high standards. He spent very little time inside. "Why do men never take care of themselves?" Alice bustled over to the chair, straightening the cushions, peering inquisitively through the darkened doorway into his bedroom beyond.

Lucas shrugged. "Because there's no need." He swung his booted feet down off the table and reached for the basket. There was cheese and bread rolls and a meat pie. His mouth watered.

"Thank you," he said indistinctly, through a mouthful of Scottish cheddar.

She laughed and walked back toward him. "There are other ways in which to thank me, Mr. Ross," she said.

Their eyes met. Lucas felt his stomach churn. There was such avid heat in her gaze as it slid over him, so different from Christina MacMorlan's cool sweetness.

"You flatter me," he said.

"I don't think so." She was coming toward him, sliding the cloak from her shoulders as she did so. He could feel the heat of her body now, feral and eager. This was awkward; he could not afford to alienate her. She could make life at Kilmory very difficult for him.

"I don't want to trespass," he said.

Alice's gaze widened on him. "You know about me and the duke?" she said. He saw a second's calculation touch her eyes. "I can manage him. He need not hear about us. I'd like someone younger and more energetic."

Looking at Alice now, with the top buttons of her practical housekeeper's gown undone and a predatory gleam in her eyes, Lucas wondered what on earth the scholarly Duke of Forres wanted with her. But perhaps the answer to that was all too clear. The duke was a man like any other, and his wife had been dead a very long time. This, then, was the reason why the duke preferred Kilmory to his other estates. Alice was here; it made his philandering easier.

Alice was almost on top of him now. In a moment she would be sitting in his lap.

"I'm sorry," Lucas said. He stood up.

She stopped, her eyes narrowing. "You prefer men?"

"No," Lucas said. He smiled in spite of himself. It was a confident woman who thought that. He liked her for that confidence, even if he did not want to take advantage of it.

She saw the smile and misinterpreted it. Her eyes narrowed still further, then she laughed. "You're playing for higher stakes! I knew it!" A broad, appreciative smile crossed her face. "Well, I'll be damned."

She put her hands on her hips, looking at him thoughtfully. It felt as though, suddenly, her attitude had shifted. They were coconspirators now whether Lucas wanted that or not.

She circled behind him. Her demeanor felt like that of a horse trader approving the stock. Lucas was not sure whether to be amused or disgusted.

"With a face and body like yours," she murmured, "why not aim high?" Her polite vowels had slipped a little with excitement. Perhaps she saw no need to feign gentility with him now. "Do you think you can pull it off?"

"I'm not sure," Lucas said truthfully. He wondered who she imagined his target to be. Allegra? It would be the most obvious choice. Christina? His heart bumped his ribs at the thought. He did not want Alice turning her spite on Christina.

"You're an adventurer, just like me." Alice sat down on the chair beside his, leaning her elbows on the table, watching him as he resumed his seat and reached for the bottle of ale she had brought. "Well, why shouldn't we be? I've worked damn hard on my back for any advantage I can get. If I can become Duchess of Forres..." She stopped, gave a short laugh. "Well, I can try."

Lucas raised his brows. She was ambitious indeed. "How is that going?" he asked.

She gave him a dark, disillusioned look. "Badly. The old fool is quite happy to bed me when he can get it up and he flatters me about how much he needs me, about how Kilmory needs me, but marriage—" She gave a derisive snort. "Well, he's a duke. Thinks he's above me. I'm not finished yet, though."

"I'm sure you're not," Lucas said. He wondered what the Marquess and Marchioness of Semple would do if they learned of Alice's ambitions. His lips twitched to think of Gertrude's reaction.

Alice's eyes were sharp as she watched him. "Help me and I'll help you," she said. "It's a pity the riding officer got in before you with Lady Allegra. That little miss was ripe for the plucking. Full of airs and graces, but as hot for sex as any scullery maid. But Lady Christina—" She gave a short laugh. "Well, you might be lucky there. She's gone so long without she's likely desperate. And she's an heiress, of course. But you'll have realized that."

"I have," Lucas said. He felt repulsed at the way Alice spoke so insultingly of Christina. Christina was too warm, kind and generous to be disparaged like that.

He schooled himself not to show his disgust. Even though every instinct prompted him to move away from Alice, he forced himself to sit still and finish the bread and cheese. He even nodded his appreciation.

"Thank you," he said. "That was good."

Alice smiled, putting a hand over his as he re-packed the basket. Lucas made a conscious effort not to recoil from her touch. "I'm good for something, then," she said, "even if it is only food rather than sex."

"Do I interrupt?" Christina's voice from the doorway made Lucas jump. He had had no idea anyone was there, least of all that the door was not properly latched. He leaped to his feet and saw Alice Parmenter hide a smile. She thought he was laying the respect on thick because that was what servants did. They hid their contempt and resentment behind a mask of deference.

Christina took a couple of steps into the room. Her gaze, ice-cool as a mountain spring, took in Alice Parmenter and the little sly smile on her face. Lucas cursed under his breath and took several steps away. But it was too late. Christina had definitely seen Alice touching him. Possibly she had even heard some of their conversation. Her expression was cold.

Alice stood, too, resuming her businesslike air. There was a gleam of malice in her eyes, although her tone was respectful. "My lady. Mr. Ross was working so hard on the grotto that he missed supper."

"How thoughtful of you to provide some," Christina said. Her tone was bland. "Thank you, Mrs. Parmenter."

Dismissed, the housekeeper could do nothing other than take the basket, pick up her cloak and slip past Christina through the door and out into the night. In the silence that followed, Lucas waited.

Christina did not come any farther into the room and she left the door open.

Her gaze scanned the room, very much as Alice Parmenter's had done before, then came back to his face. "There is nothing of your own here," she said. She sounded puzzled. Her eyes were a wide and candid blue. "Did you not want to make it into a home?"

"No," Lucas said. He felt a pang of some emotion he did not recognize. "I don't have many possessions," he said. "I travel light."

"But there is no warmth," Christina said. She sounded upset now. "There is nothing to make the place comfortable."

"I think it is very comfortable," Lucas said. He gestured to the bright rag rug on the floor. "Someone went to a lot of trouble to furnish it well." He took a guess. "You, I suspect, Lady Christina."

Her eyes met his and she shrugged a little awkwardly.

"It was nothing," she said. "I wanted… I try to ensure that our servants are happy here." After a moment she added, "I have been taking Mr. Hemmings some more medicines. Unfortunately his gout has come back so badly that he has asked to go home to be cared for by his niece. He leaves tomorrow."

Her tone was remote again, mistress to servant, placing him at the appropriate distance. "Mr. Grant will take the role of head gardener for the time being." She looked at him. "I hope you understand."

"Of course," Lucas said. "I have been here barely a month. I would not expect a promotion."

"I realize that we take advantage of you," Christina said. She blushed. "Of your energy and stamina, Mr. Ross…" She blushed harder and Lucas tried not to laugh. "What I am trying to say is that I know Mr. Grant is older and frailer than Mr. Hemmings and so will not be a great deal of practical use, but he would be offended to be overlooked." Her gaze pleaded with him.

"It's all right," Lucas said. "I understand."

He saw the tension leave her. "Thank you," she said simply. "I will arrange for some additional labor from the village, but these men are not gardeners. They do not know a jasmine from a rosebush." She shrugged. "I think we will have to resign ourselves to a level of neglect without Mr. Hemmings's guiding hand. Soon the estate will resemble precisely the sort of Gothic wilderness my father wishes to create. He should be pleased."

Lucas bit back a smile at her wry tone. "I will do my best to keep up to the work," he said. "And I am learning the difference between a rose and a jasmine. In fact, I wondered—" He took a breath. "Might I borrow some books on gardening from the castle library so that I can do some research?"

Christina looked startled. "More books?"

"I quite enjoy reading," Lucas said drily.

She blushed. "Of course. I did not mean to imply—" She stopped. "Of course," she said again. "You already have permission to use the library."

Lucas nodded. "Thank you."

She was ill at ease, fidgeting with the braiding on the sleeve of her coat.

"Was there something else, Lady Christina?" Lucas said.

She met his gaze, hers half apologetic, half defiant.

"It seems I need to warn you that relationships between the staff are not tolerated, Mr. Ross," she said. "It is not appropriate for you to…become involved… with Mrs. Parmenter."

It was not what Lucas was expecting. He felt a pang of shock and right behind it a swift, fierce pang of anger. He fought it down. It was irrational to be angry with her for believing that he was romantically involved with Alice. What she had seen was suggestive. But that made no difference to how he felt.

"You have no need to tell me that," he said tightly.

Christina sighed. "No? You certainly seem to be profligate with your affections, Mr. Ross."

For a moment Lucas had no idea what she was talking about, and then he remembered the previous night at the manse. Christina must have seen the MacPhersons' housemaid ambush him in the courtyard. It would explain her coldness to him later and her predisposition now to think he was the sort of Lothario who habitually made a pass at any woman who crossed his path. He cursed. The MacPhersons' housemaid was a flirt, and her brazen advances had surprised him but he had disentangled himself quickly enough. He had no interest in her and no time for dalliance.

Something of his feelings must have shown in his face because Christina's expression had changed. She did not look angry; she looked sad. Lucas realized with a shift of the heart that she had read his silence as an admission of guilt and she had not wanted to be proved right.

"I don't know what you saw last night," he said carefully, "but there was nothing in it."

"If you say so." Christina lifted a shoulder in so perfectly executed a gesture of aristocratic disdain that Lucas felt his temper soar still higher. "I am giving you a formal warning, however, that any sort of amorous relationship will not be tolerated whilst you are at Kilmory." She turned away from him. "Good night, Mr. Ross."

Lucas reached past her and pushed the door closed with the flat of his hand. Christina spun around to face him, shock flaring in her eyes.

"Are you jealous?" Lucas said softly.

Color flooded her face. "Of course not!" Her tone was icy. "I have no desire to be another notch on your bedpost, Mr. Ross. Now stand aside!"

Lucas did not move. "How contrary you are," he said, "that you cannot see that the only woman I want is you. I think about you all the time. I dream about you. I have done since that very first night."

Her lips parted on a gasp. The shock in her eyes deepened, shadowed with doubt and a sudden vulnerability. It was so unusual to see her defenses falter. Normally she was so composed, so utterly in control, but now he could see straight through that self-possession to the woman beneath.

In that moment Lucas forgot his reasons for being at Kilmory. He forgot everything in a rush of emotion so fierce he simply reached out and pulled her to him and kissed her. And when she was in his arms it felt as right as it had done the very first night.

CHRISTINA HAD WANTED to kiss Lucas Ross again. She had dreamed of it, longed for it. The reality, so hot, so sweet and so powerful, exceeded both her memories and her dreams. His tongue slid between her lips and his arms went around her to anchor her close. The room spun. She could feel the heat and the hardness of his body, one hand spread in the small of her back, holding her against him. She touched her tongue to his, her senses overwhelmed by the intensity.

Lucas tugged hard on the ribbon of her bonnet and pushed it back with an impatient hand, tangling his fingers in her hair. She heard pins scatter across the floor, landing with a tinkle of metal on stone. The stroke of his tongue was more insistent now, demanding. She was sharply aware of her entire body, dizzy with pleasure. There was urgency in the kiss, but tenderness as well, so delicious and intimate that it stole her breath, stole her very thoughts. She forgot everything except this one man and this one moment.

The ribbon on her cloak was next, unraveling between Lucas's fingers. The heavy material slid from her shoulders like a caress to puddle at her feet. She felt cold without it, but at the same time feverishly hot and shivery. She pressed closer to Lucas, giving him back kiss for kiss, sliding her arms about his neck, shamelessly eager, until suddenly, too soon, it was over.

Lucas let her go and she took a step back, resisting the need to steady herself by grabbing hold of him again. She was shivering, and she wrapped her arms about her for warmth and comfort. All her senses seemed magnified; she could hear the soft hush of the wind in the pines outside the cottage, and beneath that, distantly, the break of the waves on the beach. She could smell the oil from the lamp as the wick burned down. It mingled with the scent of dust and damp.

We should try to improve these cottages if we expect people to live in them, she thought irrelevantly. *I will speak to Papa about it. I have done my best to make them comfortable, but they are damp; probably Mr. Ross will get the consumption.*

"Are you all right?" Lucas asked gently, and she realized that she had been staring blankly ahead of her as though in a trance.

She looked at Lucas and felt a pang of longing, a skipped beat of the heart. He was looking at her, too, quizzically, with amusement. Suddenly she felt unconscionably cross that he could kiss her so thoroughly and then seem so untouched by the experience when she was trembling, her good sense fragmented by his touch.

Had he been lying to her about Alice Parmenter and had kissed her only to distract her? Very probably he had. And yet it had felt real, all too real. She shivered, confused.

"Aren't you going to dismiss me on the spot?" Lucas did not sound particularly bothered. Perhaps he really *did* go around kissing noble ladies for sport. She was not sure whether she should believe his denials. She certainly did not believe the assertion that she was the only one he had an interest in. That could not possibly be true, not her, the plain spinster sister, old, faded, on the shelf, good only to run the house and chaperone the nieces her siblings furnished her with. Lucas could have no real interest in her when he was so handsome and so charming that women were falling over themselves in the rush to warm his bed.

He smiled at her. Damn him for that, when she felt as though the world was still tilting on its axis, as though the ground she was standing on was as unstable as quicksand. She had no idea how to deal with situations like this because normally she never got herself into them. "It would be unfair to dismiss you," she said, striving to be impartial.

She sensed his surprise, although his face remained as impassive as ever.

"Would it?" he said. "Why?"

"I did not object to you kissing me." She was not sure why she was being so honest but it felt important. "I did not protest." Her face heated. "I kissed you back."

She had. With interest. And she would do it again in a heartbeat if only she could. She was not even sure if it mattered if he *was* pretending to like her. Not when he could kiss like that.

"That is very…charitable of you," Lucas said.

She was not sure whether he meant the kissing or the fact that she would not sack him, and she certainly was not going to ask for clarification in case he took it as encouragement. Her lips still tingled from the touch of his. The blood still beat hot through her body.

"Perhaps," Lucas said, "I should do it again if there is no sanction to stop me."

Christina's heart bumped hard against her ribs. She took a step back. "I would certainly dismiss you if you were to kiss me a second time."

"So it is a straight choice between kissing you and my job." Lucas sounded as though he was genuinely considering whether it was worth it. "Hmm. In that case, there is no real contest." He reached out a negligent hand and pulled her close to him. Gentle fingers grazed her cheek, tilting up her chin. "I enjoy my work," he said, his lips brushing hers, "but I adore kissing you."

And after that they did not speak for a very long time.

"I WAS NOT SURE," Christina said later, "whether the feeling was entirely on my side. I felt sure it must be."

He could ask her anything now and she could not lie. She was undone by the pleasure of his kisses, lost in bliss, heated and adrift with feelings she barely knew.

Lucas was sitting on one of the upright wooden chairs and she was sitting on his lap, cradled in his arms, a position that was not ideal for kissing, although they seemed to have managed well enough.

I must make sure that these cottages are furnished with more comfortable seating, Christina thought vaguely, her palm spread against Lucas's chest, feeling the steady beat of his heart. *These chairs are far too hard and quite unsuitable for lovemaking.*

"And now you know that it was not just you," Lucas said. "Far from it." He was toying with her hair, his fingers gentle amongst her curls, touching her as though she was infinitely precious. It felt delicious and it made her heart turn over with longing. "From the very start I found you shockingly attractive," he said. "I did not even need to see you to want you."

Christina gave a little giggle. "I could have been anyone."

"I'm not sure that would have made a difference."

"But then you *did* see me—"

"And wanted to kiss you even more."

Lucas cupped her face and kissed her again, long and slow and languorous this time, and the tight spiral of lust in her belly tightened still further.

It seemed impossible that he shared her feelings, dangerous feelings, feelings of desire and lust and need. His lips were tracing a tender path down the line of her throat now, and her skin rose to the touch, wanting more. Her bodice felt too tight. She was nearly panting. There was a constant, deep, disturbing ache low in her stomach, and her clothes frustrated her, layers of material that were superfluous. She knew a sudden shameless urge to rip them all away so that she could feel his mouth against her skin, and moaned when he slid his hand down over one breast, and her nipple hardened into a tight peak against his palm.

His mouth returned to hers and she heard him groan against her lips, a rough sound of desire that echoed hers. The kiss slid deeper into heat and fiery need. Everything was happening so quickly, but Christina did not want to stop. She did not want to think. There was no reality but this man, his kiss, his hands on her. She had fought these feelings for what seemed such a long time. Now all she wanted was to stop fighting.

She wrenched off her spencer and started to unbutton her blouse with fingers that shook.

"Christina…" Lucas covered her hands with his. He was shaking, too.

"Don't stop me," Christina said. "Please—"

He shook his head. His eyes were smoky dark with desire. "You will regret it."

"I *want* it," Christina said. "I want you."

He made a sound halfway between a gasp and a groan and she knew that for the first time she had broken through that cold reserve and reached the man beneath. A feeling took her that was part fear, part triumph, and wholly exciting. She wanted this man, needed him desperately.

He kissed her again. He tasted so good, hot and

masculine, and he smelled good, too, of fresh air and summer grass and a musky scent that was the essence of him. Her senses drank him up. Something shifted and opened within her, a willingness to recognize her own desires at last. It felt arousing, dangerous and yet so right because it was Lucas that she was with and it was Lucas she needed.

He picked her up and carried her through to the inner room, placing her gently on the bed, coming down beside her, propping himself on one elbow. She wanted him to kiss her again but he was still, leaning over her, studying her face. She sensed hesitation in him and another emotion she could not place. Confusion? She doubted Lucas Ross was ever confused in his dealings with women, yet he was uncertain now.

"It shouldn't be like this," he started to say, but she pressed her fingers to his lips.

"Hush." She drew his head down to kiss him again and felt the resistance in him melt. Through the thick material of his breeches she could feel his erection hard against her thigh. She pressed against it and heard him groan again with a harsh urgency. Suddenly it was too much; she had waited too long. She pushed the shirt from his shoulders with hands made clumsy with eagerness. She had wanted to touch him since the day she had seen him cutting the lilacs in the gardens, so powerfully built, so elegant with the slide of muscle under warm, smooth skin. She ran her hands over his shoulder and back, exulting in the sensation, then reached down to unfasten his breeches. His hands bumped hers. They were as awkward as virgins; she wanted to laugh and yet there was such a tight, sharp ache inside her that defied laughter.

"Lucas, please…"

She heard him swear under his breath as he stripped off his breeches, and then his body was hot and hard against her softness—and she was definitely overdressed. She thought of the time it would take to remove her clothes, the frustration to struggle out of all the layers, and then she felt something rip and Lucas's hands on her bare shoulders, pushing down her bodice, and she could almost have wept with relief.

"Oh, yes…" His mouth at her breast made her twist and writhe. She had never wanted anything in her life as much as she wanted Lucas now. She was the one who pulled up her skirts, shameless now, brazen. There was a moment of longing, of desperate anticipation, and then he was kneeling between her thighs and sliding inside her. It was fast, fierce and desperate. She came at once in a helpless tumble of ecstasy that would have had her crying out had Lucas not covered her mouth with his.

She had experienced nothing like this before. The lovemaking she had known as a debutante was a pale imitation of the passion and emotion she felt now. It had been the exploration of a young woman on the cusp of adulthood who had been eager to grasp at life and understand its secrets. In contrast, the depth of her feelings now scared and awed her so much she could not think about them, and she let them float away and emptied her mind to everything except sensation. She clung to Lucas as he continued to move inside her, the smooth slide of his body over and in hers an almost unendurable pleasure.

He bent his head to her breasts again and the sensation ripped through her, building, always building, toward that ultimate pleasure. She grasped the wooden bars of the bed head and clung to them as his body took hers, feeling him through every inch of her, a part of her. At each stroke the feelings intensified and she released her grip on the bed and slid her hands down over his back, his taut buttocks, drawing him in ever closer. She came again, hard, shattering with a gasp of shocked pleasure at the sheer, brilliant beauty of it. She felt the tension in him as her body drove his over the edge and at the last moment she felt him withdraw from her and collapse at her side, breathing hard.

"Oh!" She lay still in a welter of tumbled clothes and equally confused emotions. She was afraid; at the back of her mind feelings started to stir, and she did not want to confront them. Then she felt Lucas's hands moving over her with leisurely ease, unfastening buttons and untying laces. The realization that he was undressing her, stripping her, shocked her so much that everything was driven from her mind other than wanton need. She had thought herself sated. Now, though, in the darkness, with shifting shadow and patterns of moonlight, with Lucas's touch on her bare skin, she felt shameless and wicked.

Her clothes were gone. There was the kiss of the

cool air on her bare skin, and then Lucas was touching her again, exploring her with his lips and fingers and tongue, and her body seemed to open to each and every caress, each demand he made of her. He slid a hand down from her shoulder to her breast. She could feel it lie warm and heavy in his palm just as it had done on the first night he had almost made love to her. Her body jerked at the inciting memory. He ran his fingers over her nipple and she felt it harden, heard herself moan. Already she could feel her body tightening with renewed need. He played with her nipples, tweaking them, rolling them until they were tight buds of pleasure and the hot, tight sensation within her intensified.

"My breasts…" she whispered. "I always thought they were too big."

She heard Lucas laugh. The sound, so low and intimate, made her shiver. He ran his tongue up the underside of one breast and she shifted restlessly. "There is no such thing," he said, his lips against her nipple. "Your breasts are perfect. You are perfect."

His bit down gently and Christina writhed, stifling another cry.

"How do you feel?" Lucas's voice was soft. "How do I make you feel, Christina?"

"Wicked," Christina admitted. "Shameless." She could hear both pleading and pleasure in her tone. She had not quite abandoned all modesty, and lying here naked, spread beneath him, she felt utterly exposed. Her mind trembled at the wantonness of it but she did not want to stop. He had unleashed in her something so wild she could only beg for surcease.

"You can be more wicked still."

Lucas slid his hand down and between her thighs, spreading them apart. She caught her breath. His hand covered her mound, his fingers sliding over the damp folds between her thighs. She could feel herself shaking now. She did not want to give him the satisfaction of knowing how deeply he could affect her, yet there was no hiding it from him. His fingers unerringly found her swollen nub and pinched it very gently. Christina gasped, arching. He did it again, and the sensation shot through her body so sharply she cried out. She was snared by the feelings he aroused in her, captured by the powerful sensuality and the sheer wicked pleasure. He stroked her nub, rubbing gently, fueling those sensations. Her body twitched. She could not stop it. She moaned again.

"And how do you feel now?" Lucas's question was accompanied by another sly stroke that made her quiver.

"I feel so breathless," she whispered. "So strange."

"Good."

Her body felt hot and acquiescent beneath his hands. He returned to her nub, thumbing it, making her hips jerk hard. He held them down and put his mouth to her and the shock ripped through her. No one had ever done this to her before. She had had no idea.

She heard Lucas make a sound of satisfaction deep in his throat. He held her tightly and touched his tongue to her, keeping her still when she tried to roll away, flicking at her core, teasing her with long slow strokes so that the pleasure built and she writhed under his hands.

"Lucas." Her thighs were quivering. Her entire body was trembling. She gave a keening cry as she broke, shuddering and lifting her hips against his mouth in frantic rhythm.

He slid back up her body, pulling her into his arms, kissing her gently. She could smell the muskiness of her own scent on him and felt another pang of shock and sinful pleasure. Lucas cupped her face and kissed her again, his lips moving over hers.

"I want you again," he whispered. She felt the press of his erection against her thigh, hard and urgent. "May I?"

Christina made a sound of sleepy acquiescence, but all lethargy fled as he grabbed the bolster and rolled her onto her stomach, pushing it underneath her, canting her up so that she was almost on her knees. She felt his hands smooth down her back and over her buttocks, sliding between her thighs, parting her.

"I won't hurt you," he said. "Tell me to stop if I do."

He slid into her and her mind splintered with a different sort of pleasure. She was so sleek and tight and he felt so huge that it was difficult to take him all. She felt overwhelmed, invaded. He moved very gently, easing forward, allowing her body to adjust to the sense of possession. It was exquisite, overpowering. She clamped around him like a velvet glove and following blind instinct her body moved with his, pushing back. Immediately he drove into her a little harder, a little faster, and she gasped as her whole body jerked to his thrusts. He surged deep within her and she heard him groan, a harsh sound, elemental. The pleasure pushed her relentlessly onward, burning higher, claiming her until it swept her away with the force of a tidal wave, her heartbeat wild and the ecstasy pulsing through her.

For a while she lay there, aware of nothing but the shimmer of sensation fading through her body, Lucas lying at her side, and the whirl of feeling that poured through her body in a torrent. She had never felt like this; she had thought that she was experienced but instead she had been unknowing, unaware of the depth of emotion of which she was capable, ignorant of how it felt to make love with a man she…

A man she loved.

A man she loved, not with a girl's infatuation but a woman's emotion.

She lay absolutely still as she thought about it. She was in love with Lucas Ross and it did not matter who, or what he was. Servant or lord, it made no difference to her feelings.

She turned her head to look at Lucas. She was warm, lying in the circle of his arm. He was stroking her hair. It felt utterly perfect, as though they had been made for this moment. She wanted to feel happy, but instead the slide of emotion was very different, a deep, dark fall into despair. The tears prickled her throat and stung the backs of her eyes.

She had made a terrible mistake.

Again she felt that rush of emotion—dark, terrifying. Love and loss were two sides of the same coin. She had learned that when she was young.

Besides, now that she could think rationally again she realized that what they had just done had been wonderful but it was forbidden and very, very foolish. It was tempting but it was wrong. It could lead nowhere and it could cause a very great deal of trouble.

Somehow she was going to have to go back and pretend that this had never happened. She was going to have to do it because there really was no alternative. Perhaps Lucas could be her lover for a little while, but in the end the outcome would be the same; there was no future for them. There could not be. She did not want to love him. She did not want the vulnerability that love brought, nor did she want the pain. And if she continued on this foolish path, that was exactly what would happen.

She made a tiny, instinctive movement away from Lucas's embrace. He felt it.

"Christina?" he said.

"This can't happen again," she said shakily. She rolled away from him and stood up, feeling her legs tremble. It felt cold out of the shelter of Lucas's arms. Immediately she wanted that security back, that astonishing sense of belonging.

"It's wrong," she said. "We must not do it again."

"Why not?" Lucas said. He propped himself on one elbow, watching her. She was conscious of his gaze all over her as she tried to find her scattered clothing. Her hands were shaking so much she could scarcely manage to dress herself. She felt cold inside and out. Suddenly the little cottage seemed chill and cheerless and their encounter squalid and shameful, the mistress of the house seducing her gardener. What had she been thinking? Lucas was a servant, a member of her staff. It was her role to care for her people, not to use them. She felt ashamed.

"It's wrong," she said again. "It's wrong because I would be taking advantage." She avoided his gaze. She did not want to look at him or for him to look at her. She felt so vulnerable with her emotions stripped bare. She ached for him and she knew he wanted her, too. Yet she had to do the right thing whilst impossibly tempted by the wrong. "I am older than you," she said, "and I am your employer. It would be wrong to exploit that and abuse my position. If relationships between staff members are forbidden, I can scarcely expect to break those rules myself. That would be hypocritical."

Lucas stood up quickly, wrapping the blanket around his hips. He came over to her and gripped her shoulder, partly turning her to face him so that she was forced to meet his eyes. She could feel the warmth of his hands through the thin material of her blouse. His touch woke all the longing within her. She shivered.

"That isn't how it is between us," he said harshly.

She risked a quick look at him. He looked fierce, and there was hardness in his eyes she wished she had not seen because it only served to remind her that beyond desire he had no feelings for her. He could not. He was so self-contained. He needed no one.

"It is." She was not going to tell him that it was all the more impossible because she loved him. She had to finish this now, before it had begun. She had to do it for both their sakes.

"Do you really believe that?" Lucas said. "That you would be abusing your position if we…" He hesitated, as though choosing his words with care. "If we were to be together?" He was frowning now, his gaze searching her face.

"Yes, I do," Christina said. "It is my duty to protect Kilmory and all the people who belong here." She bit her lip. "To fail to live up to my responsibilities would be quite wrong. I could not place you in so difficult a position."

She saw Lucas's lips twist into a wry smile. He took her hand and pressed a kiss on her palm. "You are an extraordinary woman, Christina MacMorlan," he said slowly. "Not one man in ten would be as honorable as you."

He let her go and moved over to pick up her cloak and bonnet whilst Christina knelt down to hunt for her hairpins on the stone floor. They seemed to have scattered everywhere. Once she had found a handful she stood up and Lucas wrapped the cloak about her, his hands lingering for one long moment on her shoulders as though he wanted to pull her back into his arms. She wanted it, too; she wanted it quite dreadfully and she did not dare look at him in case he read that message in her eyes.

"Thank you, Mr. Ross." She made an effort to reassert formality, then realized how ridiculous it sounded. No wonder, after such liberties. His mouth on hers, his hands holding her, his body inside hers, so intimate, so impossible to forget. She shivered again. Part of her wanted Lucas to stop her leaving, to tell her they could be together, that everything would be all right. Yet it would not be, she knew that, and another part of her was so grateful to him for not making matters any more difficult for her than they already were.

"Good night, Lady Christina," Lucas said. And she let herself out into the cold night, wondering if she was not being honorable after all and was simply a fool to reject such pleasure in a life empty of it.

LUCAS THREW HIMSELF down on the narrow bed, put his hands behind his head and stared up at the ceiling. His body felt satisfied but his mind was tied up tight in knots, his head aching.

He had behaved unforgivably. Not since he had been in his teens had he been so at the mercy of his senses. He had never lost control the way he had done tonight with Christina.

Not such a monk now, Lucas.

The irony was not lost on him. He had not slept with a woman in a very long time, and then he had chosen the one woman he should never have touched.

He had thought himself invulnerable. Over the years he had started to believe that he needed no one, no physical intimacy, no emotional closeness. As a youth he had been as careless and thoughtless as any other young man in his attitudes toward women and sex, but as he had grown older he had found himself thinking more and more of the fact that he was a bastard, conceived out of wedlock, and that his birth had caused his mother endless shame and grief. He could never be like his father, seducing, abandoning without care, without thought. That realization alone had prevented him from ever becoming a rake.

Or it had until tonight.

Tonight he had forgotten every last one of his principles.

He thought about Christina, of the sweet vulnerability beneath her starchy exterior, of the soft appeal in her eyes, her disbelief that he would ever find her attractive. He remembered the scent of her, felt again the caress of her hands and the clasp of her body about his. It had been explosive, the most devastating lovemaking he had ever experienced; elemental, profound, all the things he did not want it to be and far too important to be dismissed easily.

Guilt lacerated him. Christina MacMorlan had been all that was honest and good, and he was a scoundrel who had seduced her when she did not even know his real name.

He sat up, put his head in his hands. He could not

tell her he was not a gardener. He could not tell her he worked for Lord Sidmouth. Least of all could he tell her the real reason he was at Kilmory. He imagined trying to tell Christina that he suspected her father of murder. She would be appalled. She would rush to defend the duke. He needed proof before he broached so difficult a subject. It was either that or abandon his quest for justice and his heart ached at the mere thought. He could not fail Peter again now, in death.

One thing he could do, though, was to write to Sidmouth and ask to be released from his role in hunting the smuggling gang. He wanted nothing to do with Eyre's work or with his methods.

Delicate tracery of shadow and light played across the whitewashed room. In the high summer, these northern lands were seldom fully dark but the sun had dropped into the sea now and the light was a deep, dark blue. Up at the house all the lamps would be lit. He wondered if Christina would be able to slip inside unnoticed so that she need find no excuse for her tumbled hair and her rumpled clothes.

It's wrong because I would be taking advantage....

He felt warmth spreading in his chest as he remembered her defiant gallantry. It was the last thing he had expected. There were any number of men who would not hesitate to take advantage of their female staff and no doubt a number of women who would do the same with their male servants. There were also many servants who saw the master's or mistress's favor as a way to advancement. Alice Parmenter was one of them. But Christina was too good

CHAPTER TWELVE

"MR. ROSS." CHRISTINA had summoned Lucas to the library first thing the very next morning. She had sent a servant; it was all extremely formal.

Christina laid down her pen and looked at him. Her eyes were tired. She looked as though she had not slept. She kept the desk as a barrier firmly between the two of them and did not invite Lucas to sit. It felt strange to see her like this, so businesslike and proper, when he had held her in his arms and made love to her with such heat and passion and need. He wanted to vault the desk and kiss her to within an inch of her life. Yet at the same time her very formality touched him. She was trying to do the right thing. He felt a wave of tenderness for her that shocked him.

"I apologize for sending for you like this," Christina said. "The truth is I am not quite sure how to deal with this matter between us…." Her voice faded away unhappily. "I do not want you to think…" She fidgeted with the quill, turning it over in her hands. Lucas noticed an ink stain on one of her fingers. Her hands were small, capable looking, like the rest of her. He felt his heart twist with an emotion he did not recognize.

"I am making no assumptions, ma'am," he said.

He saw a flash of gratitude deep in the blue of her eyes. "Thank you," she said. She took a deep breath. "Last night…" She stopped again. "I hope you realize…" She looked up. "I do not go around behaving like that."

"I think we established that last night," Lucas said.

"And I would not wish it to make any difference to our working relationship," Christina continued in a rush. She was looking extremely pink and flustered now, color in her face where it had previously been pale. "Obviously it will not happen again. But I have to maintain my authority amongst the staff here, so I would appreciate it if you did not mention—" She broke off as Lucas took a step forward and leaned his palms on the desk. Her gaze, startled and blue, met his. "Mr. Ross?"

"Lady Christina," Lucas said. He tried to erase the anger from his voice but it was difficult. "Do you even need to ask me that?"

She blushed. "I am sorry," she said. "I did not mean to insult your integrity."

She had a way of going straight to the heart of the matter that silenced him. And since his integrity was also questionable, he suddenly felt a cad.

"Do not give the matter another thought," he said gruffly.

Some emotion flickered in her eyes. "That may

be difficult," she said with devastating candor, "but I shall do my best."

Lucas felt his body tighten. So she had lain awake, as he had, thinking about everything that had happened between them. Thinking about it. Wanting it. He almost groaned aloud. She was right; it was damnably difficult to erase the memory of the previous night, particularly when he wanted to do it all over again.

Their eyes met. He saw the plea in hers and was helpless to resist.

"I promise never to do anything to compromise your authority," he said. He straightened. "I will behave with as much deference and respect as I have always done."

"Which is not saying a great deal," Christina said. "But I appreciate the sentiment."

Lucas grinned. "I am not naturally deferential."

She frowned. "I have observed that, Mr. Ross. I think—" She hesitated. "You believe that respect must be earned rather than accorded as a birthright."

Lucas was startled by her perception. He did not consider himself easy to read, and yet she had understood him perfectly. "Which is why *you* have my respect," he said gently.

Now she really did blush hard, as though his good opinion mattered to her more than anything else on earth. "Thank you," she said simply. She smiled at him and it felt to Lucas as though the sun had come out.

"Now." Her voice changed, became businesslike.

"I have a problem and I require your help, Mr. Ross." She tapped a letter that lay on the desk in front of her. "My sisters write that they will be visiting Kilmory at the end of next week."

Lucas felt a flash of alarm. If Lady Mairi Rutherford saw him at Kilmory, then his impersonation of a servant would be over. She had met him and there was not a hope in hell that she would not recognize him. Either he was going to have to skulk around out of sight in the garden grotto for the entire visit or he was going to have to work fast, complete his inquiries before the ladies arrived and get the hell out of there.

Damnation.

Ten days was no time at all to complete his mission.

But Christina was still speaking, looking down at the letter, a faint hint of asperity in her tone:

"Apparently Mairi and Lucy are bringing some friends with them from the Highland Ladies Bluestocking Society. The ladies were very excited to hear that Lady Bellingham is staying nearby. They want to meet her. I understand she is something of a bluestocking heroine. I am to invite her to tea in order for the ladies to discuss with her all manner of subjects ranging from the practical applications of trigonometry to the return of Halley's Comet."

"The Highland Ladies Bluestocking Society," Lucas said. "Is that an entirely female enterprise?"

"It is," Christina said. "The clue is in the name,

Mr. Ross. Gentlemen are not invited to the meetings unless they are attending as expert speakers."

Lucas breathed a little easier. At least Jack would not be escorting Mairi. He doubted that Jack's specialist subject was a suitable discussion topic for a group of earnest bluestocking women. On the other hand, they might be riveted to hear a lecture on the seduction techniques of the practiced rake.

"Are you a bluestocking yourself, ma'am?" Lucas asked.

Christina put her pen down with something of a bad-tempered slap. "No, Mr. Ross, I am not. It takes leisure to be a bluestocking and I have no time to spare for such fripperies." She rubbed the back of her neck. Tiny wisps of golden-brown hair escaped her chignon. Lucas wanted to press his lips to the tender curve at her nape. The impulse was so powerful that he had to clench his fists to stop himself.

"There is so much to do," Christina said, half to herself. "Everyone just assumes…" She broke off. "Well, that is nothing to the purpose. But as I said, I need your help with this visit, Mr. Ross."

"Either you wish me to make myself scarce in the greenhouses or you require me to wait at table," Lucas said, hoping it was not the latter.

Christina eyed him frostily. "Please do not attempt to read my mind, Mr. Ross. I require neither of those things from you. I could not have you waiting at table." She drummed her fingers on the desk in irritation. "There would be a riot in the dining room. The Highland Ladies are very partial to a handsome man. They have quite a reputation." She rubbed her head absentmindedly, leaving another smear of ink down her cheek. "What I would ask is that you provide appropriate cut flowers for the house on each day of the visit," she said.

"So you would require me to bring the flowers up to the house," Lucas said. "Indoors?" He could imagine himself hiding behind a huge spray of roses when Mairi Rutherford walked past. This was going to be awkward.

Christina was looking at him oddly. "Only as far as the housekeeper's room," she said. "Mrs. Parmenter and I will then arrange the flowers and display them." She tilted her head thoughtfully as she looked at him. "You are starting to know the difference between a rose and a hollyhock, I hope?"

"Hollyhocks are taller than roses," Lucas said. He grinned. "I will collect some of the gardening books on my way out. Hopefully then I will not disgrace you."

"Thank you," Christina said. She moved her papers into a businesslike pile and stood up. Clearly it was the end of their interview.

"If you will excuse me," she said. "I have errands to run in the village. Soup to take to Mrs. McGregor and medicines for the Morrison children. They have the ague. I hope there will not be a major outbreak."

Lucas caught her arm as she moved toward the door. "You look very pale," he said. "You should be careful not to wear yourself out."

His hand closed over hers and she froze, catching her breath. Her face was in profile to him and he could see the curve of her lips and a pulse beating in the delicate hollow of her throat. Beneath his hand her fingers trembled. The awareness shimmered between them like a heat haze.

"I am very well," she whispered.

"You are not," Lucas said. Suddenly he felt fiercely protective. "You never give yourself a rest."

Her gaze came up to his, cloudy with tiredness. He could see all his own confusion reflected in her eyes. "I appreciate your concern, but I do not think you should be so familiar, Mr. Ross," she said. "Only a moment ago you agreed to behave with absolute propriety—"

Lucas gave a growl deep in his throat. "To hell with propriety," he said.

He pulled her toward him. He could feel the hesitation in her but also the wicked current of temptation that swept away all her objections. He spun her around so that her back was against the door and held her there whilst he kissed her long and deep, his tongue plundering the sweetness of her mouth, his body holding hers trapped. She slid her arms about his neck and kissed him back. He felt a rush of something so elemental it could not be denied: power, possession and desire. Yet beneath the clamor of his body was an infinitely more disturbing feeling of protectiveness.

She pulled away from him, breathing hard, and he cupped her face, brushing the fragile line of her jaw with his thumb. He felt conflicted, tenderness warring with the compulsion to push her away, to keep her at arm's length before he plunged into even more uncharted waters. But it was too late. A fierce sense of need swept through him, bound up with the urge to shield her from all harm.

"Take care of yourself," he whispered, kissing her again, gently this time.

She freed herself. He could see the withdrawal in her eyes and knew she was determined to end this, no matter how much she wanted him. He caught her hand and felt her try to draw away.

"Promise me," he said, "that if you are with child you will tell me."

Her eyes opened wide, blank with shock. He could see she had not thought of that.

"It won't happen," she said. "It could not. You didn't…" She stopped, clearly unable to form the words.

"It can still happen," Lucas said grimly. He tightened his grip on her. "I will not be like my father," he said. "I won't ever abandon the mother of my child."

He saw the shift of expression in her eyes; a grief and sadness he could not understand, mingled with a longing that turned his heart inside out. She smiled, though he thought there was the glitter of tears on her lashes.

"You are a good man, Lucas Ross," she said. She touched his cheek fleetingly. "A very good man."

She turned, pulled open the library door and walked away, closing it softly behind her. Lucas listened to the sound of her footsteps fade as she went away, back to her life as chatelaine of Kilmory, laird in all but name. He knew he had no role in that; he was not a part of her life, and for the first time he disliked that intensely.

THERE WAS SO much to do; there were menus to agree with Alice Parmenter on and a meeting scheduled with the land agent to discuss the increase of rents at the home farm, and food and medicine to take to the village and calls on Mrs. MacPherson and Lady Bellingham. There were rooms to be aired in advance of the visit of the Highland Ladies Bluestocking Society and the servants to encourage and placate and stray sheep to be recaptured and a new batch of the peat-reek to distill. Yet Christina could not concentrate. All she could think about was Lucas.

She had barely seen him for a week. That very denial meant that she dreamed about him at night, dreams full of heat and longing, and woke feeling desperately lonely. Her body ached for him, but his absence was much more than that. She felt as though a part of her was missing and no matter how she tried to fill the void with activity, the pain would catch her unawares in odd moments, as it was doing now. She was seated in the drawing room full of people, a place that could have been a hundred miles away from Lucas's little cottage and the secrets they had shared.

She had not wanted to feel like this. It was one thing to give her love and her time to her people, but quite another feeling such an intensity of emotion for one man. She was afraid of that feeling, so afraid that if she gave in to it she would risk losing everything again. As a young girl her heart had been open and she had loved without reservation. That love had curled up and died when she had lost her mother and her world was shattered. Never again would she give of herself so freely.

"Christina, you are not attending." Gertrude poked her none too gently in the ribs with her fan. Her face was wrinkled with dissatisfaction, her gaze darting across the room to where Allegra was deep in conversation with Richard Bryson, the riding officer. Allegra was smiling; it was the first time that Christina could remember seeing her looking so genuinely animated. Her mother was also looking animated, but with annoyance not pleasure. It was clear to Christina that she had just missed one of Gertrude's diatribes on her daughter's bad behavior.

"I beg your pardon," she said automatically. She had been paying attention, just not to what Gertrude was saying. What scared her was that it felt too late to turn back. She was in love with Lucas and she did not know how to stop. It exhilarated her, but it frightened her, too. Loving Lucas made her want to take risks she had sworn never to take again. Loving him made her want to dare to trust that the future would not be like the past, that this time she would not be hurt. Caution warned her that she was a fool, setting herself up for further pain. She did not know what to do.

Gertrude prodded her again and Christina was tempted to take the fan and snap it in half.

"I was saying that when you chaperone Allegra during the winter season in Edinburgh, you must make absolutely sure that she does not waste her time on unsuitable men like that," Gertrude said, waving the fan in the direction of Richard Bryson. "She is not to marry below the rank of a duke's heir. Or perhaps we could tolerate an earl if we are absolutely desperate. But below that I simply will not go, Christina. Do you understand?"

"Allegra is the one you should be speaking to, not me," Christina said, a little more sharply than she had intended. Gertrude's complacent assumption that she would chaperone her daughter was deeply irritating. She had not asked her, and whilst Christina would have enjoyed a trip to the capital, the price of being at Gertrude's beck and call was a high one.

"Have you asked Allegra what *she* would like, Gertrude?" she continued. "You should consider her feelings for once, since her marriage is a decision that will affect the whole of the rest of her life. Perhaps she does not wish to marry, or at least not immediately. Or perhaps she would rather have a man who has a genuine regard for her than make a dazzling match simply to gain a duke's coronet."

Gertrude stared. Her mouth fell open a little in what Christina assumed could only be shock at having her opinions challenged. "Don't be absurd!" Gertrude snapped. She stood up, equally snappily, and walked off, her back ramrod straight with outrage as though Christina had suggested something improper. Christina smiled faintly. As someone whose father had comprehensively ruined her own prospects of marriage, she felt a little warm glow of pride to be standing up for Allegra and her future happiness. With any luck Gertrude would also realize that she was an unsuitable chaperone. Christina had heard her telling various people that it was an act of kindness, to give her something to do.

She had been deplorably lax in the past in allowing Gertrude to get away with her barbs, but not anymore. Lucas had helped her to see that her sister-in-law's attitude need not be tolerated.

She watched Thomas Wallace trying to serve the tea and cakes. Galloway was training him, but he was all fingers and thumbs, cake crumbs scattering, cups tilting at dangerous angles. Christina sighed. She had tried to do the right thing in giving Thomas the footman's job. His father had recently suffered from illness so severe that he could not longer work his croft. But Thomas was not cut out to be a footman. Lucas Ross would have served tea so much more elegantly. Lucas was not cut out to be a footman, either, but for very different reasons.

Tea at Kilmory was not usually as busy as it was today. There had been an unexpected influx of visitors, including the doctor and his wife and daughter, a sweetly pretty blond girl of seventeen who was talking with modest shyness to Lachlan. Lachlan never normally took afternoon tea, and it was a tribute to Miss Cameron that he was present. Christina sighed. Lachlan had always been a ladies' man, the indulged younger son and not the steadiest of characters. She wondered again whether she should write to Dulcibella, Lachlan's wife, begging her to come back to him, but the prospect of begging Dulcibella for anything was not appealing.

A burst of laughter drew Christina's attention back to Allegra. Allegra was looking exceedingly pretty, her blue eyes sparkling, leaning close to Richard Bryson as she made some emphatic point in their discussion. For a moment Christina thought, but could not be sure, that Allegra's fingers had brushed the back of Bryson's hand in a gesture that had looked very intimate. She frowned, feeling the first stirring of concern. It was surely impossible that any intimacy should exist between the two of them, and yet Allegra sparkled as though she was in love. As though they were lovers.

Christina had been astonished earlier in the afternoon when Allegra had returned from a ride, pink cheeked and full of repressed excitement, with Bryson in tow. She had said they had met on the cliff path and ridden back down to Kilmory together and that she had invited him to stay for tea. Gertrude had been almost speechless with outrage. Christina had not been certain that she would not rescind the invitation on the spot, and so she had stepped in quickly to reinforce Allegra's invitation, even though she did not want Bryson in the house. She supposed it was not his fault that he was a riding officer and she was the criminal he was sent to capture. He seemed to be a very pleasant young man and he had his way to make in the world. But if his future plans involved Allegra—if they were already involved—that put a very different complexion on matters.

Christina watched them again, uncertain, irresolute. Bryson was behaving with absolute propriety toward Allegra. Yet Christina's own heightened emotions told her that there was something between them. But surely she had to be mistaken. Allegra would never take a lover.

There was a commotion in the doorway. Galloway was attempting to maneuver what looked like an enormous marketing basket into the room. It was full of roses—deep red roses and white rosebuds tinged with the most delicate blush of pink. They overflowed the sides of the basket in a wonderful cascade and brought with them a scent of summer.

"Roses for Allegra!" Gertrude rushed forward, a smile emblazoned across her face as she elbowed Bryson aside and appeared to be about to snatch the basket. "An admirer! Who can it be?"

Galloway held the basket away from her. There was an expression of furtive triumph on his face that he quickly wiped away.

"The flowers are for Lady Christina, ma'am," the butler said. "They were left on the doorstep with a card." He crossed the room to where Christina was sitting and bowed deeply. "My lady."

"For Christina!" Gertrude recoiled as though the flowers had bitten her. "How inexplicable!"

Christina brushed the rose petals with her

fingers. She was rather inclined to agree with Gertrude. Such an extravagant gift seemed extraordinary. Admirers were in short supply in Kilmory. And now she looked more closely, she thought she had seen that marketing basket before, in the potting sheds. Mr. Hemmings had been using it for his seedlings.

Peering closer, she saw a gleam of bronze beneath the tangle of stems. It was her pistol.

Lucas.

She swallowed hard. She had almost forgotten that he had not returned the pistol to her and now here it was, delivered in full public view, swathed in roses, brought into the drawing room by the butler. Anyone might have seen it. But that was typical of Lucas. He liked to take risks. She sensed that in him every time they spoke, that edge of danger, and it attracted her like a moth to the flame.

Something hot and arousing tugged deep inside her and she closed her eyes for a second. She had taken the dangerous step between wanting a lover and taking one, and now that she knew how pleasurable it could be, she wanted that pleasure again. She hungered for it, for Lucas.

Belatedly she became aware that everyone was looking at her and cleared her throat rather self-consciously.

"The flowers are from Mr. Grant," she said. "I asked him to send some roses to refresh the arrangement in the library."

"Ah." Gertrude's face cleared. "I had thought it

quite impossible that you would receive roses from an admirer, Christina."

"I'm sure you did," Christina agreed.

The tea party was coming to an end. The doctor, belatedly aware that Lachlan's attentions to his daughter should be firmly squashed, was gathering up his family and making to leave. Richard Bryson excused himself with every appearance of deep regret. Gertrude scowled as Allegra gave him her hand and said airily that she would see he was invited to dinner. No sooner had the drawing room door closed behind the guests than she rounded on her daughter.

"You are *not* to encourage him, Allegra. Do you hear me? He is nobody. He is beneath our notice. How can you be so foolish? You have every advantage of birth and fortune. Use them to catch a husband worthy of the MacMorlan lineage."

All of the bright, happy color faded from Allegra's face and she stormed out of the drawing room, slamming the door behind her. Gertrude turned on Christina. "And do not think to encourage her, Christina, by inviting that young man to dinner!"

"I wouldn't dream of it," Christina said truthfully, taking the wind out of her sister-in-law's sails.

"Oh, well…" Gertrude sounded mollified. "I am glad that you share my views on Mr. Bryson's lowly antecedents."

"I don't care whether Mr. Bryson comes from the top drawer or the sheep byre," Christina said, "but I will not dine with a man whose work requires him to persecute my tenants and villagers. Excuse me, Gertrude. I have things I need to do."

She picked up the basket of roses. "Please put this in my bedroom, Galloway," she said, passing the basket to the butler on her way out the door. "I don't think I shall waste the flowers on the library—Papa never notices these things." On an afterthought, remembering the pistol, she added, "Please don't water them. I will do it later."

"Ma'am." Galloway bowed.

Christina went out into the gardens. The sun felt hot even though it was getting toward evening. Or perhaps she was the one feeling hot and flustered. She had come out without bonnet or parasol. Her mind had been on other things. She walked along the terrace, looking at the dazzling sparkle of the sun on the sea. Only the slightest of breezes stirred the pines.

At the corner of the walled garden, she got a stitch in her side and was obliged to stop and rest one hand against the wall, doubled over, whilst she tried to regain her breath.

"Lady Christina? Are you quite well?"

It was Lucas's voice. She felt him take her elbow gently as he assisted her toward a seat in the arbor. She felt like an ancient dowager. Her gown was sticking to her in the heat. She knew her face was flushed. She had never felt less attractive in her life. "I am quite well, thank you," she said. "The heat…"

"It is very hot today," Lucas agreed seriously.

"Thank you for returning the pistol," Christina said.

He smiled. Her heart did a little flip. "My pleasure," he said.

"It was ingenious," Christina said, "if foolhardy. You must not do such a thing again."

Lucas shrugged. "The matter will not arise unless I am obliged to disarm you again," he said. He spread his hands. "I could not simply walk into the parlor and present it to you on Galloway's silver tray." His voice changed, deepened. "Besides, you deserve roses. Red roses that smell heavenly, and delicate white ones with a touch of pink that look as though they are blushing."

If she had not already been in love with him, Christina thought that was the moment when it would have happened. She felt a great wash of love for him steal her breath, leaving her feeling weak. The arbor was surrounded by honeysuckle that smelled sweet and strong. It made her head swim. She looked at Lucas and felt even dizzier. He was watching her with a smile in his eyes, but behind that gentleness she saw a harder light of desire that both fascinated and almost scared her with its intensity.

"Mr. Ross," she said. "Really. You should not say such things to me."

"I know," Lucas said. He did not apologize, nor did he look remotely regretful. Her heart gave another flutter of hopeless longing.

Damn it. Simply by existing he was making this very difficult for her.

"You are well, I hope," he said. "I have not seen you lately."

"I am very well, thank you," Christina said. "There has been a very great deal to do. And you?" She added politely. "Is all well?"

She saw the smile deepen in his eyes at the ridiculously formal tone of their conversation. "All is well with me, too," he said gravely. He paused, smiled at her again. "I must go and finish my work," he said. "The grotto is almost complete."

She watched him walk away with his long, lithe stride. She was tempted to run after him and simply throw herself into his arms. The strain of maintaining such an unnaturally decorous conversation had left her feeling strangely exhausted. It was so far from what she wanted, and yet she had made herself a promise and she could not break it. She had to keep Lucas at a distance.

With a little sigh, she walked slowly back toward the castle. Inside there were so many things to do, yet she rebelled at the thought of each and every one of them. She felt restless and hot. Seeing Lucas had just made matters worse; she really should not seek him out again. She wandered through the maze—it was cooler there between the high hedges—and down to the avenue where the limes led to the fountain.

Trailing her fingers in the water, she thought what a perfect afternoon it would be for a swim. Down on the beach there was the Round House, a small stone building that her father had had constructed as a changing room for swimming. The duke had stopped sea bathing after contracting a chill the previous year, and Christina was the only one who used it, except when her sisters visited. A dip in the water was precisely what she needed. Perhaps it would help to soothe the desire she had for Lucas. Or perhaps not.

CHAPTER THIRTEEN

THE ROUND HOUSE was cool and dim after the heat outside. The duke, always mindful of his comfort, had furnished it with a great deal more luxury than his servants' cottages. There were soft rugs on the floor and fluffy towels in a cupboard, along with the rather shapeless gowns the ladies wore for bathing.

Christina slipped out of her clothes with a sigh of relief as she released the tight laces and rolled off her stockings. The long voluminous bathing chemise swathed her like a shroud. It was the last word in respectability, floor length and as thick as hessian. She would be fortunate if she did not sink under the waterlogged weight of it. For a moment she considered swimming in the nude as Mairi had done the previous year, but she lacked her sister's uninhibited ways.

On the seaward side, the doors of the building opened directly onto a deep pool scoured by the waves for centuries. Christina opened the door and the low sun struck across her eyes, dazzling her. She jumped in.

As always, the coldness of the water made her gasp. Even in the hot summer it contained an icy chill. The water grabbed at the chemise and pulled her down. She could feel the weight of the current, strong today, pulling at her. She struck out for the surface, feeling the hessian gown float out like a huge heavy balloon around her. Really, this was ridiculous. She would be drowned at this rate and all for a few scruples of modesty. She rolled around in the water, pulling at the stubborn material, floundering like a beached seal, until she was free of the wretched gown and it floated away on the tide.

It was then she heard the laughter.

Shaking the water from her eyes, smoothing her hair back, she blinked into the sun. There was someone there, someone who was floating in the pool at her side; someone who most certainly should not be there.

"Mr. Ross!" she said.

"Good afternoon again, Lady Christina." Lucas's deep drawl seemed even more pronounced than usual.

"What on earth are you doing here?" Christina said. "I thought you were working."

"I've just finished," Lucas said. "I needed a bath."

"But why?" Christina wailed. She was acutely aware both that she was naked and also that he had seen her thrashing around in the water like an ill-coordinated porpoise. "Why would you do such a thing?"

Lucas's teeth flashed white as he smiled. "It's a hot day," he said. "I needed to cool off." He paused.

"You yourself can take part of the blame for that, Lady Christina."

Oh.

He was looking at her and just the looking made her feel so hot and self-conscious that she thought she might sink under the weight of it.

"I thought," she said, trying to sound normal, "that it might have been because digging the garden is a dirty job."

"That, too," Lucas said. "Mr. Grant told me I could come here to bathe, although he seemed to disapprove of the idea. He thinks that a dousing under the pump is quite good enough."

"A lot of people think sea bathing is unhealthy," Christina said. "You could have called out when I jumped in," she added. "I could not see you here because of the sun."

"If I had called out, you would not have joined me," Lucas said with maddening reasonableness. "I had no incentive to stop you." He grinned. "Particularly when you started to undress."

"Oh!" Christina had never previously had the experience of her face radiating heat whilst her body was chilled. She did not dare look down. She had no idea how clear the water was here, but she was sure that Lucas could see every naked inch of her. Somehow it did not make an iota of difference that he had already made love to her. In fact, it only made her more ill at ease, more aware of the prickle of excitement running over her skin and the pulse of arousal deep inside her.

This was not good.

This was precisely what she had been trying to avoid.

"At least I know you are not armed at present," Lucas said. "Or I assume not."

Christina gasped and almost swallowed a mouthful of water. "Mr. Ross!"

"My apologies," Lucas said. He shook his head. "I am afraid I find the thought of you with a pistol almost too erotic, Lady Christina." He tilted his head toward the hessian gown, which had snagged itself on a rock on the other side of the pool. "Why on earth were you even attempting to swim in that sack?"

"It's what ladies do," Christina said, relieved that the conversation had taken a slightly less improper turn. "We swathe ourselves in material for respectability."

"And then you promptly unswathed yourself." Lucas sounded amused. "I cannot blame you. Another moment and you would have drowned. I really thought I was going to have to rescue you."

"Fortunately there was no necessity," Christina said. "I can swim like a fish."

"An unusual skill in a woman," Lucas said. "Girls are not normally taught to swim."

"We can all swim well," Christina said. "We learned as children. I know the sea and the lochs around here as well as my ancestors did." She turned away and swam toward the other side of the pool. When she looked back, Lucas was nowhere to be seen. A moment later he surfaced beside her, rivulets of water running down his torso, his black hair plastered to his head like an otter's pelt.

"I suppose it is forbidden for servants to swim with members of the family," he said.

"Certainly it is not encouraged," Christina said.

"Then I had better leave you." Lucas placed his palms on the rock and started to haul himself out. The sun caught the water streaming down his back and gilded his skin to bronze. Christina stared. He was magnificent. The muscles bunched smoothly in his broad shoulders. Her gaze swept down to his narrow waist and lower…

She gave a squeak. It had not occurred to her that he, like she, might have been bathing in the nude.

"You are naked!"

Lucas paused, then continued to pull himself out onto the rock. Christina floundered, almost swallowing a mouthful of seawater.

"Men do tend to swim naked," Lucas agreed, turning to face her. "There are no foolish rules about clothing as there are for women. Put your hand down," he added as Christina shielded her eyes. "You will go under if you do not swim properly."

He was laughing at her. In response she dived down deep into the clear water, feeling it close over her head, enjoying the shock of it on her skin, the sting of the cold. When she surfaced, Lucas had disappeared. She saw a shadow moving about in the interior of the Round House. A moment later he appeared in the doorway, a towel slung low about his hips. He settled himself on the flat rock above the water, watching her.

"Are you going to stay in there forever?" he asked. "You will catch an ague."

"I cannot come out until you are gone," Christina said. "It would be unseemly."

Lucas made no reply, only raised his brows, and she was reminded of all the downright unseemly things she had done with him the previous week and ached to do again.

She wondered why temptation was so very difficult to resist. It seemed unfair when she was trying to do the right thing that Lucas sat there looking the epitome of dark masculinity and perfect musculature. She shivered and realized for the first time that the water was very cold and she was getting chilled.

"I am giving you a direct order to put your clothes on and go away now, Mr. Ross," she said.

Lucas grinned. "Alas, I am so very bad at following orders."

"Please," Christina said, her teeth starting to chatter.

His smile vanished. He stood up and without another word disappeared into the Round House. Christina started to pull herself out of the water. Only now, as her muscles locked and she started to shiver almost uncontrollably, did she recognize quite how cold she had become. Her knees buckled and for a moment she teetered on the edge of the pool, terrified she was going to slip back into the water. Dizziness gripped her; she reached for a handhold on the rock and felt it slide beneath her fingers.

"Oh, for pity's sake!" Lucas was beside her, lifting her to safety. Material enveloped her, rough against her chilled body. For a moment she could barely feel it, then the rub of toweling against her skin woke her senses, half painful, half welcomed as her blood started to beat warm again. Lucas carried her into the Round House and set her on her feet, securing the towel more firmly about her.

She felt horribly embarrassed. Common sense might have prompted her to keep Lucas at a distance, but her dreams and fantasies had been quite different. She had wanted to appear elegant and alluring, a mermaid rather than a beached seal. Taking one end of the towel, she wiped the water from her eyes with fingers that were numb with cold. Her hair was a heavy weight about her shoulders. It was impossible to untangle it. For some reason that was the final straw. It made her eyes smart with tears of frustration and annoyance.

"Let me help you," Lucas said gently. He turned her around, and after a second she felt his deft fingers sliding through her hair, straightening the tangles. She could feel the warmth of his body; she could smell him, too, a scent of fresh air and cold water and something that was Lucas alone. It made the last of her defenses crumble; she felt dizzy and shaky, as though her knees were going to give way again.

No one had ever cared for her like this since she had been a child. It was so gentle, so tender, and so irresistible. She turned to face him. He was very close; she was almost overwhelmed. There was a quality of stillness in him now that was intensely exciting. It made her shiver. She reached up and put a hand on the back of his neck, pulling his head down so that his mouth would meet hers. He hesitated for only a moment, and then he was kissing her with the same gentleness he had shown a moment before.

It was not what she wanted. She felt impatient. She wanted the heat and the urgency of their previous kisses. Greatly daring, she bit down gently on his lower lip, then slid her tongue over the swell of it and into his mouth. She could feel the tension in him and the self-control that was wound so tightly. He opened to her, allowing her to slide her tongue languorously over his, and then, just as she was wondering what she had to do to provoke a stronger reaction, he deepened the kiss and pulled her to him so that she could feel the hard ridge of his erection through the layers of material between them.

Desire exploded in her, the heat spreading out from her pelvis to wash through her entire body. She pressed herself against him and felt him shudder with an answering need. He took her mouth again and plunged his tongue deep, stealing her breath, ravishing her. She placed her palms on his bare chest and felt his heat and the thunder of his heart.

"Christina," he whispered.

Her heart surged at the intimacy with which he said her name. It felt so right.

She slid her palms down his chest and lower, over

the flat plane of his stomach to where the towel was still loosely knotted about his hips. His breath hissed in; he clamped a hand about her wrist, staying her.

"Are you sure you know what you are doing?" his voice was hoarse. "We agreed—"

"I know." She stood up on tiptoe to kiss him again. She had never been surer of what she wanted. There was such longing in her for everything that he could give her. Dimly at the back of her mind, a voice warned her to caution. This time she ignored it. She had been shackled by duty for so long, so careful, so afraid to take the risk. Now she felt as though the restraint had snapped.

"I know what we agreed," she whispered. She licked the corner of his mouth delicately and heard him groan. "But I cannot help myself."

A laugh shook his chest. "Yes, you can," he said. "We both can, if we try hard enough." He sounded shaken.

"The truth is that I do not want to try," Christina said. It was shameless of her, outspoken to voice her desires like this, yet she felt compelled to be honest with him.

His hands came to rest on her waist, holding her hard, away from him. In the shadows of the Round House, his face looked stern. "I don't want you to do anything you'll later regret—"

"Then don't worry." Her impatience almost overwhelmed her. She did not want to talk. "I won't." She tugged at his towel and it fell to the floor. She ran a hand over the small of his back, down to the curve of his buttocks, feeling the hot, smooth skin against her palm.

He crushed her to him then, plundering her mouth with his until they were both gasping. Her towel had slipped and fallen from her in the tumult and every last inch of their bare skin was now pressed together, hard against soft, hotter than she could have imagined. It was two steps to the wide sofa that stood before the window. The light flowed in, bathing it in a golden glow. Lucas laid her down on it and straightened to look at her as she lay tumbled in naked abandonment. She felt a flash of self-consciousness then and was about to cover herself with her hands but he caught her wrists again and spread her arms wide.

"How beautiful you are," he said softly.

Her shyness fled. Beautiful? No one had ever called her that. No one had even thought it.

She reached for him but he shook his head, going down on his knees beside the sofa, running his hands softly down her body, from her shoulders over her breasts to the flare of her waist. Christina gasped, arching upward.

"I have so wanted to see you like this." He repeated the caress and she writhed. "It was dark before," he said. "I need to see you in the light."

Christina made a little sound of desire and supplication and he smiled, kissing her collarbone, then taking one nipple in his mouth to suck and pull. She felt it clear through her body and it settled in a low, pulsing throb between her thighs. Each tug, each lick had her squirming until the sensations threatened to drive her beyond all thought. She had never known this, the slow, exquisite build of passion, the tantalizing way she hung on the edge of bliss.

Lucas's fingers slid into her secret folds, found the entrance to her body and slipped inside. Her body twitched at the intrusion, welcoming it but wanting more. Then his thumb found her swollen nub and pressed down, sliding over her with wicked precision, and her body shattered as easily as that, spiraling into ecstasy so hard and fast that she cried out as a wave of blinding brilliance carried her away.

She was floating, the sound of the sea soft about her, the waves of pleasure still beating through her body. She half opened her eyes. Lucas was holding her, cradling her in his arms, his mouth pressed to her hair. She felt wonderfully cherished and almost satisfied. But she doubted that he was. Smiling a little, she slid a hand down his body and curled it around the long, hard length of him, hearing him suck in a breath.

"Please," she said.

Gently he rearranged her so that she was propped against the high back of the sofa, lying back against a pile of cushions, her bottom on the edge of the seat. Her body was still thrumming with the lovely lambent afterglow, but she felt a new need now, more urgent, pulsating through her. Lucas pushed her thighs apart and knelt between them. She lay back, feeling exposed and suddenly nervous, aware of how she must look, her breasts flushed, her limbs tumbled. He spread her wider and she trembled.

With one plunge of his hips he buried himself inside her. She was tight from before, and the shock of it had her gasping with sheer need. Her body closed about him and she felt him surge into her, over and over, the powerful rhythm of it lifting her up, driving her hard back against the cushions, her hands braced at her sides, her body arched as she took each thrust. He cupped her head and drew her forward for his kiss and it was as fierce and tender and demanding as the pulse of his body in hers. He held her by the waist so that he could caress her breasts with his lips and tongue, and she felt the pleasure start to expand again and light up and fill her. Heat and light and love and need and Lucas... Her body clenched hard, taking her by surprise, so much sharper this time, spasm upon spasm of bliss. She was conscious of Lucas pulling out of her, of his own shout of pleasure, and then he was wrapping her in his arms and she was sliding down into the darkness, held close against his heart.

When she woke, she was warm and sleepy and wrapped in blankets. She was also alone. For one terrible moment, she thought that Lucas had simply dressed and left, and her heart shriveled and cold struck through her body. Then she saw a glimmer of light in the open doorway of the Round House, a flare of orange against the darkening blue of the sky outside. Evidently Lucas had collected some driftwood and built a fire.

Christina wrapped the blanket around her and walked barefoot over the floor to the doorway. Lucas was sitting staring out across the sea. His expression was somber and her heart missed a beat.

He regrets what we have done.

She did not. It surprised her, but this time she had no regrets at all. She felt light and happy and satisfied, and for once her mind simply refused to grapple with the consequences or implications of her actions.

Lucas got to his feet when he saw her. He came across and took her hand.

"Are you all right?" he said. He drew her down to sit on the stone beside him and did not let go of her hand. The fire was warm; it held at bay the cool of the evening as night started to fall over the sea.

"Yes," Christina said. "Thank you," she added, and saw him smile. He pressed a kiss to the palm of her hand.

"You are so polite," he murmured. "So very well-bred."

"Not really," Christina said. "Not at all." She hesitated. Perhaps she was wrong to pursue this. Perhaps she should just let matters be, ask no questions. But she disliked pretense and she could see no way forward now if they were not honest with one another.

"I am not sure what to do now," she admitted with painful honesty.

Lucas smiled. His gaze had been on their entwined fingers. Now it came up to her face. "Neither am I," he said.

"You've never had an affair with your employer before?" Christina asked, and saw the black of his eyes turn as hard as obsidian.

"I don't have affairs." He sounded curt. He threw another branch on the fire, and it snapped and hissed as the flame caught it. "My parents' example taught me not to take such matters lightly."

"Of course," Christina said. The smile had died from Lucas's eyes and something dark and hard took its place. He got up and moved a little away from her. Nothing could have emphasized more his separation from her, his rejection of intimacy. She felt emptiness yawn inside her.

"I told you that my mother bore me out of wedlock," Lucas said. "I was aware from the youngest age that I was different, shameful in some way, an outsider. I hated my father for the way that he behaved. I still hate him, even though he is long dead."

Christina felt another pang of shock, and hard on its heels a swift rush of empathy. Perhaps his mother had been a servant girl seduced by her employer, or a woman betrayed by the man she loved. In the end it did not really matter; her shame, her unhappiness had evidently scarred Lucas deeply. Christina had no idea what it would be like to be born not having a place in the world, but she knew that people could be cruel. Lucas had survived the stigma of his illegitimacy, but it would not be something he would forget or treat lightly.

"I'm sorry," she said softly. "It must have been wretched for you. I am so very sorry."

"It was more wretched for my mother," Lucas said. "I do not believe she ever recovered from his desertion." He looked up. In the firelight his face was illuminated in hard lines and dark shadows. "I don't want to make my father's mistakes," he said. "I don't want to be like him, weak and cowardly, siring a bastard out of marriage and abandoning its mother."

"I can't imagine you ever doing such a thing," Christina said. She could sense the anger in him but also the determination; he would never be a man to abandon the woman he loved. For a moment she felt a huge pang of loss to think of the woman who would win Lucas's love. That would be a love worth fighting for, full of tenderness and loyalty and respect. Except she wondered if Lucas was capable of such a love, if he would ever take that risk.

She wanted to reach out to him, but there was something about him that forbade it, something cold and self-reliant. She remembered the occasions on which she had tried to reach him, offering him her help, and he had rejected it. Experience had taught him to trust no one, to accept comfort from no one. Even so, she felt a little chilled by the distance between them. Not long ago they had been as close as it was possible to be. Now she could feel a chasm yawning.

"You should marry," she said impulsively. "You have cut yourself off from all human comfort. It cannot be good for you." And even as she said it she felt a jealousy and possessiveness that she knew she had no right to feel.

Lucas's smile was so tender that her heart turned over. "I do believe that once again you are trying to help me."

"I'm sorry," Christina said.

"Don't be," Lucas said. "It is one of the nicest things about you, Lady Christina. You are so generous."

It should have made her happy, but instead Christina felt a pang that was close to despair. She was angry with herself for thinking that it would be different this time. Nothing had changed in their situation since the night in the cottage. Lucas was still a servant; she was still behaving in a way that was reprehensible and wrong. Yet one thing *had* changed. She knew she loved him, and that made the situation all the more impossible.

This is not good enough, she thought suddenly. *I want more than this. I do not want stolen meetings and to skulk around as though I am ashamed.*

But there was no way in which she could have more. There was nothing for her here.

The firelight shimmered before her eyes. "I must go," she said. "I need to be back before dinner." She stood up.

"Wait," Lucas said, and despite herself, despite knowing that they were back on formal terms, employer to servant, Christina felt a jolt of anticipation. She looked at him. There was a quizzical look in his eyes. Then he smiled at her, the sort of smile this time that sent quite a different reaction skittering down her spine.

"There is something I want to know," he said. "I want to know how you lost your virginity."

CHAPTER FOURTEEN

LUCAS FULLY EXPECTED Christina to tell him to mind his own damned business. He had put a distance between them, withdrawing from her, telling her as clearly as though he had used the words that he did not want intimacy, that he could offer her nothing. Yet despite that, he did not want to let her go. He needed her; he felt an urgent desire to keep her with him, to delay her when he knew she should be gone, back to the castle, back to her family, back to a life in which she played no part.

He looked at her. Her hair was loose about her shoulders, a rich auburn-brown tousle in the firelight. She was so beautiful, her face serene in repose, her blue eyes so honest and her skin so creamy smooth he ached to touch her again. There was a scattering of freckles across her shoulders. He wanted to kiss them, to kiss her, to feel that lush mouth against his. His body tightened simply at the thought.

"I'm not sure that is an appropriate topic for discussion," Christina finally said.

She looked at him, then smiled, a smile that was part shy and part wanton, and the lust kicked him hard, and at the same time he felt his heart twist with emotion. He cared about Christina. She was too special, too lovely, not to care about. It felt strange and unfamiliar to acknowledge his emotions; he was not sure how he felt about them, but he was not going to deny them. There was no point in self-deception. He wanted Christina and he needed her and he had not the first idea in hell what he was going to do about it.

"You're right," Lucas said. He put out a hand and pulled her down beside him, pressing his lips to the sweet hollow of her throat. "It is perfectly appropriate to make love," he murmured against her skin, "but we simply must *not* talk about it."

She laughed but there was a hint of uncertainty in it. "Lucas…"

"Yes?" He traced the freckles on her shoulder with his tongue. He could not help himself. He needed to touch her.

"It *isn't* appropriate, is it?" She eased away from him, drawing her knees up to her chest, resting her chin on them. Suddenly she looked young and afraid and it made his heart turn over. "It isn't appropriate for us to make love."

"It feels right to me," Lucas said truthfully. On impulse he reached out and drew her back into the curve of his arm. It felt good to have her there. He felt good and whole and complete.

"It does to me, too." She looked puzzled. She reached up to kiss him, a little tentatively, a brush of the lips that had him wanting more. "I don't want this to end," she said. "I tried. Truly I did. I know you did, too. But…"

"Then don't think about it." He pulled her to him and kissed her for a third time, the rush of desire between them instantaneous as wildfire. Lucas knew he should tell her the truth about himself, now, immediately, before any more damage was done, but here, now, in the quiet of the Round House with the wash of the sea against the rocks below and Christina in his arms, he felt the first peace he had known since Peter's death. Later, he thought as he lost himself in the kiss. Later he would tell her everything, explain everything.

"I used to think that I was wanton for desiring such things," she said softly, her hand sliding beneath his shirt to find the warm skin beneath, "but now I can only believe that something that feels so right cannot be wrong." She frowned slightly. "I wonder if it is always as good as that? Somehow I doubt it can be."

"No," Lucas said truthfully. "It isn't." He smiled at her seriousness. "It's seldom as good as that."

She laughed. "I thought you did not make a practice of this?"

"I never said I had always lived as a monk," Lucas said mildly. "When I was young I too was curious and hot-blooded."

"And now that you are older," Christina teased, "matters are quite different."

Lucas tangled a hand in her hair, savoring the soft satin of it as it slid between his fingers. Tilting her head up, he kissed her again, running his tongue over her lower lip, sliding it inside her mouth. He deepened the kiss, feeling a shock of pure need that cut as fiercely as a knife blade. She tasted sweet and hot and he could think of nothing but how much he wanted her.

"Oh." Her voice was little more than a sigh. "I know I should not do this again, but it feels so very good...."

Lucas swallowed hard. Her open enjoyment made him feel as though he could conquer the world. "I am glad," he said. "Glad that you liked it." His voice was a little rough. The fire felt hot.

She traced lazy patterns over his chest even as they kissed. Her hand slid lower, over the flat planes of his stomach, and he felt a quiver of response. She nipped gently at his throat, his shoulder, the hollow beneath his ear, and he shut his eyes and let the sensations flow through him, without thought now, simply feeling. It was exhilarating to abandon himself to seduction. She was flicking her tongue over his chest now, tasting him, exploring his body with an innocent sort of boldness and pleasure that was intensely arousing. He reached for her, but she slid down his body, frustrating his attempts to hold her, shedding his clothes as she went. The slight clumsiness of it only served to make his heart ache all the more and stoke his arousal higher at the same time. Her lips and tongue danced across his stomach and brushed his thigh with inquisitive enjoyment, and he groaned and tried to roll her beneath him, but she turned the tables and straddled him, sliding back up his body, rubbing sinuously against him.

His breathing was unsteady. He could not control it, nor the urgency with which he pulled her head down to his, tangling his hand in her hair as her mouth came down on his. Her body slid over his, and down, sheathing him, so hot and so tight that he would have shouted aloud had she not been kissing him. He gasped, arching up into her and tempted beyond endurance.

He rolled her over so at last he could take her as he wanted, plunging into her, filled by the taste of her, driving them both on until there was nothing but the whirl of sensation and desire. But suddenly he did not want this impatience, this greed. He wanted to bank down the passion that blazed between them and give them time. His hands slowed. He moved with a leisurely pleasure that had her murmuring broken pleas for satisfaction. There was tenderness with a sharp edge of desire and gentleness that still aroused. He explored her the way he had always wanted to do, learning each curve and contour of her body, each dip and hollow. She moved with him and against him, and for the first time in his life he allowed himself to surrender completely to the need he had for a woman, this woman, body and soul. He felt her body shatter with pleasure and she arched beneath him, crying out his name. Still he moved with the same deliberate control, feeling her quicken again, her body sheened golden in the firelight, her skin flushed with passion. He kissed her and felt her body grasp him, and this time he allowed himself to fall, too, into the shuddering relief of fulfillment.

He had known that taking her again would make no difference to his hunger for her. If anything it was more acute each time he touched her. He pulled her close, resting his cheek against hers, breathing hard.

He did not know how long it was before he stirred again. He felt no need to move, no need to think. He had drawn the blankets over them and they were lying entwined in the warmth and light of the fire, and he would have been happy to stay like that forever. The sense of peace inside him had strengthened. So had the sense of belonging, as though he was bound fast to this woman and never wanted to let her go. It should have frightened him, yet it did not. It felt entirely right.

When he opened his eyes, hers were already open and she was looking at him.

"You asked me a question," she said. Her palm was flat against his chest. "Do you want to know the answer?" She was hesitating, blushing. She did not meet his gaze. All he could see was the downward curve of her lashes against her cheek.

"Yes." He shifted her more comfortably into the crook of his arm. He remembered that he had wanted to know how she had lost her virginity because he was certain that it was connected in some way to the one thing that she had never talked about, the one thing she pushed away—her mother's death, her broken betrothal and the sacrifice of her future for her family and her clan.

"It's true that I have had a lover before." The look she gave him was sweet and shamefaced, full of defiance, exactly like the innocent virgin she was not. "But you knew that from the first, didn't you?"

"I guessed," Lucas said. He pressed his lips to the top of her head.

Christina's blush had deepened. "No one expects virginity in a man. But in the unmarried daughter of a duke…" She let the sentence fade away.

"Society has double standards," Lucas said, "as well as unreasonable expectations of women." He shrugged. "Half of the human race joins without the blessing of marriage. No one knows that better than I. Women have needs and desires the same as men do."

She tilted up her head so that her blue gaze scanned his face thoughtfully. "That is a very enlightened attitude," she said drily. "Especially for a man."

"I don't judge," Lucas said. He spread his hands. "How could I? I am a bastard, the child of an unmarried mother. And—" he smiled, wanting her to understand, wanting her to know he meant what he said "—it does not make you any less special, Christina. It does not make you any less *you*. All our experiences make us the people we are. And you are very lovely."

Her eyes lit up like stars and he felt a huge thump of emotion literally knock the breath out of him. *Hell.* He was losing his detachment, losing *himself* in his feelings for her, and he was not sure he even minded.

"Thank you," she said simply. "You said you had

guessed," she added. "How did you know I had had a lover?"

"From your kiss, I think," Lucas said. "You responded like a woman who had been kissed before."

"Kissing is one thing." She sounded rueful. "Any number of debutantes will steal a kiss from a beau. Making love is another matter. That is the line over which we are not supposed to step."

"But you did?" Lucas asked.

She sat up, wrapping one of the blankets around her, and placed some more twigs on the fire. She did it neatly, without fuss. Lucas realized that he liked that in her, that lack of fuss. It was just one of the many things he found so appealing about her.

"I was betrothed," she said with the same matter-of-fact honesty she always gave him. "I was young, curious…" Her shoulders lifted in a sort of humorous half shrug as though she was deploring the impatience of her girlish self. "We were soon to wed so I thought it could do no harm."

Lucas was thinking of his mother. She had been young, too, and passionate, careless of the consequences of her actions. She had loved his father; she had told him so. It was just a pity she had trusted him.

"Did you love him?" he asked.

Regret shadowed Christina's gaze, and it was so vivid it made his heart miss a beat. "Yes," she said simply. "I loved him with all my heart, with everything that was in me. I was young and I had nothing to compare it with, nothing to prepare me." She broke off. "He was handsome, and young, and I found him very pleasing." The firelight illuminated her smile. It was a little secret smile that made Lucas's heart pound with jealousy. "And I wanted to know what sex was like." She traced a pattern on the rock with her fingers and avoided his eyes. "I was in love with lust as well as with him," she said after a moment. "We met as often as we could. My mama was sick and she was a lax chaperone. I regret that I took advantage of her sickness to do as I pleased, but I imagined that I would soon be wed." She hesitated. "I thought nothing could happen to alter that. I did not realize how easily life can change, in an instant, everything—" she snapped her fingers "—blown away."

"What happened?" Lucas asked.

She shifted and her gaze slid away from his. For the first time he had the sense of something painful that she was holding back.

"My father broke my betrothal," Christina said. Her voice was colorless now. "My mother died and he decided he needed me to help care for the younger children. They had nursemaids and governesses and tutors but it was not enough. They needed the love of a mother."

"Which you provided." Lucas could feel his anger catch and burn. "Why could he not provide the love you all needed?" he demanded. "Why not remarry if he wanted a wife and mother?"

Christina made a slight gesture. "Papa was not really capable—"

"Of loving anyone other than himself?" Lucas said.

"I was going to say capable of coping," Christina said. "He never could care for himself, or for anyone else."

"So he took your dream of marriage and broke that instead." Lucas's fury was so intense he had to make a conscious effort to keep his voice quiet. "And your betrothed?" he said. "What did he do?"

"He didn't fight for me, if that is what you mean." Again her tone was dry and he liked her for that tartness, that refusal to show self-pity. "He told me I had to abide by my father's wishes, and then he went to London and married an heiress with sixty thousand pounds. It was then I recognized that I had wasted my love on a man who did not deserve it."

"He was a worthless scoundrel," Lucas said.

He wanted to find her spineless fiancé and kick his teeth in. He wanted to punch the coward who had been happy to take Christina MacMorlan's virginity but who, when it came to the point, was not man enough to claim her for his own.

Claim her...

His body tightened with a blinding wave of possessiveness and lust.

Christina MacMorlan was his to claim now, and he would not let her go. She was his in every way that mattered.

It felt as though she had wrapped herself about his heart.

The thought was terrifying, and yet at the same

time, instinctively, in the very depths of his soul, he knew it was right, inescapable, destiny.

"I am sorry," he said.

She smiled, but it did not reach her eyes. "I was unprepared, I suppose," she said. "These things hit you harder when you have no experience to help soften the blow. When I loved I never held anything back. It was a mistake."

"No," Lucas said. "Your only mistake was to trust a man who was not worthy of you."

He allowed his gaze to drift over her, over the slope of her bare shoulders and the curve of her breasts beneath the soft folds of the blanket. He wanted her, not only in the physical sense but also in a far more complex way. For the first time in years he felt fear, fear that he would lose something so infinitely precious, so important to him, that the loss of it would push him as close to breaking as he had ever been. And he sensed in that he and Christina were alike.

Christina caught his glance and a little frown touched her eyes.

"Lucas?"

He moved closer to her, took her hand in his. "Both of those were appalling betrayals," he said carefully. "Your father breaking your betrothal, your worthless fiancé failing to stand up to him… They must both have hurt you a great deal."

She shrugged, but he sensed the tension in her now, wound tight, as though she knew he was not going to let this go this time. "I was disappointed in them," she said expressionlessly. "McGill was weak and my father was selfish. You have said so all along—" a faint smile curved her lips "—and I know that you are right. But…" She stopped.

"But that was not what hurt you the most," Lucas said.

She stiffened. It felt as though he had suddenly come up against the most forbidding barrier of all, utterly solid, impossible to breach, a deep, terrible grief that she would never allow herself to release.

"Christina?" he said.

She turned toward him and he was shocked to see the fierce glitter of tears in her eyes. She looked angry and forlorn at the same time, a furious angel, and a heartbroken child.

"None of it would have happened if she had not left me," she said. The words burst from her. "I loved her. I needed her! I was only eighteen."

"Your mother," Lucas said. He felt a huge rush of sorrow and compassion for the girl she had been. "You needed your mother."

"I never thought things would change." The glitter in Christina's eyes intensified. A big teardrop splashed onto the rock by her hand. "I was happy. I thought I knew what the future would be and then, in an instant—" her voice faltered "—I wasn't safe anymore," she said. "Everything had gone."

"Sweetheart," Lucas said. He gathered her into his arms. He could feel her trembling, little sobs that racked her whole body.

"You tried to take her place," he said. "You have

been caring for people ever since." He drew her closer, stroking her hair gently as her tears dampened his chest. "Hush, it's all right." He kissed her wet cheeks and she clung to him as though he was the only safe thing in a stormy world. "You're safe now. Everything will be all right."

She burrowed closer still. "I was so frightened," she whispered. "There was no one to help me. Papa, McGill…"

"They failed you," Lucas said. He brushed the damp hair away from her hot cheeks. "I'm sorry for that," he said. "I'm sorry that they let you down when you most needed them."

She shook her head but she held on to him all the more tightly.

"Christina," he said, knowing he meant it, "I'll never leave you. I swear it."

She went very still. "Lucas…" She sounded shaken, and when she looked up her gaze was wary. "But—"

"There are no buts," Lucas said, "no reservations." He kissed her. "Marry me," he said. He had meant to wait to ask her but he could not. He knew he should give her time but suddenly it felt as though he did not have any. He wanted to tell her everything, to lay the whole truth before her and at the same time reassure her that he would always be there for her.

She was quiet, and for one terrible moment Lucas thought that she was about to refuse him, and the world felt a very empty place indeed.

She sat up, drawing her knees to her chest again. "Lucas, are you sure?" She still sounded uncertain.

"Yes," Lucas said. "Very sure. I want you. I want to marry you." Urgency possessed him with the need to tell her the truth. "Listen, Christina," he said. "There are things I need to explain—"

She pressed her fingers to his lips. "In a moment." She hesitated. "It will be difficult for you." Her tone had changed. She sounded brisk and practical. "You do realize that? People will talk. There will be slights and sneers. Society will demean you at every turn. You have already endured the stigma of being a fatherless bastard." She looked wretched all of a sudden. "I cannot ask you to become an outcast again for my sake."

She was still thinking of him. With a rush of understanding Lucas realized that she was anticipating a huge scandal, people calling him a fortune hunter and ripping his character to shreds with their malice. She had not even considered what they might say about *her* because she was so considerate of his feelings. Protectiveness stole his breath.

"You are the sweetest and most generous woman there is," he said. "But if I had to walk barefoot through hell, I would still want to marry you. It would still be worth every step."

"Thank you," she whispered. "Then I will be honored to be your wife."

They sat there for a while clasped in each other's arms, and then Christina got to her feet. Lucas felt a sense of loss, a feeling that he was not complete without her.

"I really must go," she said. "We will talk about this tomorrow. I need to go to the whisky still this evening." She was hunting for her clothes, dressing haphazardly. She sounded brisk, efficient. Lucas was aware of a very strong urge not to let her go, as though this moment between them could never be recaptured. He felt a sense of dread, formless but powerful, in the pit of his stomach.

"Christina," he said, suddenly urgent, "please promise me that you will give up the whisky smuggling."

He saw the faint light shimmer on the expression in her eyes, the astonishment that he should broach this here, now. Urgency grabbed him, drowning out all the other things he was going to say.

"One day," he said, "it will be you Eyre is coming to arrest, not one of the other members of the gang. Get out before it is too late."

She touched his cheek. "I will," she said. "This is the last batch of peat-reek. I promise."

"You say that," Lucas said, "but Eyre—"

Something came into her eyes then, a shadow of puzzlement and suspicion. Lucas knew at once, with a lurch of the heart, that in his fear for her he had given himself away. He had robbed himself of the chance to tell her the truth in the way he wanted.

"You seem very well acquainted with what Mr. Eyre thinks," she said quietly. "How can that be?"

Lucas took a deep breath. "Because I've been working for Lord Sidmouth," he said. "I am the man he sent to bring your smuggling gang down."

CHAPTER FIFTEEN

"No," CHRISTINA SAID. But she already knew that it was true. She could see the guilt in Lucas's eyes. For one long, terrible moment she wished the question unsaid, wished just to be ignorant, and happy in that ignorance. But it was already too late. A swarm of memories was pressing in on her; she remembered the smugglers capturing Lucas on his very first night in Kilmory when he had been spying on the cliffs. She thought of all the questions he had been asking and the fact that he had met openly with Eyre.

Lucas was not a servant. He had never been a servant. No wonder he had not been remotely deferential. He was a man accustomed to decision and command, authoritative, forceful and powerful.

Everything fell into place, forming a pattern of deception so bright and painful Christina was only astonished she had not seen it before. Lucas had hidden in plain sight and she had been so foolish, so besotted, not to see it.

She felt cold. She started to shiver and wrapped her arms about her. Suddenly her clothes seemed too thin, too flimsy to protect her. She needed something as a defense against him, and against the terrible, appalling images that were in her mind of the way she had made love without holding back, and in return he had lied to her.

"Let me explain—" Lucas started to say, but she shook her head, putting her hands over her ears. She felt so sick she could not even look at him, and she did not want to hear any more of his lies.

He had said he respected her and cared for her. "Don't say a word," she said. "Please. Don't speak to me."

Disgust and despair swept through her, making her shake with mingled anger and mortification. She felt hot; her stomach ached with sickness. Those who said that there was no fool like an old fool were correct. She had been dazzled. She had fallen in love with Lucas and it was all a fantasy. What hurt the most was the self-delusion. She had wanted it to be true and so she had believed it. She had seduced herself with an illusion. She blamed herself even more than she blamed him.

"I don't suppose that your name is even Lucas Ross," she said quietly. "And you are most certainly not a gardener—or a footman." Anger flared in her, sudden and hot. It felt good, better than cold misery.

"I should have seen it from the first," she said. "You were the worst damned servant there ever was—you did not even *pretend* to keep to your place. But I was so besotted I couldn't even see it!" She made a sound of disgust. "Well, you are *sacked,* Mr. Ross, or whatever your name really is. You will pack your bag and leave Kilmory at once." Then, realizing that she was about to be sick, she rushed into the closet, slamming the door behind her. She only just made it in time.

She was dimly aware that Lucas had followed her into the room. She wished she had bolted the door. But it was too late; he wrung out a cloth in the cool water from the bowl on the dresser and held it out to her, then when she refused to take it he went down on one knee beside her and wiped her face as though she was a child. She hated to admit it, but it did help her to feel better. He picked her up then, again as easily as though she was a child, and carried her back into the main room, putting her down on the sofa and crossing to the Armada chest where he started to rummage through the contents.

"Go away," Christina said.

He ignored the instruction. "I am looking for a shawl for you."

Christina slid off the sofa and fetched one herself. She saw his face darken at her refusal to accept his help. She ignored him, wrapping it tightly about her.

"Christina." He had come back to her. "Please—hear me out. Let me explain to you why I came here—"

"I don't think that there is any possible explanation that can excuse you, Mr. Ross," Christina said. She looked into his eyes and felt another wave of despair.

"How it must have amused you to play me," she said, trying to hide her hurt behind sarcasm and hearing the hollowness in her own voice. "You are a fine actor, Mr. Ross, but what a role, making love to the old spinster aunt. I hope they pay you well."

"Stop it," Lucas said. He sounded angry. He caught her elbows and drew her close. She tried to resist but it was hopeless; she was too tired and miserable, and anyway her body betrayed her, recognizing his touch, softening under it, wanting him still. She could have screamed in frustration. He was the last man she wanted to comfort her and yet she longed for him to take her in his arms and hold her and tell her he loved her.

"It was not like that," Lucas said. "It was never like that."

"It doesn't matter," Christina said wearily. "Let me go," she added quietly. "Let me go now."

Lucas released her at once and she felt even worse, cold, alone and so lonely it felt as though her heart was cracking in half.

"It matters," Lucas said fiercely. "It matters more than anything in the world. I regret nothing that happened between us, Christina."

Almost, she believed him. He looked so sincere. She had thought she could read his face so well, but she did not know him at all. She had not recognized his lies for what they were.

"You put at risk everything I cared about," Christina said. She felt the protective fury surge through her again. "You endangered the people I love, the clan I work so hard to protect." Her voice shook. "They are my life, Lucas, and you wanted to destroy it all."

She saw Lucas's eyes darken with anger. He was holding on to his temper with an effort and somehow the knowledge made her even more furious when he had no reason to be angry and she had every reason.

"I protected you," Lucas said. He spoke very quietly. "I did not tell Eyre about the whisky still. He could have arrested you days ago if I had spoken up."

"Am I supposed to thank you?" Christina snapped. "I am sure you had your reasons."

She saw some expression flicker in his eyes and knew she had hit on the truth. She felt another wave of sickening misery.

"What was it?" she said. "What was that reason?"

For a moment she was not sure he would answer. She saw a muscle tighten in his cheek. The line of his mouth and jaw was set hard, inflexible.

"I did not come here solely because of the smuggling," he said. He spoke slowly, as though he was reluctant. She understood that. So much damage had been done already that she shuddered at the thought of more devastation. He looked up; met her eyes.

"I came to find out what happened to my brother," he said.

She saw it then. She saw it in the slant of his cheek and the angle of head and the gaze of his dark eyes. She saw it and wondered how she could have been so blind before. Peter Galitsin had been a boy, and Lucas was most definitely a man, but the resemblance between the two of them was undeniable.

"Peter Galitsin," she whispered. She put out a hand to steady herself. The wall of the Round House felt chill against her hot palm. She remembered the questions Lucas had asked about Peter's death. He must have believed that the smugglers were connected to the murder. She felt sicker still, but there was nothing left in her stomach to be sick with.

"What is your real name?" she asked. It felt like a trivial question in a way, particularly when she had no idea whether he would tell her the truth or not. Desolation chilled her again. He had misled her in more ways than she could count.

"My name is Lucas Black," Lucas said. "Peter and I were half brothers."

Christina felt another flash of bitterness so sharp it felt like a dagger thrust. "So the tale you spun me about being illegitimate—"

"Was true," Lucas said harshly. "I was born out of wedlock to a Russian princess and a Scottish laird."

Christina gave a slight negative shake of the head. She did not know how to believe him now. She could not disentangle truth from falsehood. She remembered Lucas talking about a misspent youth on the streets. She thought of the passion with which he had spoken of the scars of illegitimacy. Could it all be lies? She was not sure if it even mattered. She could never trust him now.

"I suppose you suspected me of killing your brother," she said with a flash of pain she could not hide. "That was the reason you did not denounce me to Eyre before. You were waiting to find out if I was guilty."

Lucas squared his shoulders. "I cannot deny that

was how it started," he said. "I thought that the smugglers had something to do with Peter's death. You are their leader. So yes, that was what I believed to begin with." He gave her a very straight look. "But I had not been more than a week in your company before I knew that could never be the case. You would never do such a thing."

"If that is so, why did you not tell me the truth?" Christina demanded. She knew the answer almost as soon as she had spoken and did not wait for his reply. "You were afraid that if I learned you had deceived me, I would sack you," she said flatly. "You wanted to stay at Kilmory. So you kept lying, kept using me, pretended to care for me and all the time you were hoping I would lead you to your brother's murderer." She was ashamed of the way that her voice broke. "Damn you, Lucas," she said more quietly. "Why could you not have come here openly to ask about Peter? I would have helped you."

She turned away. She did not want him to see her like this, in pieces. "You were right," she said. "I want you to go. Leave Kilmory."

"No," Lucas said. His jaw had set stubbornly. "Christina—"

"Please," Christina said. "Stay at the Kilmory Inn if you wish to continue your inquiries. I don't care. But if you have even the smallest degree of respect for me, do not, I beg you, pester me with any more excuses."

She pushed blindly past him out of the Round House and stumbled down onto the beach. It was only then that she realized she was barefoot and had left her stockings and shoes behind. The sand felt cool between her toes. The breeze had a sharp edge. The blue twilight wrapped about her, but for once the timeless beauty of Kilmory could not touch her. She felt cold to the soul, with what was left of her heart shattered into a million pieces. She had been right all along about love. It hurt. You could lose it in an instant, and then everything changed.

DAMNATION, BLAST AND bloody hell.

Lucas ran an exasperated hand through his hair.

That could not have gone much more badly. It had been far too little, far too late. He could see that now, now that the damage was done. His quest had blinded him to the hurt he would cause Christina when the truth finally came out. He had made some disastrous miscalculations, proving nothing to her other than that she could not trust him.

Fool. Bloody fool.

She had been hurt so badly before. Her whole life, all her certainties, had been destroyed in one moment. Now he had unwittingly done the same thing, taken her certainties, taken her world, and broken it.

He went outside and sat on the flat stone facing the sea. The driftwood fire had burned down to a glow of smoldering ashes now. The sky over the sea was rose and gold. The breeze felt cold. He sat there for a long time, thinking.

In pursuing his search ruthlessly to the end he had

lost the one thing he had come to care for above all else: Christina, and the promise of a future with her.

Yet Peter deserved justice, too. He could not simply abandon his brother's cause, not when Peter's murderer was still out there, not when no one else would ever bring him to justice. He felt horribly torn. He could not leave Kilmory without doing all he could to discover the truth. But more important still was the need to prove to Christina that she could believe in him.

I would have helped you, Christina had said. He wondered if, even now, she might be persuaded to do so. She had such a passionate belief in natural justice. He had to trust that her goodness, her generosity, would help him now, even though he did not deserve it.

Lucas got to his feet slowly. The urge to go after Christina, to override all her objections, was strong, but equally powerful was the respect he had for her. He could not force her to help him. This time he had to earn her trust. He had to win her all over again.

It was as he emerged onto the beach that he saw Eyre galloping across it on a rangy gray, the sand kicked up by its hooves into a spray. As Eyre saw him he reined in and drew to a halt. He did not dismount but sat looking down on Lucas from a great height, his eyes narrowed.

"Out late, Mr. Ross."

"I've been swimming," Lucas said with a shrug. "Gardening is a dirty business."

"So is spying," Eyre said pleasantly. "I hear you've

been busy seducing the duke's daughter as part of your investigation. Nice work, Mr. Ross. I hope it was worth it."

With the greatest effort of will Lucas kept his mouth shut and his hands from Eyre's throat. The excise officer only wanted to provoke him; Lucas knew that. But it was almost impossible not to defend Christina and give the man the confirmation he sought.

"Is there something I can help you with, Mr. Eyre?" he said coldly.

"Not really," Eyre said. "I've got an informer in the castle now. I don't need your help." The horse sidestepped as Eyre's hands tightened on the reins. He looked up at the cliff and following his gaze, Lucas could see a number of other riders on the track at the top. "We're on our way to the whisky still now," Eyre said. "Word is we'll catch the smugglers in the act tonight."

"Best of luck," Lucas said, feigning boredom over the sudden pounding of his heart. Surely, he thought, Christina would not have gone straight from him to the whisky still. Yet angry, disillusioned and miserable, she might well have wanted to hide away from the prying eyes of her family. He felt the tension grab him like a vise.

Eyre raised a hand in a mocking salute and galloped away. Lucas forced himself to walk slowly back along the beach toward the castle as though he had not a concern in the world, but as soon as he was out of sight he broke into a run.

There was a spy at Kilmory, someone who had betrayed Christina and her smuggling gang to the excise officers. He wondered who that person could be. The irony was that Christina would believe that he was the traitor. She would never believe his protestations of honesty now, assuming he ever had the chance to see her again. He thought of Eyre and his cohorts heading along the loch to the whisky still and he ran faster.

He pounded on the front door of the castle and it felt like hours before Galloway came, stately as a galleon, to open it.

"Mr. Ross?" The butler's face was set in lines of deep disapproval. "This is the front door. The servants' entrance—"

"I'm aware of where it is," Lucas said tersely. "I need to see Lady Christina."

The butler looked both affronted and wary, and in that moment Lucas knew that the servants were all aware of his affair with Christina and that Galloway utterly deplored it and would never in a hundred years allow him to see Christina or pass on any message to her.

"Her ladyship is not at home," Galloway said, and started to swing the door closed, but Lucas blocked it with a slap of his palm on the wood. The butler jumped.

"Has she gone to the whisky still?" Lucas demanded.

Galloway blinked at him, impervious, silent.

"Damn it, man," Lucas roared. "Tell me!"

"Mr. Ross!" Galloway was shaking with fury. "You are insolent. You will be dismissed from your post."

"Too late," Lucas said. "Lady Christina has already sacked me." He turned away. He could not afford the time to see if Christina was inside the castle. He did not want to draw further attention to the fact that she might be missing or indeed to their relationship, though it seemed it was too late for that. The only thing he could do was go to the whisky still and hope against hope that she would not be there.

He knew that if she had gone there he would be too late. The excise officers had fifteen minutes advantage and they were on horseback. They would be at the bothy already.

He turned and ran.

Too late...

The stones slid beneath his boots. The heather and bracken whipped at his legs. As he came around the headland toward the loch, he saw smoke rising into the still blue of the night sky. His heart gave a huge thump of fear. Eyre had set the bothy alight.

Lucas ran up the slope. It felt as though his lungs were bursting, but he drove himself on. He could not see the excisemen anywhere. The bothy door swung wide, hanging off its hinges. The lock had been smashed. The interior was alight and burning fiercely; the smoke was thick and choking, glass shards everywhere from the broken window.

Lucas rested a hand against the splintered door frame and drew in deep gulps of fresh air.

Christina. He had to find Christina.

Then he heard shouts and the drumming of hooves. Fresh fear gripped him. Pushing away from the door, he ran out onto the path. The moon was up now and it illuminated the hunt below. He could see the figure of a woman, cloaked and hooded, fleeing through the heather down toward the edge of the loch. She was sure-footed and did not stumble or hesitate once. Her cloak billowed out behind her like a sail, black against the inky blue of the night and the purple haze of the heather. But for all her speed, she was not going to get away. Lucas could see the trap. Behind her the riding officers were fanning out, a half dozen of them on horseback in a semicircle, some of them driving her downhill toward the water, some of them coming in along the shore of the loch.

Soon she would have nowhere to run.

She reached the edge of the loch and half turned to look behind. Eyre was thundering down through the bracken at her back, the others shouting, circling, drawing ever closer, their blood lit with the excitement of the chase, all except Bryson, who appeared to be having a short, sharp argument with Eyre. Eyre raised his pistol and the breath jammed in Lucas's throat on a shout. He saw the riding officer try to level the pistol and heard the snap of the shot. Christina checked for a second in her headlong flight along the edge of the loch.

Eyre was trying to kill her.

He did not want to capture her. He did not want to take her prisoner. He wanted her dead.

Sheer, atavistic terror grabbed Lucas by the throat. He set off down the hill toward them, knowing it was hopeless, that there was nothing he could do to save Christina and that Eyre would surely have shot her before he got there. But he would take the man down and kill him for what he was doing, for the hunt, and the terror and the cold-blooded execution.

Christina had reached the point where a spit of shingle ran out into the waters of the loch. Eyre was so close at her back that Lucas saw him reach out to grab her cloak and only just miss. Christina did not hesitate. She walked into the loch. Lucas saw her skirts billow out, her cloak spreading across the water.

She would rather drown than give herself up to these thugs and bullies.

He cried out then; his voice caught on the wind and blew away. The heather roots tripped him but he stumbled on, trying to reach her, knowing in his heart it was too late but not prepared to give up, to give in.

Christina was walking steadily onward, out into the waters of the loch. It had to be an optical illusion caused by the moonlight, but it appeared that she was walking *on* the water. Eyre had urged his horse into the loch behind her and as Lucas watched the creature plunged up to its chest in the water and Eyre gave a shout as he was almost unseated. A moment later the horse was swimming and Eyre had fallen off with a loud splash and a howl of invective, yet Christina continued to walk out into the darkness until the moon disappeared behind a cloud and the spread of her cloak on the dark water vanished. When the moon came up again there was no one there, nothing but Eyre splashing out into the shallows, soaked and still swearing, leading his horse, and the other riding officers circling on the beach, milling around, bewildered.

Lucas stood, staring at the breeze ruffling the top of the water. He did not know what to think. Hope and desperation warred inside him. And then he remembered, like the whisper of the breeze, Christina's voice telling him how well she knew the sea and the lochs and the landscape, the way her ancestors had.

Lucas gave a great shudder. He felt his knees weaken and he crumpled to sit in the midst of the heather and bracken, head in hands. Christina knew and loved this land in a way that Eyre and his men never would. She understood it. And tonight that had surely saved her. He did not know how. He did not know where she had gone, but he felt hope and faith catch alight inside him and burn steadily.

The riding officers still had not seen him. In all of the fray they had not noticed he was there. He lay a bit lower in the heather, feeling the sharp prickle of the stems against his skin, listening.

"Where did she go?" Lucas heard Bryson ask.

"She drowned," Eyre said shortly. He was shaking himself like a dog.

"But—" One of the others, a youth called Austin, was pressing closer. "We all saw. She walked away. She walked *on* the water."

Eyre glared at him. "What do you think she is? A bloody witch? A ghost? She drowned, I tell you!" His voice was rising. "And in the morning we shall see who is missing and then we will know."

"We've nothing, though," Bryson said. "No whisky still, no arrests, not even a body—"

Eyre turned on him. "We've a woman missing, and I think I know who she is..." He stopped abruptly. It was clear to Lucas that Eyre's vanity could not allow him to share his suspicions of Christina. In the same way that he could not countenance that she had outwitted him again, he alone wanted to claim the triumph of breaking the news of her drowning and of her secret life as the smugglers' leader.

Lucas stood up a little stiffly and started to edge toward the track. He had to find Christina, help her. When Eyre came to Kilmory Castle expecting to tell her shattered family that she was dead, Christina had to be alive and well, waiting to refute everything Eyre said.

The excise officers were cantering away along the edge of the water. They were subdued, looking over their shoulders. One superstitious fellow even crossed himself. Lucas waited until the last echo of the horses' hooves had died away, and then he walked down to the water's edge. He was not sure where Christina would come back to dry land, but it had to be along the western edge of the loch.

He followed the shoreline along to a place where the silver birch trees grew thickly, their pale trunks reflecting the moonlight. There, amongst the tangled roots, he saw the huddle of a body lying motionless in the shallows.

Christina.

He had lost count how many times that night he had felt despair. He waded into the water and caught hold of a waterlogged fold of cloth, pulling her toward him. She felt heavy and reluctant to come to him but he struggled, swearing, until his grip on the sodden material was sufficient to be able to lift her.

She was still breathing. Whispering a prayer of thanks under his breath, he started to drag her out of the shallows. Immediately she stirred and started to struggle.

"That's my girl," Lucas said. Relief flooded through him as fiercely as the terror had before.

"I'm *not* your girl." Her voice was scarcely more than a croak.

"Let's not argue about that now," Lucas said. "Give me your hand. We need to get you out of there."

She hesitated for only a moment, then her hand grasped his outstretched one and he pulled her toward him. Her clothes were saturated and the water was reluctant to give her up, but he grasped her other arm and lifted her. She was clinging to him, soaked through, but beneath the sodden layers of material, she felt warm and alive, and he crushed her to him and felt the fierceness with which she held him. He felt relief, thankfulness—and anger with her for putting him through such an ordeal. It was so strong it took his breath away.

"I warned you," he said. His voice was rough. He wanted to shake her; he wanted to do something to vent all the fury that was inside him. "I told you it was dangerous." He pulled her hood back so that he could see her face. Her hair spilled in glorious disarray about her shoulders. She had the pallor of exhaustion, her eyes wide and frightened, a smear of dirt down one cheek. There was blood, too. He could see it now in the pale moonlight, a smear of it on her sleeve. His anger fled as quickly as it had come.

"You're bleeding," he said. "The bullet hit you."

"It's only a scratch," she said. She sounded faint with fatigue. "I should have realized you would be here." She had freed herself from his grasp now and stepped away from him, wariness in her eyes.

"Have you come to arrest me?" she said.

"Don't be stupid," Lucas said shortly. "I came to warn you, but I was too late. Come on," he added, trying to encourage her up the shore and onto the path. "We mustn't waste any time."

Still she hung back. His patience snapped. "Look," he said. "A moment ago you clung to me. You trusted me."

She turned away so that he could not see her face. "I was glad to be safe," she murmured. "I forgot."

"You should trust your instincts," Lucas said.

She gave him a look of weary disillusionment. "They have not served me so well in the past," she said. Ignoring his outstretched hand, she clambered up the hillside and onto the track.

They did not speak as they walked back to the

castle. Christina had put up her hood again and held the sodden material of her cloak close. Lucas could see that she was shivering. It was as they neared the castle ruins that he heard the furious beat of hooves on the road and grabbed her, pulling her into the shelter of a tumbledown wall, one hand clapped over her mouth.

"Eyre," he whispered in her ear. "He is going back to try to find your body."

He felt the shudder that shook her, and drew her closer, arms wrapped about her, trying to instill a sense of security and protection into her as she trembled. He pressed his cheek to her hair and flattened his hands against her back and held her shaking body to him.

"You're safe," he whispered. "Don't be afraid."

Christina drew away from him slowly.

"I don't understand," she said, when the sounds had faded and the night was still again. "Why did you not betray me? I thought you must be the one who told Eyre where to find the whisky still."

"There is a spy at Kilmory, but it isn't me," Lucas said. He caught her by the shoulders. "Do you really think I would betray you? Dear God, Christina—"

"I don't know," Christina said dully. She tried to twist out of his grasp. "Don't you see, Lucas?" she said. "I don't trust you. I can't trust you. I thought I knew you and you were someone else entirely."

Lucas could feel her shaking. "I did not betray you to Eyre because I have been trying to protect you," he said harshly. "I've seen what you have tried to do to help the people of Kilmory and I admire you for it even if I don't agree with what you do. And I don't like Eyre's methods," he added grimly. "I wrote to Sidmouth to say so."

"Did you?" He could feel her gaze on him, weighing his honesty. The light flickered on the expression in her eyes. For a moment she had looked hopeful, as loving and candid as she had been before, then the shadow of disillusion swept into her eyes and her expression closed again.

"Thank you for tonight," she said. "I can manage well enough on my own now." She swayed, exhaustion and shock clearly taking its toll, and Lucas swept her up into his arms.

"I'll carry you back."

"Please don't." There was an edge to her voice. "I can manage quite well on my own—"

"Rubbish," Lucas said roughly. "You almost fainted just now. Lie still."

He thought she was going to argue further but she gave a little sigh and turned her face into his neck. He felt her breath on his skin. Their faces were so close; he had to resist the fierce urge to take her mouth with his. He knew how she would taste, and the memory sent a fierce jolt of lust through him. Her eyelashes flickered. He saw the flash of answering heat in her gaze. So she was not immune, then. The knowledge gave Lucas hope.

He carried her across the swath of grass that separated the ruins from the main building. Eyre was evidently confident; he had set no watch on the castle. Nothing moved in the silent grounds. Behind the shuttered windows, the lights still glowed.

"How did you get away from the riding officers?" he asked. "It looked as though you were walking on the water."

"Oh…" Her lips curved into a smile. "There are ways across the loch, a shingle path just beneath the surface of the water, hidden from sight…."

"Thank God," Lucas said. "Even so, you almost drowned."

"The water was higher than normal because of the summer rain." She sounded exhausted now. "Please put me down. I will go to my chamber via the door in the tower so that no one is aware of what has happened tonight."

"I'm not leaving you on your own," Lucas said. He placed her gently on her feet as he bent to retrieve the key to the tower door. "I'm staying with you."

"That's ridiculous." Through her exhaustion he could hear the crackle of starchiness in her voice. Lady Christina, daughter of the duke, was standing on her dignity. Except that he was not going to let her, not anymore.

"We are betrothed," he said. "We exchanged vows only a couple of hours ago. It is my right to protect you. I am not leaving."

CHAPTER SIXTEEN

"Betrothed?"

Christina was so outraged that she forgot that she was cold, tired, wet and exhausted.

"I asked you to marry me and you agreed." Lucas sounded maddeningly reasonable. He had found the key now and was sliding it into the lock. "That constitutes a trothplight under Scots law."

"But that was before I knew who you were," Christina said. "I withdraw my consent."

"Then I will sue you for breach of contract." Lucas held the door open for her with as much courtesy as a gentleman helping her from her carriage at a ball. "We are betrothed. I have the right to protect you."

"No, you do not." Christina could not remember the last time she had felt so infuriated. "Lucas, this is not funny." She glanced at his face as she passed him in the entrance; he was smiling at her, a smile that reminded her of all the things that had happened in the shadows of the Round House and made her feel very hot and bothered. She was definitely getting a chill.

"I'm not joking," Lucas said, the smile dying from

his eyes. "I want to marry you, Christina. That has not changed."

"You can't expect me to marry a man who lied to me," Christina said. "How can I trust you after that?"

"I did not lie," Lucas said. He sounded annoyingly matter-of-fact. "I admit that I concealed certain facts from you—"

"Such as your identity and your reason for being at Kilmory!" Christina burst out.

"And I am sorry for that," Lucas said steadily. He turned to close the door behind them and Christina stared in frustration at his broad shoulders. She wanted to slam a fist against them, show him how much he had hurt her. "But nothing I did was intended to harm you." He turned so suddenly that she caught her breath, almost overpowered by his nearness. "On the contrary," he said, "I tried to keep the truth from you to protect you. That was a mistake."

"I'm glad that you acknowledge it," Christina said stiffly.

Lucas spread his hands in a gesture of appeal. "I had to find my brother's murderer," he said. "I still have to do it. It is a sacred trust to me. I hope you understand."

Christina was getting dizzy going up the spiral stair. Her feet dragged, and despite herself she was grateful for the strength of Lucas's arm guiding her upward.

"I suppose I do understand," she said after a moment. "That is, I understand that you are committed to discovering who took your brother's life."

"And will you help me?" Lucas said directly.

Christina paused. She had had time to think now and she could see, even through her sense of disillusion and betrayal, that to Lucas it was a matter of honor to achieve justice for Peter. She thought of the joy with which Peter had spoken of his reconciliation with the older brother he had not seen for so long. That brother had been Lucas. It had been Lucas who had received the unendurable news of his death, Lucas whose hopes for a future rebuilding the relationship with his brother had been snuffed out on the track by Kilmory. That knowledge in itself broke her heart. She knew Lucas must be hurting badly.

"You may stay here at Kilmory until the perpetrator is found," she said. "Then I want you to go."

Lucas stood aside to allow her to precede him into her chamber. He did not argue with her, but his face was dark and cold again, forbidding, determined. She shivered. Yes, he would hunt down his brother's murderer. He would see justice done.

"Whom do you suspect?" she said. "You seem convinced that the culprit is here in the village, or perhaps even in the castle. You must have some basis for your suspicions."

She saw some emotion flicker in his eyes and had the distinct impression that he was keeping something from her. "I have a few ideas, but nothing definite," he said, "and I would not wish to accuse an innocent man."

Christina let it go. She was too tired to argue anyway, and she did not want further proof that Lucas did not trust her with his secrets.

"You said that you are half Scottish, half Russian," she said, remembering. "It's a ruthless combination."

For a moment, humor lit Lucas's black eyes. "I hope I have the best of both."

"Why do you call yourself Lucas Black?" Christina asked. A part of her did not want to talk to Lucas when her feelings toward him were still so raw, but she was curious, too, curious about the man he really was.

Lucas shrugged. "I use the name Black because I am laird of the Black Strath," he said. "Strictly speaking, my name is Prince Lucas Orlov, but I do not use the Russian title."

Shock robbed Christina of breath for a moment. She wondered how much more there was that she did not know. An entire life story, she supposed. He had given away so little about himself.

"Laird of the Black Strath," she said. "That is near Perth, is it not? A Sutherland estate?"

"My father was Niall Sutherland." Lucas sounded curt. "He left the Black Strath to me, but I do not go there. I am no laird. I am a businessman with no understanding of the land."

"That's a pity," Christina said. "Especially for your people."

She saw the flicker of something in his face, something of shame or guilt. "I make sure they are well cared for," he said. "My land agent is good and they lack nothing." He took a taper from the fire and the lamp burst into light.

"So the Duchess of Strathspey is your aunt," Christina said. "I see." More pieces of the puzzle clicked into place, more pretense. Her heart ached and suddenly she felt very tired. She wished she had not followed instinct instead of reason. Instinct had betrayed her. It had told her she could trust Lucas; that it was safe to love him. Instinct had been wrong. She had lost again. The foundations she had been building had proved as shifting as sand. She had no intention of giving Lucas a second chance, not when everything she had thought she knew of him had turned out to be a sham.

"We need to get you out of those wet clothes." Lucas had stoked the fire to a blaze and was coming back across the room toward her. Her heart bumped against her ribs. She clutched the sodden cloak to her neck in a futile gesture of modesty.

"I can undress myself," she said, but her fingers were shaking so much with cold and reaction that they fumbled the ribbons of the cloak.

"Let me," Lucas said.

"No!" She backed away from him. "I don't want you to see me naked."

"I saw you naked about three hours ago," Lucas said. He took the cloak from her fingers and drew it away from her, spreading it across the back of one of the armchairs. His gaze searched her face. He frowned. "Do you want me to send your maid to you?"

"I can manage," Christina said.

"Then I'll help you," Lucas said.

"I meant that I can manage if you go away now."

Lucas smiled. "Someone needs to be with you in case you are taken ill," he said. "You may well have caught a chill from tonight or inflamed the bullet wound. You could develop a fever." He turned her gently around and she felt his fingers on the buttons of her gown.

"No wonder you are so autocratic," Christina said, shivering as he slid the soaking material from her, "if you are a prince. What rapid social advancement from gardener to nobleman, Mr. Black. Or should I call you Highness now?"

Lucas laughed. "You may call me whatever you wish."

"Don't tempt me," Christina said.

"As I said, I don't use the title." Lucas turned her around to face him, his hands warm on the chilled skin of her bare arms. His gaze slid down her body and Christina suddenly realized that the fine material was plastered against her, leaving absolutely nothing to the imagination. She saw a muscle flicker in his jaw. His gaze came up to hers, fierce and hot, sending a deep pulse of need beating through her. Then he turned abruptly away.

"You had better take the rest off yourself," he said shortly. He strode across the room, returning with the robe that Annie had laid out for her by the fire.

Christina's fingers shook as she tugged on the stubborn laces of the chemise. Lucas had gone back to the fireside and was adding another log to the grate, his back ostentatiously turned to her.

"How is it that you are a prince if you are illegitimate?" she asked as she struggled to peel off her chemise and petticoats.

"My grandfather asked the Czarina Catherine to legitimize me." Lucas's tone was level but she wondered how many hurts and humiliations it concealed. "He did it for my mother's sake. He thought it would make matters better."

"And did it?"

"No." There was dark humor in his voice now. "It made matters much worse. I was still a bastard by birth and most people would not let me forget it." He shifted, stretched. "Once I was big enough to fight, though, the taunting stopped soon enough."

It would not have been as easy as that, Christina thought. There would have been a hundred snubs and slights, a thousand. Not only to him but also to his mother. Those were the insults that would have proved impossible to ignore.

Lucas turned his head. His dark gaze snagged with hers and Christina felt her heartbeat increase. She felt so vulnerable beneath that gaze. It felt as though some small, fragile link in the chain had been reforged between them, a bond that frightened her and that she did not want.

"Get into bed," Lucas said. "You need to rest."

She had wanted him to leave but now, suddenly, she did not want to be alone and she was too tired to question why. She smothered a yawn as she swung her legs under the covers and lay back against the pillows.

"Tell me about Peter," she said. "Tell me about your brother."

Lucas's expression softened. He came back to the bed and she felt the mattress sink a little as he sat down beside her. Her eyelids were already closing. Lucas started to tell her about his mother's marriage to Prince Paul Galitsin, about Peter's birth, their childhood in the Galitsin Palace, vivid details of his life before the death of his mother had seen him thrown from his stepfather's house and sent him over a thousand miles across the world to Scotland. His words were soft and mingled with the stroke of his fingers against her cheek or her hair; her head swam with tiredness and the beginnings of fever. She felt hot and thirsty. Lucas brought her a glass of water and held it gently to her lips. Then his voice resumed again, with tales of life on the streets of Edinburgh, and his voice mingled with the sound of the sea and the wind in the pines outside, and she slept.

She woke some time later, still hot and confused, with dreams and reality merging. She was running through the loch, the water dragging at her skirts, Eyre reaching to grab a handful of the material of her cloak. She felt darkness and panic. She sank like a stone and felt the waters close over her head. She could not see, could not breathe.

She opened her eyes. The lamp had burned down low and everything was in shadow. For a moment she was confused, then she recognized the familiar contours of the room: the fireplace, the chest of drawers by the window, the high-backed chair over which was draped a shapeless pile of clothes. Relief chased through her that she was safe. Her racing heartbeat slowed and instantly she became aware of other things that the fear had blotted out: the warmth and reassurance of another body beside hers, the strength of the arms that held her.

Lucas.

She was so shocked that she tried to sit up. Immediately her head swam and she lay back down, letting the pain ease to a dull ache, allowing Lucas to draw her closer to his side as he murmured something in his sleep and pressed his lips to her hair in a fleeting kiss.

Her memory came flooding back.

She felt warmth steal through her as she remembered how Lucas had saved her life, and turning her head slightly, she breathed in the scent of his skin. It felt wonderful, so familiar and yet so exciting. She ran a hand gently over his hair. It felt soft and silky beneath her fingertips. Lucas stirred a little but did not wake. For a moment she thought that her heart would break with such a poignant mixture of love and pain. She had wanted to lie with Lucas like this. Before their quarrel, she had ached to be able to openly share such love and intimacy. Now she did not know what to do, what to think. He had hurt her and misled her, yet her instinct still whispered that he was an honorable man, that everything he had done had been for his brother's sake, that beneath the lies and the deception she knew him still, knew him in her heart.

Reason told her that that was sentimental nonsense. She had trusted Lucas and he had broken her heart. She would have been prepared to marry Lucas Ross, and no barriers of status or age or wealth would have stood in her way. She did not know this man, Lucas Black, Prince Lucas Orlov, laird of the Black Strath.

Lethargy stole through her, weighing her down. She did not know which to believe, head or heart. She lay awake for a while. She wondered if Eyre really did know her identity and if he would come in the morning to see if she was dead or to arrest her for smuggling. She wondered who had betrayed her. Gradually, though, the reassurance of having Lucas beside her and the steady sound of his breathing helped her to relax. She was warm and she was safe. Anything else could wait until the morning.

LUCAS WOKE WITH the distinct impression that something was wrong. There was a rattle of bed curtains and then Annie's cheerful voice. "Good morning, my lady. I thought you might like your breakfast up here and a bit of peace and quiet to start the day before…" The words ended in a shriek, hastily suppressed. Rolling over in the bed, Lucas saw that the maid was standing staring at him, one hand pressed to her mouth, the other over her heart in the time-honored gesture of shock. Thank God he still had his clothes on, or her shock would have been larger and so would her scream. And thank God she had already put down the breakfast tray.

"Ma'am…" Annie said. "Mr. *Ross!*"

Lucas heard a sudden, urgent rustle of bedclothes beside him as Christina woke. Her gasp echoed Annie's. He put out a hand and grabbed her, knowing she was about to bolt.

"Don't leave," he said pleasantly. "It is your room."

Christina was staring at him with eyes full of sleep and confusion. She looked soft and tumbled and completely adorable to him, her face pale and her blue eyes huge.

"What—" she began.

"Please don't ask me what I am doing here," Lucas said. "Unless you have lost your memory."

Color came into her face and her gaze snapped awake. She looked like the starchy duke's daughter now, except that behind the haughty facade he was certain he saw a glimpse of fear. She had been vulnerable the previous night. She had allowed him to help her. Now she was regretting it, but he had no intention of letting her step away from the intimacy between them.

"How are you?" he said. "Has the fever gone?"

"I am very well, thank you," Christina said shortly.

"Ma'am," Annie said again, almost beseeching, looking from one of them to the other. "Oh, ma'am!"

"It's all right, Annie," Christina said, reaching for

the robe Lucas had passed her the previous night, a practical affair of figured silk. "Mr. Ross is—"

"Lady Christina's betrothed," Lucas finished for her.

"I was going to say leaving," Christina said.

"That isn't going to solve anything," Lucas said. He looked into her stormy blue eyes. Again he saw that flicker of vulnerability behind the confusion.

"Christina," he said fiercely, "I am not going to hide away. I am not going to pretend that nothing happened between us. We are betrothed and I am not going to leave you."

Again their gazes clashed. "You have to go," Christina said, but he could hear the fear in her voice now.

"Stop pushing me away," Lucas said harshly. "Yes, I misled you and I am sorry for that, but you are using it as an excuse to run from me. You trusted me before and you can trust me again. I swear it."

"Begging your pardon, milady, Mr. Ross…" Annie's nervous voice cut straight across the tightly spun tension. She had drawn back the curtain, letting bright sunlight flood into the tower room. It brought with it the sound of carriage wheels rumbling over the gravel, doors slamming, voices.

"Your sisters are here, milady." Annie shot Christina a nervous glance out of the corner of her eye.

This time Christina did leap from the bed. Lucas caught a glimpse of creamy skin as she grabbed the robe close, knotting it about her waist with hands that shook. "They aren't supposed to be here until later this afternoon!" She was looking seriously upset now. "How can I…" Her gaze skittered to Lucas, then veered away. "Lucas, you really must go." She made shooing motions with her hands. "We'll discuss everything later. If you go down the tower stairs—"

"I'll appear directly in front of your sisters coming out of the secret stair that leads to your bedroom," Lucas said. "Yes, that would work."

Christina pressed her lips together in a thin line at his sarcasm. "Then take the main stairs," she said.

"And risk Galloway thinking I'm a thief creeping out with the family silver? No, thank you." Lucas stood up, reaching for his jacket. He might have wished for something a little more sartorially elegant when making his debut in front of Christina's family, but it could not be helped.

"Accept it, Christina," he said. "I am your fiancé, and I am going downstairs with you to meet your sisters, and I will not skulk around pretending that I am just the gardener."

Christina gave a sharp sigh. "Annie," she said, ignoring him, "please would you bring me my cream muslin with the crimson ribbons?" She turned to Lucas. "I am sure you are acquainted with the correct etiquette on these occasions, Your Highness. It is customary for a gentleman to leave a lady's chamber whilst she dresses."

"Highness?" Annie squeaked, looking as though she was about to faint. "Oh, my lord!"

"No," Christina said, "a prince. The cream muslin?"

"Yes, ma'am, right away." Annie threw Lucas a dubious glance over her shoulder as she scurried toward the chest of drawers. "A prince!" he heard her say under her breath. "Only fancy!"

"I'll wait for you in the dressing room," Lucas said. "And, Christina—" He touched her wrist lightly. "We are engaged."

"To save my reputation," Christina said frostily. "Yes, I do understand that we must maintain that pretense in public, at least for a while."

"To hell with that," Lucas said. He bent his head and took her mouth in a hard kiss, allowing his feelings to show, the frustration and the desire and the need. He felt her hesitate, and then she kissed him back with the same turbulent passion. He could sense anger in her. She nipped at his lower lip and it felt as though she wanted to hurt him, but there was a longing there, too. He kissed her deeper, more fiercely, and she responded with a fire that drove all other thoughts from his mind. He had his hands on her shoulders, about to push her back on the bed and tear the robe from her when Annie's loud clearing of the throat recalled him to sanity. Breathing hard, he released Christina and stepped back. Her eyes were dark and hazy and her lips were swollen from his kisses, and he felt such a violent pang of lust that he swore under his breath.

Annie closed the door of the dressing room pointedly behind him, and Lucas threw himself down into an armchair to wait. He could hear the low voices of Christina and the maid through the door but could not distinguish the words. He sat back with a long sigh, feeling the tension wound up tight inside him. He was going to use every means possible to win Christina back. He would fight for what he wanted. He had not been sure that he would get a second chance. Now that he had one, he was not going to waste it.

CHAPTER SEVENTEEN

CHRISTINA LED THE way downstairs, very conscious of Lucas's tall figure at her side. She had not wanted to accept his support. She had wanted to push him as far away from her as possible, because she was afraid. But Lucas had refused to go.

She had woken earlier that morning and found herself lying in his arms with her head against his chest and his heartbeat strong and steady in her ear. It had felt so good, so right, despite everything that had happened. She was so unaccustomed to being cherished. She wanted to open her heart to the sensation, to give herself up to it, and that was why she was afraid. To open her heart to Lucas again, to risk loving him, to give him her trust, was too dangerous. Twice now she had seen her world torn apart. It was better, safer, not to take the risk again. Yet even so she felt as though she was fighting a battle she might lose. She could still feel Lucas's kiss and the urgency of his hands on her body. She shivered with longing.

There was mayhem in the hall. Gertrude was barking orders at a harassed Galloway whilst Thomas the footman ran ineffectually back and forth, confusing everyone's luggage. Angus was doing nothing, as usual. Christina's sisters Lucy and Mairi were talking to the duke, who had evidently been disturbed from his studies by all the noise. Richard Bryson was speaking urgently to Allegra, whose face was pale and set.

"Tina!" Mairi spun around when she saw her sister. She grabbed Christina and pulled her in for a hug against her enormous pregnant belly. "There you are! We had almost given you up!"

"Where have you been, Christina?" Gertrude demanded. "There are a hundred and one things that need doing! I cannot be expected to organize this all on my own! How are you, Mairi," she added, eyeing Mairi's bump with disapproval. "I cannot imagine why you thought it appropriate to travel in your state of health. Anything might have happened!"

"It's lovely to see you, too, Gertrude," Mairi said. "You seem gloriously the same as ever."

Her gaze had moved to Lucas, and she was staring. So was Lucy, who had come over to greet her. Christina knew that plenty of women stared when they saw Lucas, but she could see that there was a different quality to her sisters' interest. Mairi looked surprised, Lucy interested.

"Ah, Ross!" Gertrude pounced before anyone could speak. "Help Thomas with the luggage, would you?" Her eye fell on Richard Bryson. "What is he doing here?" She sped away.

"Well!" Mairi said. "I know that you are very democratic in your beliefs, Prince Lucas, but I think that Gertrude asks a little too much of her guests."

"Good morning, Lady Mairi," Lucas said, smiling as he took her hand. "It's a pleasure to see you again." He turned to Lucy. "Good morning, ma'am. You must be Lady Methven. I apologize for the lack of a formal introduction."

"This is Prince Lucas Orlov," Christina said tightly, "or Mr. Black as he would prefer to be known." She absorbed another pang of shock as she realized that Mairi and Lucas knew each other. That must mean that Jack and Lucas must be acquaintances, or perhaps even friends. She did not know what to think about that except perhaps it was a close-run thing which of them she would like to shoot first.

"How do you do?" Lucy said, smiling charmingly. "Robert has mentioned your name. He and Jack are joining us later," she added. "They will be delighted to see you again."

"Robert, as well!" Christina burst out. "How marvelous! The entire *family* knows Lucas except for me!"

"I think you know me fairly well," Lucas said, with a smile that brought the color up into her face.

"Lady Christina and I are betrothed," he added. "I hope you will wish us happy."

Mairi gave a little whoop. "Christina, darling!" Her eyes were bright with interest and speculation. "You are a dark horse. I didn't know you even knew Lucas!"

"I'm not at all sure I do," Christina said drily.

"Did he say *betrothed?*" Gertrude's voice cut across them all like a knife through butter. She rushed back across the hall, eyes bright with the excitement of scandal. "Did I understand you right?" she demanded of Mairi. "Christina is *betrothed to the gardener?*"

"Are you feeling quite the thing, Gertrude?" Mairi asked. "Lucas may choose not to use his title, but he is scarcely a gardener. Whatever gave you that idea?"

"Probably the fact that Lucas has been tending the garden here at Kilmory for the past six weeks," Christina said.

"My name is Lucas Black, Lady Semple," Lucas said, "and I am—"

"A Russian prince," Mairi said mischievously. "So you need not worry that the family escutcheon will be blotted, Gertrude. Prince Lucas outranks us all."

"Russian?" Gertrude said, looking down her nose as though Lucas had announced he was something appalling. "A prince may be all very well, but not if it is a foreign title. That does not count."

"I don't think Lucas needs to account to you for his antecedents, Gertrude," Christina said. She had spoken without thinking, rushing to Lucas's defense, her mind already jumping ahead to the hurtful vulgarities Gertrude would utter once she knew Lucas was illegitimate. She saw him looking at her. The warmth had deepened in his eyes, and he took her hand in his again.

"Thank you," he said, nothing more than that, but his touch and his smile made her feel hot.

"Will someone please tell me what is going on?" the duke said plaintively. "A Russian prince? In my garden?"

"I apologize for the masquerade, Your Grace," Lucas said easily. "I wished to be incognito for a while and it seemed the easiest way. I hope I did no lasting damage to your magnificent roses."

"Delighted, of course, old fellow," the duke said vaguely. Christina wondered with irritation whether her father was so wrapped up in his studies that he was not really paying attention. "You certainly worked wonders in my grotto," the duke continued. "The benefits of a classical education, what? Eton and Oxford, was it?"

"No, Your Grace," Lucas said. "The back streets of Edinburgh. The fact that I now have a substantial business empire I ascribe to all I learned in that period."

Christina noted that Gertrude's lips were now so pursed she looked like a tightly pulled reticule drawstring. "Trade!" She sniffed. "Well, it may do very well for Christina at her age, but nothing other than an English duke will do for my Allegra."

Allegra stepped forward. Her face was set. She looked pale but determined. She had Richard Bryson by the hand.

"Actually, Mama," she said, "I am already married. Richard—" she pulled Bryson forward "—is my husband."

There was a thud as Gertrude fainted.

"MY DEAR OLD FELLOW," the duke said to Lucas. "What can I do for you? Come to ask my permission to wed my daughter, what?"

"Yes, Your Grace," Lucas said. He had a great deal more than that he wanted to ask Christina's father, but he thought he would start with the easy questions first. They were in the ducal library, supplied with plenty of coffee by a sullen Alice Parmenter. Jack Rutherford and his brother-in-law, Robert Methven, were present, as well. They had arrived in the early afternoon; Jack had at first seemed inclined to punch Lucas when he had discovered what had happened with Christina, but fortunately Robert had a cooler head and talked him round. Lucas had then told his future brothers-in-law of his suspicions that the duke had been involved in Peter's death, and they had agreed to support him in a confrontation. Lucas wanted no further deceit or secrets. The matter had to be resolved now.

"Well," the duke said, his gaze riveted on his coffee cup, "it's all rather difficult, don't you see? I'm not at all sure I can give permission."

"I beg your pardon, sir?" Lucas, whose mind had jumped ahead to how he might phrase his questions about Peter, was brought up short.

"It's tricky, you know." The duke still appeared fascinated by the coffee and would not look Lucas in the eye. "Y'see, I need Christina here with me. So much to do at Kilmory, don't you know, what with the estate and the household and everything...." He waved a vague hand around. "I'd be lost without her."

"You have an estate manager and a housekeeper and an army of servants, sir," Lucas said, holding on to his temper with the greatest effort. He wondered if this was what had happened when the duke had broken the match between Christina and Douglas McGill. Except he was no McGill and he was not giving her up.

"Not the same at all," the duke groused. "No, indeed, not the same. So you see..." He spread his hands. "Can't allow it, I'm afraid. All there is to it."

"You do appreciate, Your Grace," Robert Methven intervened swiftly, shooting Lucas a warning glance as he half rose from his chair, "that Mr. Black does not need your permission to wed Lady Christina? He is asking out of courtesy only. She is of age and so may make her own decisions."

"Well, we'll see," the duke said comfortably. "Can't imagine Christina wanting to leave me. Far too set in her ways, y'know. We'll see."

Lucas was starting to dislike the Duke of Forres even more than he had done previously. The man was self-absorbed to a shocking extent. He itched to grab Forres by the neck cloth and shake him. He caught Jack's eye. Jack looked as though he wanted to intervene, but Lucas shook his head slightly. He would fight this particular battle later, and he would fight it to the end. But for now he had another issue he wanted to raise.

"There is another matter I wished to discuss with you, Your Grace," Lucas said. He felt Jack and Robert draw a little closer, felt the tension build in the air. "The brooch that you gave your daughter as a birthday gift—a very fine brooch of silver and amethysts—where did that come from?"

For a moment the duke looked utterly blank, but then his face cleared. "Oh, by Jove," he said, "I remember that! Elegant piece. I found it in a shop in Edinburgh. I picked up my little icon there, as well!" He jumped to his feet and scurried off to fetch the icon, putting it into Lucas's hands. "Splendid, isn't it?" He was beaming with uncomplicated pleasure. "Couldn't believe my luck."

"A shop in Edinburgh," Lucas said. His voice was not quite steady. "What sort of shop?"

The duke looked slightly shifty. "A pawnshop," he admitted. "I like to buy gifts on the cheap if I can, but I didn't want Christina to know that."

Lucas put the icon down slowly. There was a ring of truth in the duke's words. The man was completely guileless. He might be tight with his fortune, but he was no criminal. Yet this had to be more than a coincidence. Lucas looked at Robert, who was frowning.

"When did you make the trip to Edinburgh, sir?" Robert asked.

The duke rubbed his head absentmindedly. "Let me see…was it November? No, December. Christmas!" He looked as though he was expecting a reward for this triumphant feat of memory. "We spent Christmas in Edinburgh," he repeated. "You remember, Methven, Rutherford." He glanced across at Jack. "You all came to join us."

Jack nodded. "We did."

December. Less than a month after Peter had died. Lucas felt a shiver as though the ghost of the past had brushed him. Could someone from Kilmory have robbed and murdered Peter and seen the trip to Edinburgh as a means to rid themselves of the stolen goods, not foreseeing the terrible coincidence that had led the duke to the very same pawnshop?

"Who else went with you?" Lucas asked.

"Took my valet," the duke said, rubbing his chin. "No need to take the other servants. We have a staff at the house in Charlotte Square. Christina came, too, of course," he added, as an afterthought. "There was no one else."

Christina.

Lucas would never, ever believe that Christina was guilty. It simply was not possible.

"I think there was someone else," he said slowly. "Wasn't there, Your Grace?"

The duke flushed. "No," he said sharply. "No one."

"Alice Parmenter," Lucas said. "She is your mistress." He heard rather than saw both Jack and Robert shift with surprise. "I suspect Mrs. Parmenter did not travel with you," he continued. "She certainly would not have stayed with you, but I think she was in Edinburgh, too. Did you install her in a house somewhere nearby, Your Grace? Somewhere convenient to visit?"

The duke looked shifty. "What if I did? No law against a man keeping a mistress, what? We're all men of the world." He looked around at Jack, at Robert, looked as though he was about to make some infelicitous remark about them probably keeping mistresses, too, and then thought better of it. "This is nothing to the purpose," he said testily. "What if Alice was there? Damned if I see why I have to account to any of you for it!"

"You don't, Your Grace," Lucas said, standing up. "But Mrs. Parmenter does. She needs to account for the murder of my brother."

CHRISTINA STOOD IN the doorway of the Great Hall. It had been decorated for dinner and then a ball afterward and it looked stunning. Vases overflowed with fresh flowers in tumbling profusion. Banners of green and gold with the arms of MacMorlan drifted down from the high rafters. Candlelight sparkled on silver. Everywhere the ladies of the Highland Ladies Bluestocking Society mingled and fluttered like so many exotic birds.

The only problem was that no one felt very festive. The household had been utterly shaken by the arrest of Alice Parmenter for murder, robbery and dealing in stolen goods. Alice had been taken away to jail in Fort William, complaining loudly that the death of Peter Galitsin had been an accident. She had seen him at the castle and thought him young, rich, naive and ripe for robbery. She had followed him back to the inn that night and sent him a message to meet her on the track above the cliffs. She said she had only taken a knife to persuade him to part with his money. He had been stabbed in the scuffle because he had tried to stop her when she'd taken the icon from him. She added bitterly that had the duke been a little more generous to his mistress she would have had no need to steal, but he was as mean as an old miser and inadequate in bed into the bargain.

Galloway had looked as though he was about to keel over with shock when he heard the news. Gertrude had been appalled, more by the fact that the duke had stooped so low than the news that the housekeeper was a murderer.

"The housekeeper!" she kept saying. "How could he?"

"Never mind, Gertrude," Lucy had said. "It could have been much worse. I hear Alice was trying to persuade Papa into marriage—imagine her as Duchess of Forres!"

Gertrude had looked even more horrified and had rushed off, perhaps, as Mairi mischievously said, to find Angus in the hope that it was not too late to produce an heir. The news that the duke might yet consider remarriage had also seemed to spur Lachlan into action as he had set off for home and a reconciliation with Dulcibella.

"We'll see how long that lasts," Lucy said darkly.

Christina had wanted to cancel the ball, but the members of the Highland Ladies Bluestocking Society were already arriving and Lucas had assured her that he wanted the event to go ahead. He had even brought her the flowers he had promised to decorate the Great Hall: great armfuls of scented roses and hollyhocks, jasmine and anemones, acorns and pinecones that smelled sweet and fresh.

"It's a triumph, Christina," Lucy said, patting her sister's arm. "Of course, Gertrude is taking all the credit, but I think we all know who did the hard work."

Mairi eased herself onto a chair with a heartfelt sigh. She might be seven months pregnant but Christina was quick to note that she still looked like a fashion plate from *La Belle Assemblée.*

"I feel like a whale," Mairi complained. "There will be no dancing for me tonight."

"I should think not, Mairi." Gertrude, at her most matronly and disapproving, with a puce turban and pheasant feathers, gave her sister-in-law's pregnant stomach a look of profound disapproval. "You are not fit to be seen in public! I cannot imagine what you are thinking, parading about in this state!"

"Thank you, Gertrude," Mairi said. "I don't believe in hiding myself away just because I am pregnant. It is a perfectly natural state. Allegra looks very pretty tonight," she added, nodding to where their niece, celestially fair in a modest spangled cream gown, was talking with her husband and a couple of the bluestocking ladies. "Marriage suits her. She glows. Perhaps," she added, "she is *enceinte,* as well."

Gertrude made a sound like a horse snorting and sped off across the room to accost the happy couple.

"Mairi," Christina said, trying to suppress a smile, "you are very bad."

"Well, it could be true," Mairi said, easing herself more comfortably onto the chair. "It seems they have been wed at least a month and Angus and Gertrude had no notion."

"That is not surprising," Christina said. "They notice nothing beyond themselves."

"You didn't realize, either," Mairi pointed out.

"I did wonder if they were lovers," Christina said, "but for all her sophisticated airs, Allegra is very young. I thought I was imagining things."

"At least with Allegra's marriage to occupy her, Gertrude is not harping on at you about yours, Christina," Lucy said with a giggle. "I think in time she may take quite well to having a Russian prince as a brother-in-law. I have already heard her boasting to Lady Dorney that he is a relative of the czar."

"Lucas will hate that," Mairi said. "You know how he shuns his aristocratic lineage." She broke off as Lucas came in. "Oh, my goodness," she said, fanning herself. "Christina, you are *such* a lucky girl."

Lucas was flanked by Jack on one side and Robert on the other, but he did not look like a man who needed the support. In fact, the three of them looked what they were: shockingly handsome, slightly dangerous and enough to make the Highland Ladies Bluestocking Society members swoon. Christina realized, with a catch of her breath, that she had never seen Lucas in formal evening attire. She had seen him in livery and in his working garb, but now in the stark black-and-white of formal dress he looked magnificent. He was looking around the ballroom. He was looking for *her.*

They had had no opportunity to talk since that morning, and now her heart turned over at what might happen next. She had told Lucas he could stay at Kilmory until he had solved the mystery of Peter's death. With Alice arrested, that mystery was solved. She wondered if Lucas would leave. She wondered if she really wanted him to go. She did not know the answer to either question and she felt hopelessly confused.

Her breath trapped in her chest. What scared her was not the way Lucas could command a room, nor even the spectacular good looks that still had the ranks of the Highland bluestocking ladies buzzing, but the way he could make her forget all reason. There was a dangerously sensual gleam in his black eyes that made her toes curl in her satin slippers. She desired Lucas Black, but she was not sure she could trust herself to love him again, or trust him not to betray her.

He showed every sign of crossing the room to join her but was waylaid by several ladies clamoring for an introduction.

"Lucas is most shockingly handsome, isn't he," Lucy said. She giggled. "If Lady Dorney gets any closer she will practically be *wearing* him. She always was a woman who believed that a cause was not lost until the knot was tied."

"And not even then in some cases," Mairi said drily.

"If he were mine I should not let him out of my sight," Lucy said.

"You are missing the material point here," Christina said sharply. She had spent a part of the afternoon explaining Lucas's deception to Lucy and

Mairi, and it infuriated her that they seemed to have already forgotten everything she had told them.

"Lucas came here pretending to be a servant—"

"And I wish I had seen him in livery," Mairi put in.

Christina ignored her. "He misled us all," she said. "I slept with him—"

Both her sisters sighed enviously in unison.

"Would you marry a man you cannot trust?" Christina demanded.

Mairi pursed her lips. "If he looked like Lucas, then, yes, I probably would. I'm shallow like that."

Lucy touched her arm. "I understand, Tina. Really, I do. You know that Robert tried to compromise me into marriage because he had to do what was right for his clan. He put the needs of his people first because that was what his honor obliged him to do."

"You are saying that Lucas's honor obliged him to bring his brother's murderer to justice," Christina said.

"Yes," Lucy said. "I think you already know that. Lucas is a man of honor. He did what he had to do."

"Besides," Mairi said. "You love him. Don't throw that away."

"I loved him before," Christina admitted. "Now I am not sure I even know him."

The thought of handing Lucas her heart a second time made her terrified. It was not like when McGill had refused to fight for her, when he had refused to stand up to her father's will. That had hurt badly at the time. She had loved McGill with a girlish infatuation and she had had no experience to draw on to soften the blow. Now she had the experience, but the pain was greater because the love she had had for Lucas had been so much more powerful than anything she had felt before. She knew with certainty that she could not survive such a betrayal again.

"He's the same man," Lucy said. "In your heart you know it."

Galloway sounded the dinner gong.

"Oh, my goodness," Mairi said. "You have placed Lucas next to Gertrude at dinner." She opened her blue eyes wide. "Perhaps you don't love him after all. That's the first time I've seen a table plan used as punishment."

"Lucas is the highest-ranking male guest," Christina said. She felt a stab of guilt. Mairi was right; she had thought, if not to punish Lucas, then to test him. "It's only appropriate that he should escort Gertrude," she said by way of an excuse. "She is the highest-ranking female guest."

"I'm a marchioness, too," Lucy complained. "You could have given him to me!"

Jack came up at that moment to escort her in to dinner. Normally Christina found him an entertaining companion, but tonight her attention was frequently drawn to the other end of the table where Lucas sat. She was slightly chagrined to see that he was handling the situation rather well; he gave Gertrude all his attention so that by the end of the first course she was positively simpering and Christina was feeling quite cross.

"You can trust Lucas to handle anything you throw at him," Jack said in her ear.

Christina watched as Gertrude leaned over and touched Lucas confidentially on the back of his hand to emphasize a point she was making. Lucas smiled and nodded and Gertrude beamed at him.

"Was I staring?" Christina asked. "I simply cannot believe he has charmed Gertrude," she added.

The note in her voice betrayed her and Jack laughed. "I see," he said. "You wanted him to fail."

Christina bit her lip. "I suppose I still feel angry with him," she admitted.

"Of course you do," Jack said easily, "but Lucas won't oblige you by falling flat on his face in polite company, so perhaps you had better change your ambitions."

Christina glanced back at Lucas. He was watching her. There was something in his eyes that was hot and possessive.

"He's doing all this for you," Jack added. "Lucas hates his titles, he never uses them. Did you not wonder why you hadn't heard of him? It is because he never took up his place in society until now. When he first came to Scotland, the trustees of his father's estate refused to grant it to him. They threw him out. He had to fight for his lands." Then, as she stared at him, "Did he not tell you?"

"No," Christina said. She cleared her throat. "That is, he told me that he doesn't care for the aristocracy, but I had not thought—" She stopped. She should have realized, she thought. She had known that Lucas was illegitimate, that society had shunned him. He would not want to be a part of a culture that had condemned his mother and turned its back on him because of his bastardy.

Suddenly she felt swamped by emotion. She picked up her knife and fork again and made a pretense of eating, but she was not even sure what the food was. She felt too confused, too disturbed.

Dinner was long and elaborate. Lucas had Lady Bellingham on the other side of him and courteously turned his attention to her during the second course. Gertrude sulked but brightened up when the dessert was served and she had Lucas's attention once again. When dinner was over and the dancing started, though, Lucas came straight across to claim Christina's hand.

"At last," he said.

"You are supposed to open the dancing with the Countess of Cromarty," Christina said.

"I shall beg her pardon later," Lucas said. "I want to dance with you."

Gertrude was dancing with Richard Bryson and actually looked as though she was enjoying herself. Christina was so shocked that she almost missed her step.

"Your doing, I think." She looked up. Lucas was watching them, too, a faint smile playing about his mouth. "What on earth could you have said to Gertrude that would have persuaded her even to give Richard the slightest chance?"

"Merely that he seemed like a resourceful fellow

who was wasted on the revenue service," Lucas said. "I suggested that I might have a place for him managing some of my business interests."

"I would not have thought that Gertrude wanted a son-in-law who worked at all," Christina said.

Lucas smiled. "Well, of course, it is not ideal. But I implied that Bryson was also related to the Sutherlands, my father's family. Since my aunt is the Duchess of Strathspey, that put a different complexion on matters."

"Is he?" Christina asked. "Related to you, I mean?"

Lucas shrugged. "I would not be surprised. My father's family is related to almost everyone in Scotland if one goes back far enough."

There was some element of reserve in his voice that reminded Christina forcibly of what Jack had said.

"It was kind of you to draw on that connection to help Richard," she said impulsively. "It must hurt to have to speak of your father and—" she hesitated "—have people pick over your birth and your mother's reputation and your history."

Lucas's jaw was rigid. "No one would dare to mention my illegitimacy directly to me now," he said, and there was a thread of dry humor in his voice. "It is not the same as when I was a child."

And yet, Christina thought, in some ways that child was still there. The child who had lost everything and been reviled was still there, and her heart suddenly ached for him. She looked around the ballroom and understood for the first time. Jack had been right. Lucas really was doing this for her, stepping into a world he had rejected fifteen years before so that he could be with her. He was doing it because he loved her, and the only question was whether she dared to love him back.

The music changed, swept into a waltz. Lucas carried on dancing with her.

"You have this dance with Lady Dorney," Christina said.

"Who?" Lucas said. His hold on her tightened. "Christina," he said. "I have something to ask you." Then, as she tilted her head back to look at him, he said, "Will you marry me?" He looked formal, a little severe. "No secrets," he said, "no deception, no convenient betrothal just to save your reputation." His lips brushed her ear, sending a wicked little shiver down her spine. "Always, Christina. Forever."

The music spun onward, a whirling spiral of sound that echoed the whirling spiral of her thoughts. Christina felt the tears close her throat because it only made her feel worse, more afraid, standing on the edge of danger, not ready to take the leap. She realized that this was all about her, not about Lucas. It was about whether she could trust herself to love him again. It was whether she was prepared to take that risk.

Lucas's mouth hovered over hers. "I love you," he murmured. His eyes were full of tenderness and desire. "I'll never stop loving you. I cannot promise not to die, but I have no intention of leaving you for a very long time."

Christina almost lost herself then, trapped by the fierce black gaze that held hers, her heartbeat racing and the rest of the world forgotten as he held her close. Then someone bumped against them and apologized and she realized that the waltz still went on and that people were staring. Her hand came to rest on his chest. "We are scandalizing the ballroom," she whispered.

"Now, that," Lucas said, "is where I do not give a fig for society's opinion."

Before Christina was aware of what he was about, he had whisked her out of the doorway into the hall. It was quiet here, with the noise and chatter of the ballroom muted. Lucas drew her behind a group of statuary and kissed her. There was no gentleness in it, no hesitation, nothing but raw, explosive passion, so fierce and dangerous that her head reeled. Still kissing her, he started to pull her toward the stairs. They stumbled in their haste and she heard him give a mutter of impatience against her mouth, and then he had scooped her up in his arms and was taking the stairs two at a time. He put her down outside her chamber door and they kissed again, hungry, desperate, then crashed through the door with Lucas slamming it shut behind them.

"I gave you a chamber in the east wing," Christina said as his mouth finally lifted from hers.

"At this precise moment, I can't remember where that is," Lucas said, "and I don't care."

He tumbled her down onto the bed and Christina reached for him. Everything she had been feeling in the past few days, the hurt, the anger, the confusion and the longing, fused into one huge burst of need. She had felt it that morning when they had kissed. Now she ripped his jacket and shirt off, the beautiful formal evening clothes she had admired him in only hours earlier, and then she realized that they did not even belong to him.

"I've just ruined the evening clothes Jack loaned you," she gasped as she smoothed her hands over his shoulders and chest, exulting in the warm slide of skin on skin.

"It was only his second-best suit," Lucas murmured. His lips brushed the hollow at the base of her throat. "I'll buy him a new one." His hands were busy on the fastenings of her gown, tugging, struggling with the buttons and bows. "Damn it, why must you wear so many clothes?"

With a growl of frustration he pulled them off haphazardly and threw them to the floor, leaving her naked.

Then everything changed and became slow and languorous. Lucas ran a hand down her body with lazy pleasure and she tilted her head up so that her lips found his. She opened to him without holding back, and they kissed gently, yet there was a feverish edge of need to it as though any moment they might fall beyond control. Lucas bent his head to her breast and Christina arched against him, feeling her breath fracture and the desire inside her wind ever tighter. His tongue flicked her nipple and she groaned aloud.

"Trust me," he whispered against her hot skin. "Give yourself up to me."

Again his tongue flicked over the sensitive tips of her breasts and she squirmed helplessly. Pleasure was a deep, dark tide inside her now, washing through her, demanding release. Lucas pressed his lips to the hollow of her stomach and she gasped, reaching for him, but he held her hands fast so that she had no choice other than to lie still.

She closed her eyes. Light danced across the backs of her eyelids, fantasy and pleasure merging as she focused on the sensations he was arousing in her body. His lips and tongue trailed a path across from one of her hip bones to the other. Tingles chased across her skin and her hips lifted in desperate appeal. At once he slid a hand between her legs, his fingers seeking and finding, stroking with such knowing skill that she cried out. Her body rippled and clenched, but he felt the response and drew back, leaving her hanging tantalizingly on the edge.

"Not yet."

She made a sound of appeal and frustration and he laughed, rolling on top of her, sliding a leg between hers. She could feel the hardness of his thigh and the thickness of his arousal and she tried desperately to draw him in to her, but he resisted. The strength of him held her trapped as he returned to kiss her again, deep demanding kisses that only served to build the heat and the fever higher. He drew back and stroked the damp hair from her face.

"Trust me." There was such an intensity of emotion in his black eyes that she felt dizzy. "I won't let you fall."

He kissed her again, carnal, sensual, so that her body twitched with desire and she shifted in another vain attempt to pull him closer to her. He held back; she could see his smile, and he bent his head to her breasts again, the brush of his stubble against her sensitive skin an exquisite torment.

"I know what you are doing." She gasped the words. "You want…"

"Everything." His fingers caressed her again and she jolted. "I want you to give yourself to me without reservation."

His hand pushed her thighs wider, and then he was inside her and she almost cried out with relief as he possessed her. He held her hips, withdrew a little and then plunged deeper. Her body rose to meet his at each stroke. It was fierce, terrifying and glorious. She felt as though she was abandoning something of herself and yet finding something she had never imagined. The fear that had dogged her steps, the refusal to trust was destroyed forever in the intensity of her emotions. She wanted to give her heart freely. She wanted to share her life with him.

"I love you," she said. "Lucas…"

The world shattered into tiny, brilliant fragments. She felt him holding her, heard him say her name and felt him shaking as much as she was. He drew her close and she curled into his side, too exhausted to think, dazed. And then she drifted gently into sleep with her body and mind entangled in him.

CHAPTER EIGHTEEN

LUCAS WOKE TO a sensation of warmth and contentment. Christina was lying with her body curled into the shelter of his. Her hair fanned across his chest and tickled his nose and chin. She was smiling, fast asleep. It felt as though she belonged in that precise place, in his arms, resting next to his heart.

It felt as though they belonged together.

Strange that now, after so many years of cutting himself off from any sense of belonging, he should feel as though he had come home, not to a place but to a person, Christina, the other half of his soul.

There was the sound of the door opening, a rattle of bed curtains, no scream this time.

"You again!" Annie said cheerfully. "You had better get down to the kirk. This can't go on."

Christina was stretching, yawning, her eyes soft with sleep and so much love that Lucas felt his heart turn over.

"A good idea," she murmured, smiling at him.

"We will speak to Mr. MacPherson this very morning," Lucas said.

"Papa—" Christina said, sounding suddenly uneasy.

"He will not stand in our way," Lucas said. "And if he does—" he kissed her "—we will elope."

"I rather like the thought of eloping with the gardener," Christina said. "But before that, I will see you for breakfast."

Somehow Lucas managed to find his way back to the chamber in the east wing that Christina had had prepared for him the night before. Jack's valet had thoughtfully laid out another set of clothes for him. Lucas vowed to take rather more care of this set. He washed and dressed and made his way downstairs. A number of the guests were already gathering for breakfast, but before they could go in to eat there was a peremptory knock at the front door. When Galloway opened it he was swept out of the way like flotsam on the tide as a posse of soldiers marched in with Eyre at their head.

Lucas felt a cold, solid weight of dread settle in his stomach. When Eyre had not troubled them the previous day he had hoped it was because the riding officer had heard that Christina was alive and well and that in the absence of any evidence he could not touch her. Now he saw how deeply he had underestimated the man. Eyre had merely been biding his time.

"Lady Christina!" Eyre boomed, and turning, Lucas saw that Christina was just coming down the broad staircase and into the hall. Eyre, puffed up with self-importance, strutted toward her.

"What the devil is this?" Lucas demanded. The dragoons stood awkwardly to attention, a half dozen of them under the command of a captain who barely looked old enough to be out of short trousers.

Lucas looked at Christina. She was standing on the bottom step, very straight, very pale. Her gaze touched his briefly and Lucas saw a welter of fear and anger there and felt his skin crawl with hatred. This man had tried to kill her. He had hunted her down and tried to shoot her. He saw Christina lace her fingers together tightly to stop them from trembling and felt a wave of protectiveness so fierce it shook him.

"Perhaps we should speak privately, Mr. Eyre," Christina said. Her voice was very steady. Lucas was proud of her. "As you can see—" she glanced around at the shocked crowd of guests milling in the hall "—we are hosting a party here today. It really is not appropriate for us to discuss business in front of everyone."

Eyre gave a derisive snort. Lucas could see the gathering through the riding officer's eyes: the aristocratic house, the opulence, the flowers, the servants and the privilege, all of the things that Eyre resented most in the world. Even his nephew had been accepted into this gilded world now, into the one place where Eyre would never be welcome. Lucas knew Eyre would not back down. On the contrary, this would give him the stage he wanted to humiliate and ruin Christina before everyone. He could see it in the gleam of anger and triumph in Eyre's eyes. The riding officer was relishing this. He was enjoying every moment.

"I am sure you have no secrets from your family and friends, my lady," Eyre said. "I am sure they are all aware of your criminal activities. But if not—" he braced his legs a little wider, leaning back, a self-important stance full of confidence "—allow me to tell them all about it."

Lucas saw Lucy and Mairi exchange a frankly incredulous look. Gertrude's mouth had fallen open. Under other circumstances, Lucas might have found it amusing that Christina had shocked her family so comprehensively, but this was no laughing matter. Eyre was intent on destruction.

"A couple of nights ago," Eyre said, "acting on information given by an informer, we instigated a search for the whisky still that we knew was operating illegally on the Kilmory estate. We discovered a bothy in Loch Gyle that we believe had recently been used to brew the peat-reek."

Robert Methven gave Lucas a meaningful stare. Lucas knew he was telling him to keep quiet, that he would deal with this. Lucas could see the sense in that, since he was Christina's betrothed and hardly impartial, but the need to defend her burned into him like a brand.

"Do you have any evidence, Mr. Eyre?" Robert said politely. "Did you recover any of the apparatus of distilling?"

Eyre shot him a look of intense dislike. "No, my lord," he admitted, "but we have the informer's word for it that the whisky still was there."

Jack shrugged. "Informers will say a great deal

if they think it will gain them material benefit," he said. "Was your informer Mrs. Parmenter, by any chance? I think it is fair to say that she has quite a grudge against this family and will say anything to cause trouble."

"The informer," Eyre said grandly, "was Lord Lachlan MacMorlan. He also laid information to the effect that Lady Christina was the leader of the Kilmory whisky smugglers."

Lucas saw Christina sway and took the steps to her side in one bound, sliding an arm about her waist.

"Lachlan?" she whispered. "Lachlan was the spy?" She looked utterly devastated. "Why would he do such a thing?"

"For money, I imagine," Robert said. His mouth was set in a very hard line.

The hall was in uproar. Gertrude appeared to be having the vapors. Allegra was crying. Richard had his arms about her, comforting her, swearing that he had not known. Lucy and Mairi looked completely stricken. Mairi groped for a chair and sat down hard. Jack took her hand in his.

"Lachlan," Mairi said. "The low, scheming, deceitful *worm*. I always thought he would sell his own family for profit, and now he has."

Eyre, Lucas noted grimly, was grinning, delighted to have caused such chaos. "You may be interested to know, sir," he said, turning to Lucas, "that my suspicion is that Lord Lachlan was also instrumental in the death of your brother. He and Alice Parmenter were lovers. They were in it together."

Lucas felt Christina's fingers tremble in his. Her expression was agonized as her eyes met his. "No," she said. "Oh, no. Lucas…"

Lachlan, Lucas thought. A drunkard, a fool, dismissed as negligible by everyone because they thought he was lost in wine. He felt dizzy with the shock and he felt a fool for not seeing it sooner, for not realizing. He remembered the look Lachlan had given him at the stables that day, sharp and appraising. He remembered the duke saying that the whole family had gathered in Edinburgh for Christmas. He remembered Alice saying that she wanted a younger lover. He had not known that she already had one in the shape of the duke's son, a man who had been a conniving criminal under the disguise of a drunken sot.

The duke was looking perplexed. "But Alice was my—"

"Your Grace," Robert said sharply, and the duke fell obediently silent.

Eyre was still speaking, and Lucas snapped out of his thoughts as he heard Christina give a little gasp. She was the one who mattered now, he thought. Christina was the one who needed protection from Eyre. Everything else could wait until later.

"You are the woman we hunted into the waters of Loch Gyle on the night we went to destroy the still," Eyre was saying. "You were the leader of the smugglers, just as your brother said. You will pay for those crimes."

There was absolute silence in the room, a silence

that rang with hostility. Lucas felt it and with it a
fierce pride. Not one member of the MacMorlans,
not Gertrude, not Richard Bryson, not the Duke of
Forres himself was going to make this easy for Eyre.

"I thought," Jack said gently, "that you had no
evidence, Mr. Eyre? You can scarcely arrest Lady
Christina on no more than the word of her brother,
who may well be a murderer."

Lucas saw the angry color come into Eyre's face
at the challenge. But the man was dangerous still. He
knew Eyre had not finished yet. He still had Christina firmly in his sights. The dragoons stood drawn
up to attention, blank faced, awaiting their cue.

"I think that Lady Christina can be persuaded
to confess, sir," Eyre said confidently. "Lord Lachlan gave us the names of each and every one of the
smuggling gang. They are all in custody now, and
their families with them. If Lady Christina helps us,
then I am prepared to be generous and let them go.
If not—" he shrugged "—they will bear the punishment for her crime."

Christina had turned paper-white.

"That is iniquitous, Eyre," Lucas said. He could
not keep silent any longer. "It's no more than blackmail."

"It's persuasion, sir." Eyre's gaze rested on Lucas
with disdain. "Lady Christina understands."

Lucas saw Christina close her eyes and take a
deep breath. He knew what she was going to do. He
knew it with a sense of inevitability that made him
feel sick and cold inside. Christina was not the sort

of woman to allow others to take the responsibility for her actions. She would take Eyre's devil's bargain because she would feel she had no choice, and Lucas would love her fiercely for it whilst feeling utter despair.

"Christina, please, no—" he started to say. Their eyes met and she smiled at him, though he could see the sparkle of tears in her eyes.

"I'm sorry," she said, speaking directly to him, as though no one else were present. "I'm sorry, Lucas. I love you so much."

She turned back to Eyre. "You are quite correct, Mr. Eyre," she said. Her voice was icy cold and steady. "I was the woman you hunted into the waters of Loch Gyle. I was the woman you shot and tried to drown. There are plenty of men who were witness to that, including Mr. Bryson and Mr. Black." She inclined her head toward Richard, who nodded grimly in return. He was looking at his uncle with undisguised loathing. Lucas felt a ripple of unease pass through the ranks of the dragoons. "You have already illegally imprisoned innocent children and burned people's property to the ground," Christina continued. She turned to the captain of the dragoons. "You must arrest me for smuggling, captain," she said. "I quite see that. But I accuse Mr. Eyre of attempted murder, so you had better arrest him, too."

"Ma'am—" The captain was completely out of his depth now.

"I'm ready to go with you now," Christina said, "but you must honor Mr. Eyre's agreement and release those Kilmory villagers who are now in custody. I take full responsibility for everything. Now take me away."

Lucas watched the dragoons escort her to the carriage that was waiting. He felt as though a part of him was being wrenched away.

He was losing her before they had barely made a beginning.

Jack had his hand on his arm and was speaking to him urgently but his words rolled off Lucas as no more than sound. He watched the carriage down the drive and out of sight. The soldiers had turned to Eyre now. He was blustering and protesting, but the young captain stood firm. A moment later they had snapped him in manacles and marched him away, too.

"Are you going after Lachlan MacMorlan?" Jack asked. "Bringing Peter's killer to justice was always the most important thing for you."

"It was," Lucas said slowly. He realized that Jack was right; until very recently he would not have hesitated. "Yes," he said, and as he spoke he felt something open up within him and fly free. It was as though he was finally able to let go and mourn Peter's memory rather than being driven by his need for vengeance. "But not now. I've got something more important to do first." And he saw Jack grin as he ran toward the stables, shouting for a horse.

CHRISTINA SAT IN the parlor of the magistrate's house in Fort William. She had been staying with Sir Anthony and Lady Medway for approaching six weeks now. They maintained the polite fiction that she was a guest but everyone knew she was in fact under house arrest until the authorities in London decided what to do with her.

It was not an uncomfortable imprisonment, at least not in the physical sense. She was confined to the house but had the use of the library and the run of the gardens. What was uncomfortable was being an unwanted visitor in the house of strangers. Lady Medway had sent her daughters away, ostensibly to visit relatives for a few weeks, but Christina was sure it was because she was considered a bad influence. The magistrate's wife treated her with great politeness, but every so often Christina would catch her looking at her out of the corner of her eye as though Lady Medway thought of her as an unpredictable animal who might suddenly do something outrageous and shocking. She supposed it was no surprise; stories of her exploits and those of the Kilmory Gang had run like wildfire through the small Highland community. She was notorious now.

Through the unseasonably long, hot days of August, she reflected on whether she could have done anything differently but always came to the same conclusions. She could not have pleaded ignorance and left the other members of the gang to face the law alone, abandoning them to their fate. It was not in her nature. She had had no choice other than to take responsibility.

In doing so, though, she had sacrificed her own

happiness and hurt Lucas, too. She thought of him every waking moment. It seemed the cruelest irony that she had come to love and trust Lucas completely and then she had had to turn her back on him in order to save those who depended on her. It had been the hardest decision of her life, and even now she felt sick in her soul to think of what she had done, but she could not see any other way.

She had not heard from Lucas. She was allowed no letters and did not know if he would even write to her if she was permitted to communicate with him. Lachlan had betrayed her and had killed Peter, too. It was horrific. She had had no chance to talk to Lucas about it, but she knew she could not blame him if he wanted nothing to do with her family ever again.

She dreamed of Lucas every night and woke in the mornings with a dull thud of disappointment when she realized that the man who had walked through her dreams was a ghost, no longer beside her. She knew that people said that in time such pain grew easier, but it did not feel like that to her.

One morning Lady Medway came into the parlor where she was playing a solitary game of cards. The weather had turned cold and dull, too chilly to sit out in the garden, and Christina was feeling cooped up and miserable. Lady Medway's demeanor, though, was full of repressed excitement.

"There is a gentleman to see you, my lady," she said.

Christina's heart did a giddy swoop only to dive down to her feet again when she saw the gentleman in question was not Lucas. This man was older, spare, sandy, travel stained as he handed his cloak to the overawed housemaid.

"I am Sidmouth, Lady Christina," the man said, appraising her with sharp gray eyes. "I am not at all pleased to make your acquaintance." He came into the room and strolled over to warm his hands before the fire. Lady Medway's housekeeper bustled in with a tray of tea and biscuits. It was clear that Lady Medway herself wanted to be party to the conversation, but Lord Sidmouth dismissed her with a very courteous inclination of the head and a word of thanks.

"I am honored to meet you, my lord," Christina said when they were alone. Her heart beat hard. She had never expected that the home secretary himself would pass judgment on her case, least of all that he would come all the way to Scotland to do it. "Will you take a seat?"

"Think I'll stand," Sidmouth said peremptorily. "I've been sitting down for the past several days." He laid an arm along the mantel. "You've caused me a great deal of trouble, young woman," he said. "I don't appreciate being obliged to leave London and come haring up to the Highlands like this. Scotland ain't my favorite place, y'know."

"I'm sorry for that, my lord," Christina said politely.

"Ah, well..." Sidmouth took a long swallow of the tea and selected a biscuit from the tray. "It was the only way I was going to get any peace. I suppose I should tell you first—" he sighed "—that your brother Lachlan has escaped justice and fled abroad. That problem, at least, was taken out of my hands." He looked at her from beneath lowering brows. "A pity that you did not see fit to do the same, madam. But I suppose one member of the family at least had to show a bit of backbone."

It was the closest to a compliment she was going to get out of Lord Sidmouth, Christina thought.

"You have powerful friends, ma'am," Sidmouth continued, "and they wouldn't let the matter rest. Methven and Rutherford." Sidmouth sighed. "Petitioning me all the time for a pardon for you. Damned nuisance they made of themselves."

Christina felt a flicker of warmth. "That was good of them," she said. She had had no notion; it had been strange and disorienting to be so cut off from her friends and family, but now she realized that all the time they had been working to help her. She swallowed a lump in her throat.

Sidmouth had not mentioned Lucas yet. She tried not to care.

"As for your sisters!" Sidmouth's brows snapped down. "Two more determined women would be difficult to find. Do you know what they did? Sent me a bottle of your finest peat-reek, madam. Told me the crime was not the distilling of it but my attempts to ban it!"

Christina smothered a smile. That sounded very like Lucy and Mairi. "Did you taste it, my lord?" she asked.

Sidmouth glared at her. "I might have done.

Whisky ain't my tipple, but I have to admit it was damned fine." He sighed again. "Which is nothing to the purpose. You've given me a damned problem, ma'am. Wanted to make an example of the Kilmory Gang, but I can't imprison the daughter of a duke and you won't let me imprison the rest of the gang without you. So—" his glare became even more ferocious "—seems you'll all have to go free, which is most unsatisfactory. But Mr. Black has given surety against your good behavior. He is the one who will pay the fines if you renege, and the rest of the gang, as well."

"I beg your pardon?" Christina said. Her hand shook she refilled the teacups and handed Sidmouth's to him. The spoon rattled loudly in the saucer. "Mr. Black?"

"Lucas Black," Sidmouth repeated impatiently. "He was worse than the rest of them put together! Came all the way to London to speak with me on your behalf. He threatened to expose Eyre's behavior to the press if I didn't release you. I almost had to arrest him for blackmail."

"That was foolish of him," Christina said faintly.

"Well, there's no fool like a man in love," Sidmouth said, suddenly and unexpectedly sentimental. He put a hand inside his jacket and drew out a letter. "He asked me to give you this." He smiled at her. "There's a carriage waiting to take you home when you are ready, Lady Christina." He looked at her. "It would be good to know that in future you turn your talents to a more domestic sphere, madam. I don't want to have to arrest you again."

"Whatever I do," Christina said, "I certainly won't be giving you that opportunity, my lord." Sidmouth laughed and kissed her hand, surprising them both with his gallantry.

When he had gone out, Christina looked at the letter lying so innocently on the table. She had a sudden craven urge not to open it, and when she picked it up her hand shook. She slid open the seal and unfolded it.

"My dearest Christina…"

She felt the tears catch in her throat.

By now I imagine Sidmouth will have told you that if you ever brew the peat-reek again he will lock you up and throw away the key. I have given surety for your good behavior, but there is a price for my help.

As you know, I am a businessman. I feel it would be a terrible waste if you were not to use the undoubted talent you have for whisky distilling in the future. I am therefore making available to you a sum that will enable you to establish a whisky distillery of your own, a small one, perhaps, to start with, but one where you can take that undoubted talent you have and use it legally to distill the best whisky in Scotland. When the time comes that you can afford to pay me back, I expect the sum returned in full—with interest, of course.

Christina gave a gasp that was half laughter, half tears, wholly shock. She remembered telling Lucas that it would be a dream to have her own distillery. He was giving her the means to pursue that dream. He had faith in her. He had put the world into her hands.

Except that this new world would be a lonely place if Lucas were not part of it, too. Her heart beat fiercely as she stood up and hurried toward the door. She had to find Lucas; it did not matter if he was in Edinburgh or London or Russia. She would go to the ends of the earth if she had to. She had to find him and marry him and after that she would set up her distillery and it would be the best one in Scotland, of that she was determined.

She was vaguely aware of Lady Medway's startled face as she rushed toward the front door.

"Lady Christina," Lady Medway called, "your luggage, your cloak—"

"Please send my belongings on to me," Christina said. "Although I am not sure where I am going." She stopped, turned back and hugged the startled matron very tightly.

"Thank you," she said. "You have been very generous to a stranger in your home. I'll never forget your kindness."

"Oh!" The tears started in Lady Medway's eyes and she hugged her back. "Oh, Lady Christina, you are nothing like I imagined a criminal to be!"

Out in the street there were two carriages waiting and what looked like an enormous crowd. Christina stopped, blinked. Standing by the first carriage was a tall figure she recognized.

"Lucas!" Christina threw herself into his arms and felt them close around her. All her fears and unhappiness melted like mist in the sun then. He was real and solid and he held her as though he was never going to let her go.

"I thought you had not come," she said. Her voice shook. "Oh, Lucas! I was afraid that after what Lachlan did you might never want to see me again...." She stopped as he kissed her.

"This has nothing to do with Lachlan," he said against her lips. "This is about you and me, Christina." She could feel his smile. "Your family sends their love," he added, releasing her a little but still keeping her within the circle of his arms. "They wanted to be here to witness our wedding, but Mairi has just been delivered of a baby girl and even she thought it wise not to travel quite yet. Besides, perhaps it was wrong of me, but I wanted you to myself for a little while." He kissed her again with love and sweetness and promise. "So Lord Sidmouth has agreed to give you away, and Sir Anthony and Lady Medway are to be our witnesses. I hope you are agreeable?"

"A niece!" Christina said. She felt dazed, overwhelmed, her heart bursting with happiness. "Mairi is well?"

"Perfectly," Lucas said. "She sends her love. And Jack is the most doting father imaginable. But the wedding?" Then, as Christina nodded and smiled brilliantly at him, he tucked her hand through his arm and turned toward the kirk. "I should tell you that your father withheld his consent," he added, "but I told him that no power on earth would make me give you up, so he had better get used to the idea."

Christina felt the warmth unfurl in her heart like a flower opening. "Thank you," she said. "I am pleased to have the chance to elope with you."

Lucas laughed. "With the blessing of the home secretary as well as the church."

Outside the kirk, Lucas paused, his hand on hers, and drew her a little aside so that the others could not overhear. "After we are wed," he said, and Christina sensed a sudden hesitation in him, "I thought... I wondered if we might go to the Black Strath." He touched her cheek very gently. "This is your doing, Christina. I thought I needed no one and no place that I could call home." His gaze was riveted on her face. "I hated my father's legacy and tried to ignore it, but I saw how you had transformed Kilmory, how much you wanted people to belong and how much you cared. I realized that I wanted that, too." He swallowed hard, and Christina saw that this was still difficult for him, that he was confronting the past and it was painful.

"I tried to push my heritage away," Lucas said. "I tried to push *you* away, but it was too late. I wanted you and I wanted us to have a home together." He cupped her face in his hands. "I am not very good at belonging yet," he said roughly, "but I love you and I believe we can transform the Black Strath into our home."

"I think we can do that together," Christina agreed. She reached up and kissed him. "As long as there is a suitable site there for my distillery," she added.

Lucas laughed. "There is a stream, and a bothy…"

"Then that will be perfect," Christina said. She felt the joy rise up in her and held it tightly, as tightly as she was holding Lucas's hand. "Shall we?" she said.

The door of the kirk swung open. Lady Medway put a bouquet of white roses into her hands and they stepped forward into their future.

* * * * *

An indecent proposal

Lady Lucy MacMorlan may have forsworn men and
marriage, but that doesn't mean she won't agree
to profit from writing love letters for her brother's
friends. That is, until she inadvertently ruins the
betrothal of a notorious laird…

Robert, the dashing Marquis of Methven, is on to
Lucy's secret. And he certainly doesn't intend to let
the lovely Lady Lucy have the last word, especially
when her letters suggest she is considerably more
experienced than he realised…

Can true love be born from scandal?

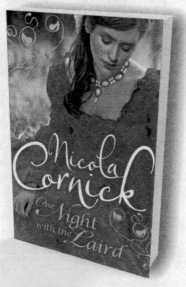

Bluestocking darling and secret scribe Lady Lucy
MacMorlan has no interest in marriage. Instead,
she makes a profit from matchmaking others and
her clandestine love letters are the hushed talk
of Scottish society.

Except now her talent is causing distress—one of
Lucy's more provocative letters has just cost Robert,
Marquis of Methven, his much-needed betrothal.
His revenge? She must marry him or he will
wage war on what is left of her good reputation…

HARLEQUIN®MIRA®
www.mirabooks.co.uk

'If you will be a great man's
mistress, you must pay
the price…'

1372. The Savoy. Widow Lady Katherine de
Swynford presents herself for a role in the household
of merciless royal prince John Plantagenet, Duke
of Lancaster, hoping to end her destitution.

Seduced by the glare of royal adoration, Katherine
becomes John's mistress. She will leave behind
everything she has stood for to play second fiddle to
his young wife and ruthless ambition, in the hope
of finding a love greater than propriety. But is
anything strong enough to face the cries of heresy?

POLAND, 1940
A FAMILY TORN APART BY WAR

Life is a constant struggle for sisters Helena and Ruth
as they try desperately to survive the war in a bitter,
remote region of Poland. Every day is a challenge to
find food, to avoid the enemy, to stay alive.
Then Helena finds a Jewish American soldier,
wounded and in need of shelter.

If she helps him, she risks losing everything, including
her sister's love. But, if she stands aside, could
she ever forgive herself?

HARLEQUIN®MIRA®
www.mirabooks.co.uk

Henry Atticus Richard Ward is no ordinary gentleman…

As maid to some of the most wanton ladies of the *ton*, Margery Mallon lives within the boundaries of any sensible servant. Entanglements with gentlemen are taboo. Wild adventures are only in the Gothic novels she secretly reads. Then an intriguing stranger named Mr Ward offers her a taste of passion and suddenly the wicked possibilities are too tempting to resist…

Covent Garden, London, October 1816

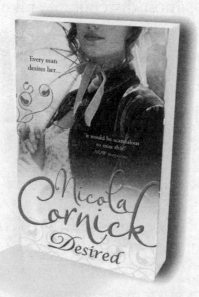

Tess Darent's world is unravelling. Danger threatens her stepchildren and she is about to be unmasked as a radical political cartoonist and thrown into gaol. The only thing that can save her is a respectable marriage.

Owen Purchase, Viscount Rothbury cannot resist Tess when she asks for the protection of his name. Will the handsome sea captain be able to persuade the notorious widow to give her heart as well as her reputation into his safekeeping?

HARLEQUIN®MIRA®
www.mirabooks.co.uk

When the *ton*'s most notorious
heartbreaker meets London's
most disreputable rake

Susanna Burney is society's most sought-after
matchbreaker, paid by wealthy parents to part
unsuitable couples. Until her latest assignment brings
her face to face with the man who'd once taught
her an intimate lesson in heartache...

James Devlin has everything he's always wanted, but
the woman who's just met his eyes across a crowded
ballroom could cost him everything.

To put the past to rest once and for all, Dev just
might have to play Susanna at her own
wicked game.